"There are no side

"Yes there are. Mine and theirs. You knew that, you knew that better than anyone and now you're choosing their side. Great, just great!"

He could see the tears in her eyes and the hysteria that was building. In two steps he was in front of her, his hands around her upper arms, shaking her a little and forcing her to look at him.

"Scout, I'm here for you. For you. And I'm not going anywhere. Got it?"

She looked at him then, right into his eyes. As though she was seeing straight through to his soul, really, for the first time.

"Until you leave me again. Yeah," she said, pulling away from him. "I got it."

There it was, Jayson thought. The final second of their time-out just ticked on the clock.

The past was back.

Dear Reader,

Hopefully, if you are reading *Scout's Honor*, you had the chance to read *The Comeback of Roy Walker* as the first book in the series. When writing that book I truly fell in love with the somewhat prickly younger sister named Scout.

Then of course there was Scout's relationship with her father and the man she once loved that she could never quite get over.

I was so excited to write this story and I hope I did right by both Scout and Jayson. This is a story of love and grief and finding a way to start over again even when everything seems lost. It's one of my personal favorites.

I love to hear from readers, so if you do enjoy this story you can let me know at www.stephaniedoyle.net or on Twitter, @StephDoyleRW.

Stephanie Doyle

STEPHANIE DOYLE

Scout's Honor

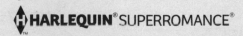

HARLEQUIN®SUPERROMANCE®

Recycling programs
for this product may
not exist in your area.

ISBN-13: 978-0-373-60929-1

Scout's Honor

Copyright © 2015 by Stephanie Doyle

Printed in U.S.A.

HARLEQUIN®
www.Harlequin.com

Stephanie Doyle, a dedicated romance reader, began to pen her own romantic adventures at age sixteen. She began submitting to Harlequin at age eighteen and by twenty-six her first book was published. Fifteen years later she still loves what she does as each book is a new adventure. She lives in South Jersey with her cat, Hermione, the designated princess of the house. When Stephanie's not reading or writing, in the summer she is most likely watching a baseball game and eating a hot dog.

Books by Stephanie Doyle

HARLEQUIN SUPERROMANCE

The Way Back
One Final Step
An Act of Persuasion
For the First Time
Remembering That Night
The Comeback of Roy Walker

SILHOUETTE ROMANTIC SUSPENSE

Suspect Lover
The Doctor's Deadly Affair

SILHOUETTE BOMBSHELL

Calculated Risk
The Contestant
Possessed

Visit the Author Profile page
at Harlequin.com for more titles.

CHAPTER ONE

SCOUT STARED AT the gathering around the grave site and tried to remember how she'd gotten here. It wasn't as if she had forgotten the past three months of her life. Of course she hadn't. Nothing would ever take away that time. That horrible beautiful time when she got to care for her dying father and be with him as he slipped away from this world.

She'd read baseball biographies to him while he slept. They'd watched classic World Series games on the MLB Network channel when he was awake. She'd even allowed her sisters to have time with him. After all they were his daughters, too, and they also loved him, so it seemed only fair.

Yes, Lane and Samantha deserved their time with Duff. But when it came time for the serious stuff—the pain meds, the oxygen and then finally the morphine drip—that had been all Scout.

With the help of Sarah, the hospice nurse. Scout was convinced the woman had been sent from some mystical land of grace and peace. A perfect companion during a dark time who seemed to make it all so easy for Scout, Sarah had given simple, clear directions that Scout had followed ruthlessly.

A drop of morphine every six hours. Then two drops, then three drops. Then three drops every three hours, two hours and one hour as required by the pain.

Slowly and gently easing Duff's way.

Duff had been spared what the nurse had told her could be truly awful pain. He'd been lucky in that regard. Or maybe the whole thing had gone easier for him because he hadn't had any thought of fighting death.

He'd said it every day until the day he stopped speaking: "Sad to go, but the game has to end."

His game ended four days and two hours ago.

Standing at this grave site, Scout could see she was wearing a black coat over a black dress, except she had no idea how she'd gotten here. Really no idea what had happened in these past four days.

She thought she remembered falling…

"Scout, it's done," Lane said now, approaching her cautiously. She wrapped an arm around Scout's waist for comfort and perhaps steadiness. Had she hurt her head when she'd fallen? Is that why she couldn't remember?

She tried to respond, but it felt difficult to form words in her mouth.

"Okay." It was conceivable that had been the first thing she'd said in the past four days.

"We need to go back to the stadium."

Jocelyn Taft Wright, the owner of the Minotaur Falls Triple A baseball team and stadium, had decided Duff Baker's funeral reception should be held there. After all it was going to be a major baseball event and probably the only place in town that would hold such a large crowd of people.

Duff Baker had been a legend in the game of baseball, first as a Hall of Fame player and then as a World Series–winning manager. His time managing the Minotaurs had just been his way of retiring while still staying connected to the game. He would joke about dying in his baseball uniform. In the end it was a close thing.

So not only was the entire town planning on attending, but also a good chunk of the

Major and Minor League Baseball world—
Duff's other family—would be there. Old
teammates. Former players he'd coached.
The current roster for the Minotaurs, a lot of
the players devastated by his death. And the
press, reporters all now writing what they
hoped would be their epic tributes to one of
the game's best.

Heck, the commissioner of baseball was
coming and planned to speak.

Scout didn't mind. Although the pomp and
circumstance were interfering with her need
to hide in her closet for oh, say, the next year,
she knew it was Duff's due.

She wanted this for him. She wanted him
to have the accolades and the speeches. And
then when the season opened in the spring it
would all start again. Duff's daughters would
be expected to make appearances at various
different events. Throw out opening balls.
Be there for tribute games in the cities where
Duff had made his biggest impact as both a
player and a manager.

They had even been called by ESPN to do
a documentary on Duff and the game of baseball. Scout wasn't ready to go there yet, but
that he warranted such a tribute meant something to her.

And just the other morning she'd heard Mike and Mike on the radio offering their condolences to the Baker family. That had been nice.

"Scout, come on," Lane said, shaking her gently. Not that it helped. Scout agreed it was time to go but she couldn't find the energy to move. It was more numbness than anything else. As if a heavy fog had settled over her brain.

"Lane, Scout. We need to go. Now."

The two of them looked over to their older sister, Samantha. Scout thought she looked way too pretty for a funeral. Her blond bob was perfectly slick to her chin and her stylishly thin body was wrapped in a caramel-colored coat that Scout knew felt as soft to the touch as fur but of course couldn't be, because Samantha loved animals.

Samantha had come and gone every weekend these past few months. working desperately to repair the relationship with her father that had broken down in the years since their parents' divorce.

It wasn't that they fought. It's just that she didn't openly adore Duff the way his other two daughters did. Knowing Duff and loving Duff, Scout found that to be impossible.

How could anyone not adore Duff?

How could anyone keep a distance from him?

How was Scout supposed to survive now that he was dead?

The idea of survival without him was a doozy that kept hitting Scout at all hours of the day. It had been on her mind throughout the ordeal of his dying. It was even more persistent now that he was gone. Because there was no going back.

The finality of death was truly a bizarre thing. For three months she'd been preparing herself for the event. For three months she'd been grieving, wondering when it would finally happen. For three months she'd been looking ahead to this day knowing it would come and knowing there wasn't a damn thing she could do to stop it.

She'd thought she'd accepted his loss on some level. She'd thought she had prepared herself.

How utterly stupid of her.

"She's not moving," Lane said.

Samantha sighed as she walked toward them.

As a rule Scout and Samantha weren't close. During the divorce Samantha, who had been just starting college at the time, had stayed in touch regularly with their mother. Sam would even go so far as to try to convince Scout that there were two sides to every story.

Given that Scout believed her mother to be a traitorous bitch, that logic was unacceptable.

But during these last few months as Scout watched Samantha and Duff find their way, she'd been trying to be high-minded about the whole thing.

For Samantha's part she would always pull Scout back to reality. To the present.

Scout could have hated her for that but she had needed Samantha's discipline to get through these last few months so she could be the caregiver Duff needed her to be.

"I'm moving," Scout mumbled. Words still felt funny in her mouth. Like what she thought she was saying wasn't actually what people were hearing.

Lane gave her another push and then Samantha was walking in step beside her. A limo was waiting for them. Roy Walker was waiting for them there.

"She holding up?" he asked his wife.

Lane was Roy's wife.

So crazy, Scout thought. They'd married…
what was it…only six weeks ago? Lane always said she hated Roy Walker, but Scout
had known. She'd always seen the truth between them.

"She's moving, which is good," Lane said
to him. "Let's get her in the car."

"Stop talking about me like I'm not here!"
Scout snapped.

She knew she wasn't herself. Fine. But everyone was treating her as if she was somehow different from her two sisters, who had
also lost their father. Different from everyone else who had been at the funeral and was
grieving.

Why were they doing that?

"It's the drugs," Samantha explained to
Roy and Lane.

Drugs. Of course. That's why she felt this
way. Numb and foggy. As if she had no power
over her mind and body.

"You drugged me?" She asked the question
of Samantha, but she could see Lane wince.

"Honey, you needed something," Lane
said, apparently defending what had obviously been Sam's call. "It's just a Valium to
relax you. Now come on. Let's get you in
the car."

They had drugged her. Her sisters had done that. Scout planned to be very angry about that as soon as she could think again.

"Was *she* here?" Scout asked suddenly suspicious of everything. Now that she knew she'd been drugged, who knew what kind of evil her sisters intended. "Yes," Samantha said matter-of-factly. "I told you she would be."

"I don't want to see her," Scout said.

"Too bad, Elizabeth," a woman from inside the limo said. "I'm your mother and, whether you realize it or not, you need me right now."

Scout shook her head. "Did someone just call me Elizabeth?"

A leg, then a body and then a head got out of the car. Suddenly Alice formerly-Baker-now-Sullivan was standing in front of Scout. The traitorous mother she didn't want to see.

Not today of all days.

She hadn't been able to stop her mother from calling these past few months. Not that Scout had had much to say to her. It seemed Duff had, though, because they'd spoken a lot.

"Yes, I called you Elizabeth. Because it's what I named you. Now let's get in the car and do this thing. You look like you could

drop at any moment. Have you eaten anything in the past four days?"

Scout looked directly at Samantha. "I'm
going to need more drugs."

Samantha had the nerve to smile.

They all got into the limo and Scout made
a point of sitting across from her mother so
she wouldn't have to touch her, but that made
it difficult not to look at her.

She'd caught a break when Alice and Bob
had been in Europe and couldn't make it for
Lane's wedding. Scout gave her mother some
credit for not causing Lane any grief over the
speedy wedding, knowing it had been important to her for Duff to see his middle child
marry.

As a result she hadn't seen her mother in
almost two years. Not since the last time Duff
had forced her to go visit. Those visits would
always end with Scout leaving early because
the sad truth was, she and her mother had
nothing to say to each other.

Alice was still beautiful for a woman in her
sixties. Duff had married later in life, and he
always said it was because he'd been waiting for Alice to grow up. He used to say he
wanted to marry the prettiest girl he ever saw

and it just took fate and time awhile for them to meet.

"Was she in the limo on the way to the grave site? Did I somehow miss that?" Scout asked Lane, trying to understand how she was now in a car with her mother. Her mother, who she had been hoping to avoid for as long as she could.

"Don't be ridiculous," Alice said. "Bob drove me to the funeral and will meet up with me at the stadium. I just couldn't tolerate seeing you standing there so lost. I thought driving over to the stadium with you would be best. I'm sure I'll say something to anger you, which might give you the jolt of energy you need. You look positively frightening, Elizabeth."

Raging anger cleared away her drug-hazed state. Her mother was right. "Don't call me Elizabeth," Scout growled. "You know I hate it."

"Yes. You do." Her mother sighed. "I'm sorry, Scout. I'm truly not here to make this day harder for you. I'm here because you need me."

Scout snorted. "I do not need you. I do not need anyone. Apparently all I need is some Valium."

"Look, guys," Sam said, "can we not do this now? We're all grieving, and we're all sad. Let's just get through the rest of this day together."

"Why is Mom sad?" Scout wanted to know. "She left Duff for *Bob*. Bob isn't dead."

Alice closed her eyes as if she were searching for inner strength. It was a look Scout knew well because she was the one who often put that expression on her mother's face.

"I know this is hard for you to believe but I did love your father for a very long time. We just couldn't make it work. We're not the first couple in history to have that happen and we won't be the last. You're twenty-nine years old. Not a child. It's time for you to understand that and grow up."

Scout shook her head. "I'm sorry...was someone saying something just then? I am, like, really messed up."

"Play your games, Scout. It won't matter to me. I'm not going anywhere and you're going to figure that out very quickly."

"Why not, when I so desperately want you to go?"

"Because I'm the only parent you have left. Deal with it."

Scout had something to say in retaliation

but the words got lost in the fog. The sadness was back.

Duff was gone.

And nothing was ever going to be the same.

JAYSON LEBEC STOOD back a little from the crowd gathering at the entrance to the stadium as mourners continued to arrive. Seats and tables had been set up. A full lunch service had been catered. Many mingled on the baseball diamond to talk about one thing and one thing only and that was the late great Duff Baker.

In some ways it still seemed surreal that Jayson was back here in Minotaur Falls. That he was now the manager of the town's Triple A baseball club and filling the shoes Duff had left empty.

"Hey, I know you. You're the Face Guy."

Jayson turned at the use of his infamous baseball name and saw Reuben, the general manager of the Rebels, and Greg, the new head of scouting. Greg was pointing at him and smiling.

"I'm right, aren't I?" Greg asked.

He was. It was Jayson's claim to fame in baseball. In his debut game in the majors he'd run down a fly ball as hard as he could and lost track of his position on the field. He ended up slamming face-first into the right outfield wall. The harsh part was that the padding that should have offered some protection had fallen off in that particular spot so his face had made direct contact with the brick behind it.

The brick won. His face lost. He did, however, manage to hold on to the ball.

The doctors had to induce a coma to allow his brain to heal. Then came the job of the plastic surgeons putting his face back together. In total, he'd had five different surgeries.

Of course, because of some lingering aftereffects like dizziness and blurred vision, he would never play again. Which was why he didn't actually like being called the Face Guy.

But in baseball once you had a nickname, it stuck.

"Jayson LeBec," Jayson said holding out his hand. He knew Greg by reputation as a former Major League pitcher. Greg was older, probably in his midfifties, and had been long gone from the game by the time Jayson arrived.

"Greg Adamson," Greg said as he shook his hand. "I guess we're both new to the Rebels organization."

"Actually, Jayson has been with us for some time, haven't you? He's just new to this job, but he's been a loyal Rebel for many years. Isn't that right?" Reuben said.

"That's right. Almost five years now." Jayson wasn't sure why but he felt as if Reuben's use of the word loyal had some other meaning behind it. As if Reuben wanted to assure himself that he still had Jayson's loyalty over anyone else.

"Couldn't be happier to have both of you as part of the team," Reuben said congenially. "My, this is some turnout. Duff would have been pleased."

"Yeah. He would have," Jayson said around a sudden lump in his throat.

"I understand you know his daughter Scout Baker personally," Greg said casually. He took a sip from the beer in his hand.

Jayson looked over to where he'd last seen Scout standing. She was still there with Lane's arm around her waist, as if Lane was holding her up, while people approached to offer their condolences.

"I do. Yes."

"I've heard some things about her," Reuben said. "From the players. Seems like she was holding things together down here for a long time. A very long time."

Jayson wasn't absolutely sure how to respond to that. He knew it was true, but he couldn't get a read on whether Reuben was being complimentary or not.

"I wouldn't know. I wasn't here then."

"I was sort of surprised by how young she is," Greg said. "I mean, a woman baseball scout, that's odd enough. But still in her twenties? Don't you think that's crazy?"

Jayson didn't like the smile on the man's face. Like Scout's position on the Rebels was some kind of joke. "She learned the game of baseball from Duff Baker starting at the age of five. I think that might make her more qualified than any other scout I know."

"Of course," Reuben said, patting Jayson on the shoulder. "Poor thing, though, losing her father. You let her know I said to take all the time she needs to recover. There is absolutely no need to come rushing back."

"Yep," Greg agreed. "No need at all. My team has everything covered. Can we get you a drink, Jayson?"

Jayson held up his still clearly full beer. "No, I'm good."

"Well, we'll see you around, then," Greg

said. "Reuben, come and introduce me to more of the players."

With a knot in his stomach, Jayson watched them walk off. It had been an innocent enough conversation. Nothing to worry over. Certainly nothing he was going to share with Scout. Reuben had been sympathetic. And the truth was Scout was going to need time.

Heck, Jayson thought he could use some time for his own grieving. Although for now he couldn't think about what losing the man who had been his mentor, the man who had given him a second chance at a career in baseball, meant to him. Couldn't let his sadness take over.

He needed to stay in control for her. Scout Baker, his ex-girlfriend.

He looked to where she stood again. She had a glass of water in her hand and a strange look on her face. If he were being truly honest she almost looked high. It wasn't unreasonable to think her sisters might have given her some kind of tranquilizer. Just to get her through the day.

Or to get her through the day and having to see and talk to her mother. Yes, drugs were definitely necessary for that. Jayson remembered well exactly what Scout thought of her mother. If she talked about her at all, it was usually with the word *traitor* thrown into the mix.

It used to make him sad. As a boy who loved his mother dearly he hurt for her that she didn't have that kind of a relationship. When they were together he remembered thinking that it was something he might be able to give her some perspective on. Being loyal to Duff didn't necessarily mean she had to freeze out her mother.

It didn't have to be all or nothing.

Then he'd gotten his job offer in Texas and he'd learned firsthand that when it came down to a choice between Duff and anyone else in Scout's life, that other person was going to lose.

Which had made every day since he'd come back to this town, back into her life, nearly impossible for him. Even now that it was over he didn't have the strength to walk away from her. He couldn't leave her when he knew the level of suffering she was going through, but he also couldn't open himself up too much to her.

She might seek him out, she might need his comfort, but Jayson would never have her whole heart. He could only ever be the second most important man in her life. With Duff gone now, there would be no way to ever prove otherwise.

So as much as she might need him, as much as he wanted to help her, he had to protect himself from getting his heart crushed all over again.

Four years. Four flipping years and still she was the only one he thought about having a future with. He'd dated. He'd screwed. He'd done everything he could to exorcise her.

Nothing had worked.

When he got the job offer to come back to Minotaur Falls it had felt as if he'd run into a wall with his face a second time. A physical pain. The first thought he had wasn't that this was yet another rung on the ladder he was climbing to get back to the Major Leagues, but that if he took it, he was going to see Scout again.

Four years and she was the first thing he thought about. Which was why he'd turned down the job offer. Until Duff had called and asked him personally to come back. Then Jayson had had no choice. There was nothing he wouldn't have done for Duff. Nothing.

Including seeing Scout again.

He'd hoped seeing her again would be the

thing to cure him. To make her less of a memory and more of a reality. That he'd built their connection up in his head and put it on a pedestal it didn't really deserve.

That initial encounter with her had been brutal. He'd taken one look at her and known to the soles of his feet that he still wasn't over her.

He'd asked her about Duff and she'd gotten defensive and then he'd found himself mad all over again. Mad because she'd chosen to stay in Minotaur Falls instead of leaving with him. She had told him she couldn't leave her father. That he needed her. Which was probably true, but Jayson had always known there was something else holding her back.

It wasn't just her life here and her father that held her back. It was fear.

She hadn't been willing to take that risk on him. On them. To reach for something and try to see if it could be as special as Jayson knew it could be. That lack of faith had crushed him. Almost as much as not being the one she chose above all. It should have also crushed his feelings for her but it hadn't. Because he knew Scout was just scared.

Hard to hate someone who was so scared.

"You're Jayson LeBec?"

Jayson turned toward the person calling his name. His real name, so not a baseball person obviously.

He'd never been introduced to Alice Sullivan, but he didn't need anyone to tell him that this was Scout's mother. Same honey-wheat hair, same green eyes. It probably irked Scout to know how much she looked exactly like her mother.

"Yes, ma'am."

"I'm told you broke my daughter's heart."

Jayson laughed. He had often wondered where Scout got her bluntness. Duff had been corny phrases and subtle innuendo. Not Scout. She was in your face with what she thought. He loved that about her. He always knew where he stood.

"Forgive me for being so blunt, ma'am, but so did you."

"I know." Alice sighed. "That's why I was hoping maybe we could be friends. We both know what it's like to be on the opposite side of team Duff and Scout."

"I'm not sure Scout would like that too much." In fact, Jayson was nervous just talking with the woman. If Scout saw them together it would layer on the pain, and he wanted to ease her hurt, not add to it.

"Probably not, but I think we both know she needs someone right now. I'm going to try to fight through her stubbornness and see if that person can be me. I was curious if you thought it could be you. Samantha said you wouldn't leave her side at the end."

"I couldn't," Jayson said and felt the grief overcome him. Standing there by Duff's bed-side watching him drift away. Feeling his pain, her pain. Watching the separation be-tween them grow.

But he'd made a promise.

"I'll…I'll do what I can. But it's not like I can be… I mean I can't be anything more than a friend to her. If she even wants that. She's let me hang around the house these last few months, but I think that's mostly because she couldn't spare the energy to tell me to leave."

"Hmm," Alice said, looking at him, clearly assessing him. He reminded her of Scout when she was checking out a new prospect. As if she could figure out if a kid could hit a curveball just by seeing how he stood. "I see."

"See what exactly, ma'am?"

"You didn't break her heart like Duff said. She broke yours."

Jayson nodded. "She's still breaking it."

"I know how that feels, son." Alice patted him on the arm. "I truly do. The thing about my daughter…when things get difficult, she likes to hide. With something like this I'm afraid she'll hide so deep no one will ever find her again. I know she's hurt you, but I think, Jayson, you might be her only hope. She's going to need someone who knows her tricks, someone who knows them and still loves her for them, if she has a chance of coming out of this. I know that's an awful thing to ask. But I'm her mother so I'm asking it anyway."

"You don't have to, ma'am. Duff already did."

Alice smiled. "Of course he did. Of course he did. Well, I imagine I'll be seeing you around then, Jayson."

"You're not heading back home after this is over?" Jayson asked. That was probably news Scout didn't know.

"Depends which home you mean. My current home, no. The home I used to have…yes. Whether she likes it or not."

Jayson whistled under his breath.

"You might think my daughter is stubborn," Alice said with a slightly evil smile. "But I'm worse."

As she turned and walked away, Jayson thought these next few weeks were probably going to get very interesting.

CHAPTER TWO

Two weeks later...

"I'M READY TO WORK."

Jayson looked up from his desk and shook his head. Scout hadn't even bothered to knock. Just opened his door and walked right in with her announcement.

Like this was still Duff's office and not his.

This transition for her was not going to be fun, he thought, but he knew if they were going to live in the same town, going forward there were going to have to be boundaries.

He needed boundaries.

The season was now officially over and he was just putting his last player evaluation forms together. Not that he would take the next few months off. Even in the off-season Jayson liked to stay involved with the stadium and its activities. He found that it connected him more solidly with the team.

Jerry, the team's general manager, and his

staff would work pretty much year-round until the start of the new season. Making concession stand changes, planning different local events and, most important, trying to figure out new and creative ways to fill the seats.

But for the players' manager there wasn't a whole lot to do other than study scouting prospects and give feedback on the upcoming draft next June. To that end Jayson had set up a tryout camp, which would start in the next few weeks. They were usually long shots, but he liked being proactive.

"Did you hear me?"

"You mean what you said after you barged into my office without knocking?"

She had the sense to look sheepish. "Sorry about that."

Jayson decided boundaries were really the least of his concerns. She was his priority.

"Scout, I don't think you are ready to work."

She was standing in front of him in a pair of ripped jeans and a stained T-shirt. Her hair looked as if it hadn't seen a brush in days, and the bags under her eyes were nearly black. He didn't need to guess that she hadn't eaten or slept in days. It was all there on her face, but he could see she'd sworn off the drugs. Her green eyes were clear and focused.

Knowing Scout, she wouldn't have wanted to take anything that might have diluted her pain. No doubt she would have thought she was being disloyal to Duff by not grieving him hard enough.

It made him ache, but he knew deep inside he had to hold himself back a little. For example, he couldn't get up and walk around his desk and hold her. He couldn't try to help shoulder the burden of her grief for her.

He would look after her, make sure she was still upright. Because he'd promised to do that. But it was as far as he could go.

Or it would happen again, like it did the first time. He'd fall for her. Hard. Jayson was fairly certain he'd never survive a second round.

"No, I can do it. We've got the tryout camp coming up in a few weeks and I should be there. Not to mention high school fall ball is starting. The Rebels are going to want me out at games."

"I talked to Greg and Reuben. They were at Duff's service, of course. Reuben said to give you all the time you needed."

Jayson didn't want to think about the

underlying tone of that conversation. Scout didn't need anything else to worry about in her current state.

Scout's jaw dropped. "Wait a minute. You talked to Greg? My new boss? What right did you have to do that?"

Jayson just looked at her and she immediately backed down.

"Okay, I appreciate you covering for me for these last two weeks, but I'm telling you I'm ready to get out there and start working. Even if I'm not ready, I still need to get out there and start working."

He leaned back in his chair. Scout moved forward to put her hands on his desk.

"Jayson, my mother isn't leaving. She's staying in my house. She's unpacked suitcases, filled up dresser drawers. I don't think she has any plans to go home. Neither does Samantha, for that matter. She just keeps waving her phone in my face and telling me she can work from anywhere. Do you know what this is doing to me?"

"They're trying to help you," he reminded her. "They are your family and they love you despite all the drama of the past. If you would stop being so stubborn, you might see that.

You might realize that we're all of us here for you, Scout."

She grimaced and crossed her arms over her chest. Typical Scout defense mode.

"I don't need their help. There is nothing anyone can do. He's gone. There is no bringing him back. What are they going to do? Wave some magic wand and fix me? They can't. I'm broken and that's all there is. But I've still got two eyes and two ears and I'll know if a sixteen-year-old hitter has the stuff."

Jayson did stand then and walk around his desk. He tried not to feel hurt when she took a deliberate step back. Sometimes when he was around her he felt like his skin was laced with some kind of poison, that the merest touch might kill her.

"Scout, you're not eating, you don't sleep. You're not…strong enough to be out on the road day in and day out. I won't let you do it."

That apparently was not the correct thing to say. For a man walking a tightrope, mistakes like that could be fatal.

"You won't *let* me?" she screeched.

And there it was. It was one of Scout's least attractive traits. When she was angry, truly angry, her voice would rise five octaves until she sounded, as her sister Lane so accurately described it, like a howler monkey.

"Let. Me," she screeched again.

"Scout, calm down."

"You don't get to *let* me do anything. Am I or am I not a member of the New England Rebels scouting team?"

She was. The decision had been made by the Rebels prior to Duff's death. Scout was to take a sabbatical to care for her dying father, but when she was ready to return she would go back to her old job of scouting, reporting directly to Greg.

He really couldn't stop her from working if that was what she wanted.

"I'm broken and that's all there is."

Finally, she'd said it, Jayson thought. As if she was never not going to be broken.

That's why I brought you here, son. You've got to fix her.

Jayson shook his head. He hated when that happened. When his subconscious called up these sentences, which sounded in his head as if Duff were talking directly to him. Which of course was ridiculous because he was dead.

Jayson's very Catholic mother would have said it was Duff talking to him from heaven.

Either way it mostly scared the crap out of him.

"Answer me!"

Yep. Full-on howler monkey.

"You are."

"Then I get to determine when I go back to work, and I say I'm ready to go back now. I'm going to call Greg and let him know myself."

"Fine. Then why did you even come down here? You obviously weren't asking for my opinion."

"Because…"

He took some satisfaction in that. She'd come down to tell him because she did want his blessing. Maybe his support, too. She couldn't help herself.

In the months leading up to Duff's death, he and Scout had basically called a time-out on their own personal drama. Neither really had the energy to deal with what they'd once meant to each other and the anger that was still there on both sides four years later. He'd been this quiet presence in her life and she'd let him be there.

In the past two weeks, though, it seemed like that temporary freeze was beginning to thaw. Scout was getting pricklier and more defensive. For his part, that tightrope was getting harder and harder to walk.

They gravitated toward each other. They couldn't seem to help it. He went to her house, she came to his. Sometimes to cry, sometimes to talk.

Never to touch. Touching was clearly forbidden.

Jayson knew why she'd really come to the stadium. She couldn't help herself and it made him feel he wasn't alone in his suffering.

Gravity. It was a hell of thing.

"I didn't think about it... I just figured I would let you know," she said softly as if realizing there was no legitimate reason to tell him about her decision to return to work. "I'll call Greg."

Again Jayson felt this heavy throb of pain. He couldn't let her do this, but he wasn't going to be able to stop her, either.

"Hey, can I tag along with you on your first few outings? I'll make sure you're doing the necessary things like eating and sleeping and at the same time I can keep myself busy. You know I hate this period."

She smiled. "Some people look forward to a little downtime in the off-season."

"I'm not one of them."

She paused for a second, as if considering her options, but then she nodded. "It might be good to have company. I get a little crazy in my head when I'm by myself. Probably the only reason I haven't kicked out Mom and Bob. Bob! Can you believe it? Him staying in Duff's house of all places."

"He's not a bad guy," Jayson told her. "Did you know he was with your mom before she met Duff? He was actually a navy SEAL. He was being sent off to some hotspot for an undisclosed duration. He didn't want your mom to wait so he decided to break up with her before he left."

Scout just stared at him. "Who told you that?"

She probably wasn't going to like this either, but it was time Jayson stopped hiding that he disagreed with Scout's decision to shun her mother. Family was family and she needed all of hers. That Alice had managed to get her foot in the door at Scout's house and keep it there meant maybe Scout somehow was aware of it, too.

"I was talking to him after the funeral. Your mom, too, for that matter. You two are a lot alike."

"We are not! She's a cheater and I can't believe you would take their side."

"There are no sides here, Scout."

"Yes, there are. Theirs and mine. You get that better than anyone and now you are choosing their side. Great, just great!"

He could see the tears in her eyes and the hysteria building. In two steps he was in front of her, his hands around her upper arms, shaking her a little and forcing her to look at him.

"Scout, I'm here for you. For *you*. And I'm not going anywhere. Got it?"

She looked right into his eyes in a way that always made his insides tighten. As if she was seeing straight through him.

"Until you leave me again. Yeah," she said pulling away from him. "I got it."

There it was. The final second of their time-out just ticked on the clock.

The past was back.

Which meant so was the pain.

Five years ago...

SCOUT WAS STILL trying to process the fact that Jayson LeBec's tongue was in her mouth. Man, he tasted good. Like sparkling water

STEPHANIE DOYLE   41

that bubbled as she drank it and made her whole body want to squirm.

The wedding of the owner of the Minotaurs, Jocelyn Taft, and the town's head sports writer—only sports writer, really—Pete Wright, was still going strong, but Scout and Jayson had decided there were other things they would rather be doing.

This night had been perfect, Scout thought. Executed one hundred percent according to plan. She'd had a crush on Jayson since the day he showed up in Minotaur Falls after her father asked him to come join the team.

Maybe before that…when she saw him as a player run smack-dab into a brick wall just to catch a fly ball. That act had captured Duff's attention certainly. He believed that someone who loved baseball so much, even if his playing career was over, should still be part of the game.

Scout was tasked with teaching Jayson everything she knew, starting with assessing the talent. The two began doing some scouting for the Rebels, and Scout knew from the moment they'd shared a three-hour car ride talking easily the whole way that Jayson was going to be someone special.

Scout had never been able to talk to boys

when she was a young girl. She couldn't really talk to men now that she was a woman.

But Jayson was different.

Which was why this wedding had been the perfect opportunity to ask him out without really asking him out. If he didn't like her, she could say she had asked him as a friend. If he did like her…

Well, then the world would be a perfect place.

In traditional Scout fashion she hadn't been subtle about her interest. The nerves of being with him while he was looking so handsome, when she'd done everything she could to look as good as she could, finally caught up with her.

"So what's the deal? Do you like me or not?"

Incredibly, the answer had been yes. Incredibly, if she hadn't asked him to the wedding, then apparently he would have asked her. Incredibly, he'd been liking her the whole time she'd been liking him.

That never happened to her!

Except it had with Jayson and now they were back in his hotel room. They had each gotten rooms at the hotel next to the venue so that they could drink and enjoy the night without worrying about driving home. Now it looked as if they were only going to need one room.

A thought that immediately took Scout out of her body and put her back firmly in her head.

"Hold on," she huffed. Things were spiraling out of her control so fast she actually felt dizzy.

Jayson took a step back and smiled. "I know, right? This is crazy. I've never felt this…needy. Wait, that was wrong. I don't want you to think… I mean we don't have to do this, Scout. We've got all the time in the world."

"No! I want to do this. I've been wanting to do this for a long time. With you."

Jayson stepped toward her again, and Scout was both excited and scared. So scared she took a step back.

Jayson tilted his head in that way he did, as if she was amusing him. After all, she'd just told him she wanted to have sex with him and then she'd moved away from him. Who did that?

"Are we going to do this the easy way or the hard way?"

He said that to her anytime they were on the road and she would start to get ornery about when and where they were going to eat. He liked steak places, she preferred fried food. When it came time to actually decide on a place he would always ask her, "Are we going to do this the easy way or the hard way?"

Her answer was always the hard way because that would make him groan and that would make her smile.

Given the circumstances she didn't think that was a very good answer.

Sex and hard. No, she wasn't really ready for that. She should probably tell him this would be her first time, but instinctively she knew that if she did that would freak him out. After all she was twenty-four soon to be twenty-five. Who stayed a virgin that long? Then they would have to talk about it, and he would be self-conscious about it and it would ruin the whole night.

It made more sense to just do it. She adored Jayson. She was hot for Jayson. His kiss alone had aroused her more than anything she could remember in her life, and apparently she wasn't the only one affected.

"Let's do this…the best way." She took a step toward him and rested a hand over his heart. She could feel how fast it was beating and that made her smile. She had done that to him.

Then he was kissing her again and once more she left her head and felt only her body. Her whole body when he pressed against her, her nipples when he lifted a hand to hold her breast, her belly when his erection pressed into her.

It was perfect.

Until it all went wrong.

Present

SCOUT WALKED IN through the kitchen and stopped when she saw Bob sitting at the table, drinking a cup of what she imagined was coffee and reading the paper. Her paper.

"Hey, Scout," he said casually without looking up from said paper.

"Hello, Bob," she said stiffly.

"I just made a pot of coffee if you want some."

She did want some. She was exhausted. What Jayson had said about not sleeping was true. She was determined to stay away from the sleeping pills, though. For that first week it had been too easy to take them and wonder if she would never have to wake up again. Duff would have been furious if he knew she'd even entertained such thoughts.

Which of course she didn't. Not really.

So she skipped the pills and dealt with all the stuff that was in her head keeping her up at night. Which meant at three in the afternoon she was about ready to collapse. A cup of coffee would go a long way toward getting her through the rest of the day.

It was the idea of taking anything from Bob that stopped her.

Although technically she had bought the coffee. So really it wasn't as if she was taking anything from him.

"Thanks," she said in the same tone that she always used with him. She'd met Bob when she was fourteen. Had lived with him and her mother for nine months until they all realized it just wasn't going to work out. So she knew to be polite and respectful because that's how she had been raised.

But hello, goodbye and thanks pretty much made up the bulk of any conversations between them.

Except today she'd learned something about him. Something she'd never known. He'd served in the military. Not only served but actually made it to the level of a navy

SEAL. She supposed it fit. Even for an older guy he was in super shape. Still, it never would have occurred to her to ask him any personal questions, so it's not like the topic would ever come up on its own.

Scout actively did not listen any time her mother even mentioned his name. He'd always just been Bob, the man her traitorous bitch of a mother left Duff for. Because of this man, her mother had hurt her father. It was probably odd that Scout didn't blame Bob more. How did she know he didn't seduce her mother? That her mother wasn't some helpless victim in the face of Bob's charm and physical appeal?

She didn't know. She didn't know anything about their relationship. Only that there was one while Alice had still been married to Duff. Which was wrong. Except now she knew that Alice and Bob had known each other even longer than Scout realized.

"Were you ever married before, Bob?"

To say that his expression was stunned would've been an understatement. It might have been the first full sentence he'd ever heard out of Scout.

"I mean before my mother..."

"I know what you mean," he said slowly.

He folded the paper he'd been reading carefully as if he were afraid any sudden movements would send Scout running like a frightened rabbit.

Scout was interested enough in the answer to sit at the table with him, her hands wrapped around her cup of coffee.

"No, I never married before your mother."

"How come? I mean you're a decent-looking guy now, so you were probably good-looking back in the day."

He smiled and when he did she could see that she was right. Bob had blue eyes and dark black hair peppered with silver. He practically wore the map of Ireland on his face. With his face and body he would have been a total babe.

"I'll take the compliment and say that this is a very strange day. You want the truth? The real story? Because you're probably not going to like it much."

Scout shrugged as if it didn't matter, but she did want the truth.

Her silence was answer enough.

"I never married anyone else because your mother was the love of my life. We were together for two years before I was called up on a particularly dangerous assignment. I thought, stupidly, that it would be easier if we weren't together. If something happened to me, then she wouldn't grieve as much. When I got back from my assignment, she was already with your father and had a baby. Finding someone else… I didn't see much of a point. Then fate brought us back together somehow."

Immediately Scout's back went up but Bob reached over to touch her arm.

"Hold on. Hear me out. This is the closest we've ever come to a real conversation about this. I know you blame your mother, and your mother alone, for her marriage to your father ending. But you have to know what happened between us wasn't some kind of sordid affair. We had history, your mother and I. And as much as it hurts you to hear it, she and Duff, they weren't happy together. She didn't understand his life and he wouldn't change it for her."

It didn't hurt to hear it as much as Scout thought it would. She'd probably been twelve years old when she had started to put it together that her mom and Duff weren't exactly a happy couple. When Duff called from the road, he spoke to his daughters first, then he would talk to Alice. When he was home, all his free time was spent with his daughters.

They never kissed in front of her, and they never held hands. They never went out, just the two of them. They only ever fought. About his schedule. His time away.

"You're a grown woman, Scout. It's time you stop holding a grudge against your mother and let her back into your life. You need her. Now more than ever."

She looked at his stern expression and wanted to tell him he had no business advising her on anything. He was nothing to her but the man who had married her mother.

A man who loved his mother so much no other woman had been able to take her place.

"I don't need anyone. Thanks for the coffee, Bob."

With that Scout left the kitchen and his advice behind her.

CHAPTER THREE

SAMANTHA STOOD IN the dining room listening to the exchange between Bob and Scout. She wasn't certain why she didn't want to interrupt. Her initial instinct was to step between them as a barrier between Bob and Scout's spite. Bob didn't deserve her sister's disdain. However, for the first time they were actually having a real conversation and Samantha thought she ought to give them their privacy.

Bob knew that Scout was in pain. He knew it because their mother told him and Samantha told him and Lane told him. And though he'd never forged a relationship with Scout, he would still try to do right by her because of his love for Alice.

"I don't need anyone. Thanks for the coffee, Bob."

And that sounded like Scout. She came out of the kitchen quickly, so Samantha tried to look as if she hadn't been eavesdropping, but she clearly failed.

"Lurk much?"

Samantha shook her head and sighed. "When are you going to grow up, Scout? Bob is a good man and he doesn't need your attitude. That he's here for you should show you that."

"Forgot, that's right. You're on his side. It's why we don't speak, remember? So when are you going back to your big-time agenting life? Living out here in the sticks must be driving you insane."

Sam winced at the thought of her large, luxurious apartment in Chicago. Which was also very empty. "I'm not going until I know you're capable of taking care of yourself. Do you know there's a huge stain of something down the front of that shirt? Did you actually leave the house like that?"

Scout looked down at her shirt and frowned. At least there was some semblance of acknowledgment of her sad state. However, she recovered quickly and flipped Samantha the bird.

"And here I thought you might have stuck your tongue out at me," Samantha said, rolling her eyes.

Scout, continuing in the same childish vein, brushed by Samantha with a shoulder rub.

Samantha had already braced herself for it, a small reminder to her littler sister she was still the oldest.

Samantha joined Bob in the kitchen and helped herself to a cup of coffee, as she already knew it was fresh.

She sat down and looked at her mother's husband. The man who had come into her life when she was eighteen years old.

"Maybe...we need to tell her."

He raised an eyebrow and shook his head. "That girl is hanging on by a thread. You want to drop a bomb on her like that?"

"I want her to forgive Mom. I want her to finally see that not everything is as black and white as she thinks it is. If she can get her head around that and maybe let us back into her life, she has a chance of getting through this."

"You love her," Bob said, gently patting her hand.

"Of course I love her! I mean she makes me want to shake her more times than not, but I love her. And because I do, I'm worried about her. If you understood how completely her identity was tied to Duff..." Samantha shook her head. "I can't imagine being cut off so abruptly from who I thought I was."

"Can't you?"

Now it was Samantha's turn to raise an eyebrow. "It's not the same thing."

"You never told me how it was here these last few months. With you and Duff."

"He knew I loved him desperately." Samantha smiled sadly. "It was all that mattered to him in the end."

Bob nodded. "Of course it was."

"Yes," Samantha said. She thought to say more, but then she didn't.

Bob was right. It was too soon.

SCOUT MADE IT to her bedroom and shut the door. It was the only place she ever felt comfortable in her own home anymore. It hadn't been as bad when it was just Lane staying with her. But Lane and Roy had found a place on the other side of town and Lane had moved out right after the wedding. Which was fine because she'd been close enough to come by every day to take care of Duff with Scout.

Now her mother, Bob and Samantha were here and it didn't look like any of them had plans to leave anytime soon. As a result Scout was rarely alone unless she was in her room.

No one would dare enter Scout's lair against her wishes. Everyone knew she needed her sanctuary. A place where she could go to close out the world. Except now her head was filled with all kinds of crazy thoughts. About Duff and her mother and Bob and her mother.

She could easily stop thinking these crazy thoughts, of course, if she started thinking about Jayson.

Scout sat on her bed, stared up at the ceiling and thought about what tomorrow was going to be like. Driving with Jayson, sitting next to him on the bleachers while the two of them watched some kid play. Desperate to impress them.

Just like old times. When they were falling in love.

Scout wasn't a psychiatrist, but she was pretty sure this trip was not going to be good for her mental health.

She thought about how she'd left him today. Reminding him that she was still upset with him even after four years. Maybe what they really needed was to sit down and have an honest conversation. She could effectively express why she was so upset with him for leaving and he could once again ask her why she hadn't been willing to go with him.

Seven months. They had been dating for seven months and he wanted her to uproot her life, quit her job and leave her father to follow him to Texas. He told her to take a risk. A risk on them.

Didn't he know she'd already taken the biggest risk of her life on him? Didn't he know what it took for her to ask him to go the wedding? To spend the night with him. To slowly and eventually give him her heart.

At the time it felt as if it was all she was capable of. He should have known that. He should have known her. He should have stayed.

"Tomorrow is going to blow," she said to her empty room. Then she made a mental note to actually look in the mirror before she left for work.

THEY HAD AGREED to meet at nine in the morning but they hadn't said where. So it wasn't exactly surprising when Scout came downstairs to find Jayson sitting at the kitchen table with Samantha, drinking a cup of coffee and eating a bagel Samantha had probably made for him.

Toasting was the only culinary skill Sam had so she liked to show it off whenever she could.

"I was going to text you to just meet me at the stadium," Scout mumbled. She hated how comfortable he looked sitting at her table. Eating her food. She hated how it reminded her how common it was for him to be around the house back when they were dating.

Which was sort of strange now that she thought about it. He had had his own place, a nice apartment over one of the clothing stores on Main Street. They had been young and in love and having sex all the time, which, considering she lived with her father, should have meant she was always at his place.

But she rarely stayed there. Sometimes when Duff was away on a road trip. Every once in a while Jayson used to grumble about it, but because he never seemed to mind hanging around her house she never changed her behavior.

There was also the Duff factor. Jayson loved her father. Anytime they got together it was like watching a kid meet Santa Claus for the first time. Because Duff had also taken on the role as Jayson's mentor, there was never a lull in their conversation. Jayson wanted to absorb all of Duff's baseball knowledge. All of hers, as well.

So it made sense that when they hung out, they hung out at her house, where Duff might or might not be, instead of at his apartment alone. Didn't it?

"I didn't want you to change your mind and leave without me."

"I wouldn't have done that." Scout grumbled some more, but if she was being honest that was exactly what she'd been thinking when she woke up. Just get in her car and go without him. What would he do? Follow her? Mostly likely not.

"Besides, free bagel and coffee. Best deal I'm going to get today."

"I toasted," Samantha proclaimed.

Scout just shook her head and poured a cup of coffee. Then she added as much sugar to it as she could and still call it coffee with sugar, rather than sugar with coffee.

"That's too much sugar," Alice said as she walked into the kitchen. She was dressed in a long satin blue robe, but somehow still made it look elegant.

"Great. The gang's all here," Scout muttered.

"You shouldn't put that much sugar in your coffee. It's not good for you."

It was an old refrain from her mother, who was always harping at her daughters to eat better. Scout couldn't count how many times they would argue over it.

"Don't put too much sugar on your cereal, Scout. It will rot your teeth."

"Duff always lets me put as much as I want."

"Well, he's not here. I am."

He wasn't here. She was.

Scout added another spoonful of the sweet granules to her coffee just out of spite. And she smiled as she took a sip even though she had to acknowledge she had crossed the coffee-with-sugar barrier.

"You can continue to be as difficult as you want to be. But I still love you and I'm not going anywhere. Good morning, Jayson."

"Ma'am," he said, nodding his head.

Alice sat and addressed Jayson. "I understand my daughter is going back to work today."

"She is."

"You'll watch over her."

"Oh, for Pete's sake!" Scout shouted, slamming her mug on the counter. "I'm not an invalid, people. I'm grieving. It sucks but I'm moving on. It's bad enough Jayson has to babysit me. I don't need you trying to go all 'caring mom' on me."

At that point Bob also joined them. He was freshly showered and dressed and he kissed his wife on the cheek before looking at Scout.

"She is a caring mom. You should try letting her be that with you sometime. You might like it."

"Pretty doubtful, Bob," Scout said, turning her back on both of them. "Are you ready? I need to go."

Jayson picked up the remainder of his bagel and brought his cup over to the sink. "Thanks for breakfast, Sam. Ma'am, Bob."

Scout didn't bother with saying goodbye or letting them know when she planned to be back. It wasn't as if they were going to sit around and have some kind of family dinner. Scout still could barely handle food. It hadn't been an issue when her day consisted of lying in her bed and crying. Not a whole lot of calories burned that way.

However, today she was actually going to work. She was going to sit outside in the fresh air and breathe it in. Maybe that would help her appetite. Maybe she was even ready to put her brain toward something that wasn't thinking about how her life was over without Duff.

With that they left the kitchen and walked

down the driveway to her car, except she stopped and Jayson kept walking.

To his car.

It was a nice car. A BMW 3 Series he'd bought when he'd signed his first major contract. It was red and slick and had been the love of his life until he'd met her.

"You don't seriously think I'm letting you drive?" he asked.

"You never had a problem letting me drive before."

"Scout, you've been a zombie for two weeks. I can't trust you to keep your attention on the road. We've got a good four-hour drive ahead of us."

He was right. She'd driven to the grocery store and had almost caused an accident when her mind had started to wander. She walked to him and thought about how it was going to feel getting into his car again. If it was going to smell like him and leather and mint because Jayson was a mint gum fanatic.

"I think I might have hit my head," she said as a way to distract herself. Yes, just the feeling of sliding into the passenger seat brought back the memory of every time they had gone out. Including that first time, to Pete and Jocelyn's wedding. She'd been excited that night.

So filled with anticipation it had practically lifted her off the ground.

"Huh?"

"I've been fuzzy with things lately and I think at some point I fell and hit my head. You know, when...he died."

Jayson looked at her. "You don't remember if you fell?"

"I know, right? That's why I think I hit my head. My memory is like totally blank from that day."

He was looking at her funny. As if he knew something she didn't. Then he just shook his head. "I think you would know if you hit your head. You would have a bump."

True. She'd actually felt around for one, but there was nothing. "It's just that I sort of remember falling. When it happened. But you're right, I would have a bump. Do you know where we're going?"

He took out his phone and placed it in the console section of the car. "Yeah, I put the address into the phone."

Scouting made easy through technology. Just plug in an address and let the GPS plot a route. Scout wondered how the old guys used to track down high schools all over the country.

Jayson looked over at her before he started the car. His smile was faintly nostalgic, and she knew he could feel it, too. The past was reaching out to grab them both and remind them what they used to be once upon a time.

"Just drive," she said. "And no talking. It's the only way I'm going to get through this."

"Yes, ma'am."

With that she turned on the radio to a sports talk station and for hours they listened while grown men called in to fight with the hosts about anything and everything related to sports.

When they reached the first stop, they parked and found the baseball diamond. "Who are we here for?" Jayson asked as they took their seats in the bleachers.

They had made it with plenty of time to spare, even after stopping for lunch along the way. The game was to start immediately after the school day ended at three. Right now they could see some of the players take batting practice on the field.

"Ronny Wells. He's seventeen and apparently has the stuff. Greg emailed me a profile of him when I let him know I was coming back to work. It seems the kid's not sure if he wants to go into the draft or go to college.

Greg wants me to determine if I think he's ready for the minors."

"That's good," Jayson said.

"What's good?" Scout asked him.

Jayson shook his head. "Nothing, just that it's good Greg is trusting you with this assignment."

"Uh, duh, it's sort of my job."

"Right." Jayson smiled.

They watched the team gather around a man in the middle of the field. Scout assumed it was the team's coach. There was some laughing and guffawing and then finally the man emerged from the pile of teenagers.

"Fine, but I'm only doing this to humor you all," they heard the coach say with a smile.

Curious what his team was asking him to do, Scout watched while the man picked up a bat and then got into the batter's box. The catcher didn't bother to set up behind him. The kids then circled the mechanical pitcher.

"How fast do you want it, coach?"

It was obvious the team had done this before. Obvious the coach knew what they wanted him to say.

"Bring the heat," he told them.

"Ninety-five!"

"Ninety-five," Jayson muttered.

"Yeah, wow. That's as fast as that machine will throw. That guy doesn't have a shot."

The first ball out of the machine got knocked over the fence in the outfield. And so did the one after that. And the one after that. And the one after that.

"Are you seeing what I'm seeing?" Jayson asked her.

Scout was seeing it. She was hearing it, too. Pure contact, hit after hit. The man had a flawless swing. "How old do you think he is?"

"Maybe a few years younger than us. Maybe not."

Eventually the coach's hitting display was over and the other team arrived. Scout took her notebook out and started doing her job on the kid. He was definitely a solid prospect, but she didn't think he warranted a high enough draft position to sway him from going to college.

Given his evident frustration at the loss of the game, which resulted in him knocking over the Gatorade cooler, Scout thought college might help a kid like this mature. Baseball wasn't always just about physical abilities. A lot of it had to do with what was between the ears. Especially when it came to pitchers.

They descended the bleachers and made their way over to the dugout. The coach came out to greet them.

"Here to see Ronny?" he asked.

"How did you guess?" Scout said.

"It's a small town. I know all the parents. When I spot strangers, I assume they're from the MLBSB."

The scouting bureau was a secondary source of scouting information a lot of the clubs used. Sometimes it was hard for one team of scouts to cover the country. The bureau hired scouts simply to track players and log data for any team to access.

"We're from the Rebels," Scout said, not bothering to mention that Jayson was really just along for the ride. Not to mention that sometimes when the coaches or fathers realized she was the scout, and obviously a woman, they immediately discounted her. It never bothered her, considering the coach or father wasn't the one she was coming to see.

"He's definitely got stuff," the coach said.

"He does." Scout agreed but didn't go into too much detail. It was her opinion that a coach would always try to sell their kid hard, regardless of what they truly thought.

"So we were watching you hit before. That machine really throw ninety-five?"

The man smiled and it made Scout think he was even younger than she guessed. "It does. I can hit a mean fastball."

"Ever play pro ball?"

"Nope. I was a football player in college. Just not big enough to make it in the pros as a tight end, so I fell back on what I went to school for, which was teaching. The school needed a baseball coach, so I learned everything I could about the game and here I am. Never knew I could hit a serious fastball until I started taking batting practice."

He laughed through this story as if it was a joke. Some oddball discovery of a talent he never knew he had. What Scout heard, however, was that the guy was a football player who had had pro-level athleticism. It wouldn't be the weirdest baseball discovery story she'd ever heard.

"How old are you?" Scout asked bluntly.

He squinted at her.

"Twenty-seven," he said finally. "Why?"

Scout looked at Jayson. She probably shouldn't have. This was her call, her job. But when they had been working together she and Jayson had always seemed to share a brain.

He always knew where she was going, so it wasn't as if she ever had to explain herself. Then he could provide his feedback without her having to ask.

Four years hadn't changed anything. "It's insane," he told her.

Scout agreed. But why not?

"What's your name?"

"Evan Tanner. And you are looking at me really weird right now."

Scout smiled. "Evan, what would you think about coming to a weeklong baseball camp we're hosting and trying out for the New England Rebels?"

"I would think what he said is right. That it's insane."

"Insane." Scout nodded, feeling some odd sense of purpose. "Well, that's sort of how I roll now. So give it a shot anyway."

Scout put out her hand and after a second, as if he was still processing what he'd just been told, Evan Tanner shook it with a definitive yes.

CHAPTER FOUR

"YOU'RE REALLY CONSIDERING HIM," Jayson said as he quickly glanced at Scout before turning his eyes back to the road. They were still about an hour away from Minotaur Falls and the ban on talking didn't seem so much like a purposeful thing this time but a result of Scout being lost in thought. The look on her face told Jayson she was still thinking about Evan and his sweet swing.

"You mean Evan? Hell, yes. It's a tryout camp. What's the worst that can happen?"

Jayson shrugged. "Yeah, but isn't it kind of getting the guy's hopes up? Bringing him to a tryout. He won't make it through the first day."

"I don't think you're giving him enough credit. You saw that swing, heard that contact, same as I did."

Jayson snorted. "Scout, we're talking about a twenty-seven-year-old former football player. I don't care if he hits it out of the park every time and makes it through all five days of camp. Are you seriously going to recommend him to the New England Rebels as a prospect for the draft?"

He could feel her eyes on him. He didn't need to look at her to know she was glaring at him. The glare was basically Scout's go-to look. It would be a huge improvement from the blank expression she'd been wearing for months.

There were times during Duff's illness he wondered if he would ever see anything in those green eyes again, or if they would remain lifeless forever...like Duff.

Saw some life in her today. Knew baseball would save her. Knew you would, too.

Jayson shook the voice out of his head. That was not Duff. Duff was not talking to him. Duff was dead. Jayson was just imagining what Duff might have said if he had seen Scout today.

Although Jayson had thought the same thing. The way her body tightened when she watched Evan swing. The way it seemed every sense was turned on. Damn, it had hurt. He remembered what it felt like to sit next to Scout while she broke down fundamentals unlike any other baseball scout Jayson had ever known.

The memories sucked. Because the memories always reminded him of what it had felt like to be in love. To be in love with Scout, who loved him, too.

It had been maddening and exhilarating. It had been soul crushing and to this day still the most important thing he'd ever experienced. Even though buying his mom her first real home had been huge, it hadn't been life changing for him.

Scout had been life changing. From the start he knew they weren't just *some* couple. He knew they weren't just two young people having some fun.

No, they were the real deal. He knew it because, four years later, she wouldn't let them have a conversation in the car for fear it would bring all the old memories up again.

He knew it because he thought that was a good idea, too. As much as he was committed to honoring his promise to Duff, he was not going back there with her. The fun and the love, the passion and the sex, the madness and everything that he felt for her. The importance of those feelings was now tainted by pain.

That crushing pain had sat on his chest for months after leaving her. Eventually it mellowed out to a dullness that he knew would never really go away.

"What is with the snorting?" Scout grilled him. "You know I hate the snorting."

He'd always snorted any time she said something he didn't believe or agree with.

"I'm sorry, but I know you. Taking a risk on a guy like Evan? That is not going to happen. You and I both know it. So I guess I'm feeling bad for him. The reality is this guy is going to come to camp, we'll send him up against some Triple A pitching talent and he won't be able to hit dick, pardon my French. But even if he does, it would take a major sell to get anyone to consider him at his age and with his lack of baseball experience. I just don't see you doing that."

There was silence as Jayson changed lanes, passed a car, then changed back.

He shot her another glance. Yep...more glaring.

"Look, what do I know?" Scout asked him.

It was an old exchange they used to share. Which meant more memories. Damn.

"You know baseball."

"I know baseball," she repeated. "I'm telling

you, I know what a natural swing looks like and that guy has it. If he'd been the golf coach instead of the baseball coach, he might be trying to qualify for the US Open, who knows. But if someone comes to me as a natural-born athlete with a sweet swing and who I think can be an asset to the team, I'm willing to make the hard sell."

"You never make the hard sell," Jayson said. The words were out of his mouth before he could stop himself. What he'd said would piss her off and he really hadn't wanted to do that. Today had been a good day. She'd gone outside. She'd worn clothes that weren't stained. He'd watched her eat three bites of a hamburger and seven French fries.

"What the hell is that supposed to mean?"

"Scout, I worked by your side for over a year. You play the numbers. You go with the odds. I'm not saying it's a bad thing. It's the smart thing to do in baseball. It's why the Rebels have you, one of only two female scouts in all of baseball, on their payroll. But don't try to convince me that you might actually take a risk on this guy."

He heard the huff and felt the flounce of her body as she shifted in her seat. She'd always been this crackle of energy and every time she moved it was as if she ruffled the air around her so he could feel the ripples of it on his skin.

"You say that like I never have. Taken a risk."

He felt a sharp pain in his chest and might have been afraid he was having a heart attack except he was intimately familiar with the feeling and knew better.

Heartbreak.

"Have you?" His tone was sharper than it should have been, but it was a particularly sore subject for him. "In these past four years since I've been gone, have you? Because I sure as heck know you didn't take them before."

"Really? Are we seriously going to have this fight again?"

Jayson didn't want to fight. Fighting her was not what he was supposed to be doing. He was here to support her, pull her out of the hole she was in, get her back on her feet.

Fix her because she's broken.

That, too. He found himself angry all over again. He remembered the anger. It had lived side by side with the heartbreak. Now he was realizing, like the pain, it too had dulled to an ache. But it had never really gone away.

"You know," he said slowly, carefully, as if this next sentence might be the most important of his life. "I don't think we ever had that fight. I remember the words. I remember asking you to go with me and you saying no. I remember asking why. I remember knowing why, so I stopped asking when you stopped giving me answers. I remember goodbye. You know what I don't remember? I don't remember the fight."

"HAVE YOU LOST your mind?" Scout asked him.

Jayson had pulled over to a gas station in the middle of nowhere. He'd stopped the car and gotten out as if to suggest they weren't going anywhere until they had it out.

Now Scout was out of the car and looking at him as if he had lost his mind.

Maybe he had, but after checking his anger while Duff was dying he suddenly found he couldn't hold it in anymore. No doubt Scout wasn't ready for this showdown, but it was hard to know if she ever would be. And they needed this.

"I loved you," he snapped. "You knew that. But you wouldn't take the smallest chance on us. Not the smallest chance and come to

Texas with me. I mean, seriously, what was the worst that could happen? If it didn't work out between us, you could have always come back home."

Scout looked stricken. So much so that Jayson considered taking it back and telling her to forget it. She wasn't ready for this confrontation. He knew that now, but he just wanted her to admit that their breakup had been her fault and not his.

"You were the one who left me!"

The shrill sound of her voice hurt his ears. Jayson imagined if there were any dogs within earshot they would be howling.

"If you loved me," she continued, "really loved me, you never would have done that!"

"It was a managing job. This is baseball. You know that's how this business works. You have to go where the openings are. What was I supposed to do? Sit around and wait for something to open up in Minotaur Falls?"

"You're here now," she grumbled.

"Yeah, but I wouldn't be back as the team's manager. With a chance to make an impression on the Rebels' GM. You know where I'm going, right?"

Scout nodded tightly with her arms crossed over her middle.

"And you, more than any other person, know what it means for me to get back there. One day. I had one damn day and it wasn't enough. Every decision I made, everything I learned was all about giving me one more shot. You knew that. Tell me you knew that."

"Okay. I knew it. I knew how important it was to you, although you really never gave yourself credit for getting to the majors the first time."

Jayson didn't want to think about that. "You knew why I had to leave and take that job. It was either that or effectively give up my career. Is that what you wanted? For me to give up baseball?"

She shook her head, again tightly as if these answers were hard to give.

"Now tell me why you wouldn't come with me. I told you I loved you. You told me you loved me. Was that the truth?"

"Yes," she said softly. So softly he almost didn't hear her, but he did and it hurt him all over again to hear it.

"You couldn't take a chance on us, though. You couldn't have just a little bit of faith in me."

Scout opened her mouth as if to argue, but this time he shook his head.

"I used to blame Duff. I told him he must have messed with your head to make you think you could never leave his side. But it wasn't him, was it? You were just too scared to change your life."

"You were asking me to change every-thing!" Scout screeched. "We had been dat-ing for seven months. It was the first time I'd been in love and everything was already changing and then you wanted me to pick up everything and move with you. What about my career? My future? My family? None of that mattered to you. You never once consid-ered staying for me, but you were mad at me for not jumping up and following your com-mand. How is that fair?"

Maybe it wasn't. Jayson felt deflated. He hadn't convinced her four years ago and he wasn't going to convince her now that she was wrong. He'd wanted Scout to prove to him he was more important than anyone else in her life.

Now she never could.

"We should go," he said. "It's getting late."

"What do you want from me?" Scout shouted at him. He could see the tears well-ing in her eyes and knew he'd torn something open in her. Their wounds clearly hadn't fully healed.

"What do you want me to say?" she continued to shout. "That I made a mistake. That I regretted my decision every day. That even after four years I still think about you and wonder what if?"

She advanced on him, her eyes still red with tears, but there was anger there, too. "Because if I did that, if I made that admission, then I would have to wonder what if I had followed you four years ago. And that would have meant that I wouldn't have had these last four years with my father. Because that was all the time he had left. So, no, I'm not going to admit that."

"Scout, I'm sorry. I don't want to hurt you."

"You do nothing but hurt me!" she howled.

The blow was more devastating than anything he'd ever felt before. It hurt more than running into a brick wall or finding out he would never play baseball again.

The only woman he'd ever loved and he did nothing but hurt her.

I should go. The thought came to him immediately. They couldn't easily stay in the same space without causing each other pain. It only made sense for him to leave.

Never thought you were a quitter.

There it was again, hearing Duff in his head. And of course he would say the one thing that would annoy Jayson enough to not leave.

"Come on," he said, offering his hand. "We need to get on the road."

They both got in the car, silence now sitting heavy between them.

"Well, that was worth it," Scout muttered.

He knew she'd said it facetiously, but he didn't agree. Those were things they had needed to say to each other. Now it was done, and the bottom line was he was either going to have to let her go and move on with this life...

Or he was going to have to find a way to stop hurting her.

Five years ago...

DAMN, HE WAS NOT going to be able to take this slow. Scout was in his arms and the need to bury himself inside her was like nothing he'd ever felt before. Jayson knew what sex was—he'd had plenty of sex—but this felt different.

This was the first time he'd waited for

something he wanted. And the wait had nearly killed him.

The moment he'd laid eyes on Scout, Jayson knew he wanted her. Something about her edginess turned him on. But he'd also sensed a vulnerability about her that was equally intriguing. The one thing he knew for certain was that he was going to have to move slowly with her.

Instinctively, he knew if he asked her out that first week he would have scared her off. So instead he let their friendship develop naturally. Which made things even harder because not only did he want to screw her brains out, but also the more they hung out together the more he liked her.

Jayson couldn't remember the last time he'd liked someone so much.

Which was why when she finally worked up the nerve to ask him out, he knew all that waiting had paid off. She was coming to him. Like a rabbit he was luring out of its lair with a little bit of sweet lettuce.

Now they were in his hotel room, and her tongue was in his mouth and he was thinking with what little brainpower he had left that he was not going to be able to drag this out.

Next time, he told himself.

Next time he would nibble and lick and suck. He would tease and torment and make her come a million times before he slid inside her.

This time he just needed to get inside her.

"Scout, I need you, baby."

She pulled away and was looking at him a little bit confused, which he thought was nice. His kiss had made her fuzzy.

"Huh?"

He ran his hand down her back until he was cupping her ass and pulling her against his aching erection. "Are you ready for me?"

He felt her still and maybe that should have been his first clue, but he was too busy stroking his cock between her legs, which was making him crazy and her whimper.

"Turn around," he told her and she obeyed. He grabbed hold of the zipper of her dress and pulled it down her body, loving the skin that was revealed as the fabric fell away from her body. He loved it more when he passed the part of her back where her bra strap should have been and it wasn't there. So much so that he pressed a kiss in the center of her back, making her whimper again.

For a second they got into a tug-of-war over the straps of her dress. Scout didn't seem to want to let them go, but Jayson wasn't going to be able to see her naked if she didn't. And Jayson really wanted to see her naked.

"Scout?" he asked, wondering if there was a problem.

Then she let her arms down and the dress fell away from her body. He helped her step out of it and then he pulled on her arm to turn her around. Except when she did, she had her arms crossed over her breasts.

"Shy?" Jayson asked, smiling at her. Her hair was long down her back. Her bare body, all flat angles, made him even harder and he didn't know that was possible. Then there were her sexy panties that she no doubt wore just in case Jayson managed to get her out of her dress.

"You are so beautiful. Let me see all of you."

Again he had to tug, this time to get her arms off her body. As soon as he succeeded she ducked her head, which again might have been a clue if he hadn't been so hyper-focused on her perky round breasts and her tight nipples.

"I'm going to suck those nipples so hard I'm going to make you scream. Next time. But right now I can't wait."

Thinking she was on the same page, he lifted her in his arms and carried her to the king-sized bed. He dropped her so that she was flat on her back and as soon as he did she covered her breasts again, which made him sad. He was going to have to break her of that habit.

Next time.

Jayson shucked off his coat and toed out of his shoes. He really didn't want to take the time to remove his tie and unbutton his shirt but this wasn't going to be a one-time thing. This wasn't just about sex, either. This was the start of their relationship. He needed to treat it with some respect.

So he did take off his tie and he did unbutton his shirt, but he did it quickly.

Then he was pulling down his pants and as soon as he stood before her he heard a slight squeak. He fished out a condom from his wallet and then kicked his clothes away.

Without thinking about what that squeak meant he crawled on the bed in between her legs. He had to use some pressure to get her to spread them. He kept his weight on his arms, but he let his dick settle on her flat stomach to enjoy the feel of her smooth skin against him.

She squeaked again and he took that as

a measure of excitement. He kissed her and was a little worried when she didn't immediately open her mouth to him. But just as the thought came to him that she felt a little stiff underneath him, she was kissing him back with all the passion he felt for her.

Her hands were on his lower back, her body was arching up to press herself against him. She was ready and he was done waiting.

He got on his knees between her legs and pulled her panties down with a little awkwardness as she was twisting one way, while he was pulling the other. But finally she was naked with him and then he was getting himself into position, using his teeth to open the condom and then rolling it in place. He lifted her so that her ass was on his thighs and he would be able to slide deep and hard in one solid stroke.

"I'm sorry, honey." He could hear how rough his voice was but the urgency to thrust inside her was nearly overwhelming. "This might be a little rough and quick, but I promise I'll get you there."

He knew he was losing it because he could hear the Louisiana in his voice and that only happened when he was really drunk or really desperate.

"Jayson, I think…"

But he was done waiting. He put his cock against her opening and started to push. He felt her wetness, knew she was aroused, but he hadn't expected her to be so tight.

"Scout…"

It was like her body was pushing back against him. It was maddening.

"Honey, you've got to open for me a little…"

"I'm trying."

Trying? What the hell did that mean, but before he could think about it, he had the head of his erection inside her and he was pushing again. Then he heard her cry out and it froze him solid.

"Scout."

"It burns," she said with her arm over her eyes.

Instantly, he slid out of her. Then he looked down on her face and saw she was in agony.

"No, don't stop. You can't stop! You have to finish it."

She was reaching for his hips and sliding her butt up his legs as if she might try to impale herself on him. He caught her body and turned her on her side so that they were facing each other.

"Please, don't stop," she cried.

Tears. Actual tears. He was the worst lover ever. Obviously he'd gone too fast for her. He thought she'd been with him. She was obviously not even close to being ready.

"Scout, it's okay," he said even though the ache in his balls was extreme. "I'll slow down. Get you more ready."

"I am ready." She sobbed. "Please, just do it. There's nothing you can do that won't hurt."

Oh, hell. Did she have some kind of physical condition? Something that prevented her from enjoying sex?

"Scout, honey, you need to talk to me. Is there some kind of problem I need to know about?"

"Yes, I have a problem. And you need to fix it," she said urgently. She hooked her leg over his hip and dropped her hand down to his cock.

He caught her hand and stopped her wiggling it. "Scout, I'm not going to hurt you. I won't do it."

"But you have to. It's the only way."

Huh? Nothing she was saying was making sense and she was getting more and more upset. What was supposed to be a night of hot, intense sex was turning ugly quickly.

"Please, I just want it done."

Not something any guy ever wanted to hear when it came to sex. Jayson rolled on his back as he tried figure out what was happening.

But as soon as he did, Scout was climbing on top of him.

"Scout, wait…"

"No, I'm done waiting. It's okay." She reached for him again and placed his erection at her core. Then she pushed herself forcibly over him, whimpering the entire time.

"Scout, stop it! You're hurting yourself!"

But she didn't stop. Not until he was fully inside her. It was a horrible moment to both see her pain and feel his pleasure. But she was squeezing him like a vice and his cock was an unfeeling bastard.

"There," she huffed out, lying on top of him. "It's done."

Done? Nothing was done. He was still hard, and she clearly was nowhere close to having an orgasm.

"What's done?" he grated out.

"I'm not a virgin anymore. You can finish now. I'm sure it will be better next time."

A virgin.

Of course. And with that sentence she wiggled on top of him and it was enough to make him come furiously inside her. Without one real stroke.

Without a doubt the worst sex of his life. All he'd done was hurt her

CHAPTER FIVE

"Scout, hold up," Jayson called to her as he pulled up to the house.

She was done listening to him. She had had the passenger door open as soon as the car had come to a stop and now she was practically running up the driveway.

"Scout, you're going to have to talk to me eventually! Stop behaving like a child and turn around."

That got her to stop and offer him a succinct nonverbal response.

"Yeah, that's mature," he sneered.

"I'm done fighting," she said. "Go home and give me some space."

"Fine, you take your space but I'm not going anywhere. Okay? Tell me you know that."

She shook her head. He'd pulled over the car to yell at her for not taking a chance on him and now he wanted her to know he wasn't going anywhere. As if to say that if she did need him he would be here for her.

Because he still cared.

I loved you...

She couldn't say how much the past tense of that phrase destroyed her. All she wanted to do was run home, lock herself in her room, put the covers over her head and stay there. Forever.

She'd been wrong to think she was strong enough to reenter the world. Wrong to think she could spend the day with Jayson without getting her heart split open.

"Tell me, Scout. So I know you believe it."

She looked at him then, really looked at him, and saw how earnest he was. It was one of his most endearing qualities.

"You're not going anywhere," she repeated.

He nodded and she could tell he wanted to say more but it was as if he'd decided he'd said enough for a day.

"I'll see you around."

"I guess," Scout conceded. Recognizing that this was her life now. There was no Duff, but there was Jayson potentially around every corner.

Her room, her bed, her blanket beckoned. She turned away from him and walked inside only to find her mother at the kitchen counter chopping carrots and Bob sitting at the table, seemingly content to spend time with his wife while she cooked. They were smiling as if their conversation had been amusing to both of them. It reminded Scout how much her mother and Bob actually liked each other. Beyond the love, they were best friends.

A real, loving relationship. A shame it had to come at the expense of Duff.

An unforgivable sin in Scout's eyes. It didn't seem right that Scout should have to suffer this on top of everything else. Losing Duff, having to deal with Jayson, living with her traitorous mother. None of it was fair.

"I want you two to leave." Scout looked at both of them to show them she meant it.

Alice and Bob exchanged a glance, communicating silently, once again showing how in sync they were.

"We've talked about this, Scout," Alice said carefully. "I'm not leaving until I think you're ready."

"Can't you for five seconds think that maybe your being here is making it worse? I mean, what am I supposed to do, just watch you and Bob living happily right in front of me? You want to show me up close how Duff was a horrible husband and Bob is the shit? Maybe I'll start to see things your way. Is that what you were thinking? That Bob and I will be buds and I'll forget Duff ever lived?"

"Don't be ridiculous. What happened this afternoon? Did Jayson do something to upset you?"

"Yes! It seems he won't leave me alone, either. For my own good, of course."

"Do you want to talk about it?" Alice asked, putting down the knife and wiping her hands with a dishtowel.

"With you? No! Haven't you been listening? All I want is for you to leave me alone."

"That's not going to happen. Some day you'll be a mother and you'll understand."

"No, I won't. Because I am never doing this love thing again. So I will never be a mother. You can bank on that."

And then it hit her. She was never going to have Jayson's baby. They were never going to teach their kids how to play baseball. Because she was never going to take that risk.

Feeling the tears coming, Scout abandoned her quest to get her mother to leave and instead headed for the safety of her bedroom. As soon as the door closed behind her, she sank to the floor and let the tears come. Tears for Duff, tears for Jayson, tears for the kids she was never going to have because the pain of loving people was just too much.

"Elizabeth?"

"Go away," Scout said to her mother, who had followed her up to her room. There was no way in hell she was getting inside, though. Back when Scout lived with her mother after the divorce this was their most common method of communication. With a door in between them.

"Honey, I know you're hurting. I know you think the world is against you right now. But I know how smart you are. So I know you're going to eventually realize there is a reason Samantha and I aren't leaving you. There is a reason Jayson wants you to know he's here for you, too."

To hurt me. That's all they wanted to do. But she was safe in her room now and no one could hurt her as long as she didn't leave.

"Go away."

"I will for now. For now. We're having pea soup for dinner. I know it's your favorite. I'll let you know when it's ready."

Then there was silence and Scout knew Alice had left. Finally, thankfully, she was alone. Which was all she wanted. Why didn't they understand that?

Instead no one was leaving and she and Jayson were rehashing old news at a gas station. Why did Jayson have to do that? Why did he have to bring all the pain and misery back? He'd left her. Not the other way around. It wasn't right of him to blame her.

Was it?

She'd heard the pain in his voice when he'd said that she hadn't been willing to take a chance on them. She knew him well enough to know that what he'd really meant was that she wasn't willing to take a chance on *him*.

Jayson's father had left him and his mother when Jayson was nine, and it had left its mark, like any father leaving would. It made Jayson feel as if he wasn't good enough for or worthy of his father's love. It's what drove him to succeed in baseball. It's what pushed him all the way through the minors until he was finally called up to The Show.

He never said it, and she never asked, but Scout always believed that his drive to get to the majors had everything to do with hoping his father might see him there. Might see his kid on TV and regret leaving him.

She wondered if that was what still drove him now.

All she knew was that back when they were together, Scout had wanted to show him he was the worthiest of all men.

There were times she'd wondered if that was why he'd asked her to leave in the first place. Had he wanted to put that choice in front of her so that she would choose him? Show him he was good enough. To prove that everything she had told him was true.

Thinking back on it, they had never once talked about trying a long-distance relationship. They could have made an effort. Long calls, long visits. It wasn't as if a baseball manager wasn't on the road a lot during the season anyway. They could have eased into the idea of her moving in with him.

Instead it had to be all or nothing.

And she chose nothing.

"Because he wasn't supposed to leave," she whispered and then sobbed, resting her head on her knees.

I'm not going anywhere...

The words he'd said finally penetrated. He wanted her to know he was staying around. He wanted her to say it back so that she understood.

But why should she trust that? How could she trust him?

The truly crazy part, the part that wanted to make her scream, is that despite everything, she really, really wanted to trust him.

Her mother called her smart.

When in truth she felt like the biggest fool alive.

ULTIMATELY IT WAS the smell of pea soup that pulled Scout out of her room. Her mother was right that it was Scout's favorite. Not just any pea soup, either. It had to be her mother's. Which meant it wasn't something Scout got to eat very often.

If her mother thought soup would thaw their icy relationship, she was dead wrong, but Scout wasn't so spiteful that she was going to pass up the meal. Besides, she was hungry and, frankly, sick of her own company. She hadn't been able to stop thinking about her fight with Jayson, which she imagined was better than being sad about Duff, but not by much.

Samantha and Bob were already at the table quietly talking. Scout was about to make a snide remark about like mother like daughter, reminding Samantha of her traitorous decision to accept Bob as part of her life, but she was out of energy for now. Maybe after she ate.

Samantha popped her head up when Scout sat down. "So how was it being back at work today? Did it help you to occupy your mind?"

"Yep. Sure did. Working is great. Doesn't it make you think you should go back to work, too? Aren't there millions you should be making someone right now?"

Sam reached into her back pocket and pulled out her BlackBerry. "You would be amazed at how many millions I can make no matter where I am in the country."

"Awesome," Scout mumbled, not really packing enough sarcasm in her verbal punch.

The soup was good and if the table was a little too quiet with so many people around it, Scout didn't really care. No one was going to blame her for not making conversation.

"See anyone interesting?" Sam finally asked her.

"Actually, I did. Although…" Scout was about to preface what she'd seen in Evan's swing with all the cautious alarms she had in her head. He was too old, he wasn't a lifetime ballplayer. It was probably just a long shot.

Then she thought about what Jayson had

said. About how she would never really risk anything on such a crazy prospect.

"Although?"

"Although nothing. He's coming to the open tryouts. I want to take another look at him there. If he shows me anything, I'll be sure to tell your competition to sign him immediately."

Samantha narrowed her eyes. "That's so wrong on so many levels."

"Hey, I wasn't talking about him."

Scout had forgotten Samantha's biggest competition was also her ex-fiancé.

That was not a topic Scout would ever joke about.

When it came to her sisters, verbal shots might be fired, heck, even physical ones, but when it came to the Baker Girls versus men, they were a united front.

It was one of the things that made accepting Lane's hookup with Roy Walker of all people so difficult. The Baker Girls were supposed to be a united front in supporting their sister and her hatred of Roy Walker. Even though Scout knew all along Lane didn't *really* hate him.

Something that she used to love to rub in

Lane's face until Duff got sick and Scout issued a ban on any humor in her world.

Unless it had been in the pursuit of making Duff laugh, of course. She had tried to do that every day until he became too sick to laugh. Come to think about it, he passed only three days after that.

It was probably the only three days since the time he could laugh that he hadn't. Not bad for a lifetime.

"Donald is engaged to someone else now," Sam said casually even though Scout understood there was nothing casual about it.

Scout froze because everyone at the table knew exactly why Donald was Sam's ex. "Are you going to tell his fiancée what kind of man he is or am I?"

Sam sat a little straighter, and Scout could see both Alice and Bob looked to each other, then to Sam. No one wanted to say it out loud. What he'd done to her.

"It's really not my place," Sam said stiffly.

"That's horseshit and you know it," Scout said. "What was his girlfriend's name before you?"

"Monica."

"Wouldn't you have liked it if Monica had given you a heads-up?"

Sam glared at her, but Scout wasn't backing down. Not about something like this.

"You don't know that he…that he did that to her. You don't know that he will do it to this girl."

"More horseshit," Scout snapped. "Abusers don't stop until they are stopped."

"Elizabeth, please," her mother scolded her. "Can't you see this is upsetting her?"

"Yeah, but getting decked in the face by your fiancé is real upsetting, too. You didn't press charges, and I understood why. You stole half his client list out from under him, so I figured that was justice enough. But letting some other woman walk into a relationship without a warning…that's not you, Sam."

Sam, who was typically tight with words, saying only what she needed to make her point, nodded curtly. "I'll consider an appropriate action to take."

It was enough for Scout.

"I'll never forgive myself for not saying something when I had the chance before you accepted his proposal," Bob said as he reached over to lay his hand on top of Sam's. That Sam accepted that comfort from Bob should have been enough to piss Scout off again, but for some reason it didn't. Because it kind of looked as if Sam needed that touch.

From a good man. Like Bob.

"I had a feeling about him. I just couldn't verbalize it. It was the way he looked at you sometimes, as if he saw how much smarter you were than him. It worried me."

"You couldn't have known," Sam said. "I certainly didn't."

"Yeah, it just goes to show the Baker Girls are not so great at picking out men," Scout said, skimming her bowl for the last dregs of soup. "You with Donald. Lane with Danny Worthless. I mean, second time around she seems to have done okay but still. Then there's Jayson."

"We love Jayson," Alice said.

Scout lifted her head. Of course her mother would like him.

"Sam said he was amazing during Duff's illness," Bob agreed. "Having gotten to know him, I can see how he would be. He's solid. Through and through. I'm glad I finally got to meet him."

"And Duff was crazy about him, clearly," Samantha reminded her. "He trusted him with this team."

"Don't be dramatic." Scout squirmed. "Duff

didn't have anything to do with Jayson taking over the team. That decision was made in the Rebels' front office."

"Uh-huh," Samantha concurred. "After Duff made the call to Reuben with his personal recommendation. The Rebels could have gone in a different direction, I suppose, but I can't see them not at least considering Duff's opinion. The man knew baseball, after all."

Scout frowned as she considered that. "How do you know that?"

"Are you kidding me? When it comes to this league I know everything. But if you don't believe my sources, ask Jayson. He knew Duff had personally recommended him. I heard them talking about it during one of his visits. I couldn't tell who was thanking whom, though. For as much as Duff loved Jayson, Jayson really loved him back."

The sentiment struck another jolt of sorrow through Scout. She'd already pledged to never love again because the pain of it sucked. But even if she retracted that statement and did find someone in the future, that person was never going to know her father. That person was never going to know what he meant to her. That person was never going to love him like she did.

Only Jayson could do that. Jayson, who her family loved, apparently. Even Bob.

"Well, you're wrong. Jayson isn't the hero you all think, okay? Let's remember that he dumped my ass."

"Gee, Scout, could that be because you're intractable, stubborn and averse to any kind of a change in your life? Sounds like probable cause to me." Samantha smiled coldly as she took a bite of bread.

Revenge slam for Scout's thoughtless comments earlier.

Scout accepted the punch.

"My understanding from Duff was that Jayson asked you to go with him when he left but you didn't want to go," Alice said.

Scout glared at her mother. Alice shrugged it off as if she'd seen worse glares from Scout. Which she probably had.

"Yes, that's right, I said his name and a thunderbolt did not strike down from the sky," Alice said, holding her arms up in the air as if to show off the lightning-free kitchen. "You'll be horrified to know that Duff and I spoke occasionally and very amicably. It was the only way I could get any information about you. He told me you were very shaken up by Jayson leaving. He was worried about you. I've always been curious about it. If you loved him so much and he loved you, why wouldn't you have gone with him?"

Scout didn't want to think for one second about that question. Her answer had always been so straightforward. So grounded in common sense. After her fight with Jayson, nothing made sense. So Scout did what she always did when it came to her mother. She lashed out.

"Maybe because I didn't think marriage could work. Given the shining example I had growing up."

"You've got the wrong shining example," Alice retorted. "It's been there since you were fourteen. You just never bothered to look."

Scout slumped in her chair, not sure how to respond without calling her mother out for being an adulteress. Seemed like a cheap shot after some really delicious pea soup.

"Why do I think if there was a vote in my family between me and Jayson I would lose?"

"I don't know," Sam said as if counting votes in her head. "I think Roy likes you."

Swell. Reduced to relying on the in-laws for support.

CHAPTER SIX

Five years ago...

"I AM SO glad that is over with!"

Scout flopped off Jayson and onto her back and felt all pressure in the world lift off her shoulders. She wasn't a virgin anymore. She wasn't cold or frigid. Or afraid. She was normal. Just a normal twentysomething woman who had sex with the man she desperately wanted.

It had hurt like crazy, but Scout was confident that was a one-time thing. Jayson was hot and sexy and he seemed to know what he was doing until she took over. She just had to get through it and from here on out it would be smooth sailing.

Maybe he could even do something to give her an orgasm.

Jayson got out of bed and Scout watched him like a satisfied cat. The physical gratification hadn't been there but the mental relief more than made up for that. Now she could just watch Jayson walk around the hotel room naked, because that's what non-virgins did.

Except when he went into the bathroom he slammed the door really hard. Scout didn't think it was a good thing when the person who did find physical satisfaction was angry about it.

Immediately, she pulled the blanket up to cover her body.

When the door opened again and she looked at his face, she was certain the slamming door hadn't been an accident. She didn't know why she'd doubted it; she was the master of the slamming door. Her mother would vouch for that.

"What the hell, Scout?"

"I'm not sure…"

"Why didn't you tell me you were a damn virgin?"

He was shouting. The only time she had ever heard him raise his voice was when they were watching baseball and he was angry about a bad call. But this was different. This wasn't mild frustration; this was real anger. And it was directed at her.

Her insides shriveled.

"It wasn't good for you," she said, starting

to realize what the problem was. He'd been expecting really good sex and she'd disappointed him. But there had been no way to fake her way through that pain.

"I don't give a crap about the sex, Scout. I care about you. I hurt you. And if I had been a little more out of control I could have really hurt you!"

"You couldn't have really hurt me…"

"Why didn't you just tell me?" He put his boxer briefs on and then his pants.

Scout didn't think that was a good sign at all. She pulled the blanket higher up her chest.

"Sometimes guys freak out about stuff like this. Case in point."

"I'm not freaking out. I'm mad because you didn't tell me. We could have handled this totally differently. I would have gone slower, got you better prepared…"

"Are you upset just because I didn't have an orgasm? Because I figure you can try again and then—"

"There isn't going to be an again, Scout. Not unless you are real honest with me real quick. Did you use me? Was tonight just about getting rid of your virginity?"

Scout couldn't believe what he was suggesting, as if it wasn't important that he was the person she chose to give her virginity to.

"No," she screeched. "I mean…yes… I knew I wanted to have sex and what that meant. But it wasn't just about getting rid of my virginity. It was about me being with you. You know I like you. I told you I liked you. Why would you think I would use you?"

He turned away from her and she could see him clenching his teeth. Tears sprung to her eyes. This was supposed to have been the best night of her life. She was with Jayson, and she had finally lost her virginity. Instead, Jayson thought she was using him and he was half-dressed as if he was about to leave any minute.

Instead of kissing and touching and ordering chocolate cake from room service there was nothing but hostility in the room.

Of course she would screw this up. Only she could make the first time between her and Jayson the worst time.

"You should go," she said, wanting to be the one to make it happen. She didn't want to sit on the bed and have him say that he was leaving. She didn't want to watch him slam another door. A door that once closed would mean the end of their fledgling relationship.

Instead she wanted to make him go. So that she could break down and cry herself sick. Having screwed up the only good thing that had happened to her when it came to guys.

He looked at her, teeth still clenched.

"Go!" she shouted at him. "Just go! You know you want to. I've clearly shown you I'm not worth the effort!"

Then he seemed to catch himself. "You just lost your virginity and I'm here yelling at you."

"Don't treat me like I'm some damn girl! Like I'm weak and need to be held or something. I should have told you. Fine. I didn't because... Because I was embarrassed, okay? Because I never trusted anyone to have sex with them before you and I thought that might freak you out."

He came over to her slowly, as if she was some kind of feral beast that he needed to calm. If Scout could have she would have pulled the blanket over her head.

He sat on the side of the bed and shook his head. "I'm sorry, Scout. You just...you're so damn stubborn. Do you know what it felt like when I knew you were in pain? That I was causing it? When hurting you was the last thing I wanted to happen tonight. Then when I discovered you were so happy to have it 'over with' I couldn't help but feel like I was just here as some kind of tool you needed to use. I didn't like it."

"Okay. Well, we both screwed up, then."

He nodded. "We did."

"Did we screw it up beyond repair? Because I'm thinking I would like some more beer and a piece of chocolate cake."

That made him smile. And that made Scout smile. Maybe she hadn't ruined them completely. Maybe she could do something right when it came to him. She probably didn't deserve a second chance, but she wanted one anyway.

"Chocolate cake, huh?"

"I did just lose my virginity. Shouldn't I get a reward for that?"

Then he laughed and that made her even happier. "Yeah, you're supposed to get a reward, honey, but it isn't chocolate cake."

He'd called her honey and when he did his Louisiana accent stood out. It made her shiver and think about the kind of reward he was talking about. She didn't think she could have intercourse again tonight, but that didn't mean there wasn't a whole lot of other stuff they could do.

After chocolate cake.

"Cake, then stuff. Oh, and I need you to teach me how to give you a blow job."

His eyes closed and the groaning sound he made in his throat made her shiver again.

Present

JAYSON STARED DOWN at the stat sheet and tried for the hundredth time to focus. Baseball was a game predicated on numbers and if he was going to identify each player's strengths and weaknesses, then he needed to understand their particular blend of numbers.

It was a solid strategy that served him well in Double A ball and had gotten him the attention from Reuben in the first place. Jayson's greatest strength as a manager was figuring out how to get the most out of his guys without counting on them to do the stuff he knew they weren't capable of doing.

As a result they always felt they were working to their best advantage rather than being disappointed by what they couldn't achieve.

Jayson had long figured out that people were just a special kind of lock and once you figured out the particular combination you could open them easily.

He considered this hilariously ironic that he'd been able to do this with every baseball player he'd ever met yet he'd never once come close to finding the combination to Scout Baker.

Maybe that's why he'd never really been able to get over her. He'd never solved her. He'd never understood her. He'd never forgiven her for not coming with him.

All this time he thought he'd been so in the right. But Scout's words from the other day were starting to leak all the way into the back of his brain and it made him wonder.

She wasn't good with change. It was something he knew about her. She liked to go to the same restaurants and eat the same foods, and when something popped up that made her have to rethink her course she did so like a wary cat sizing up this new path from all angles before moving forward.

They had only been together seven months. It was the first time she'd had sex, the first time she'd slept in a man's bed, the first time she'd had any kind of real relationship.

Maybe he should have been more cautious with her. It was just that she...sucked him in so deep, so fast.

But was that her fault? Or his?

And his all-or-nothing approach…was that about forcing her to make the right choice or forcing her to choose him over everything else? Including Duff. The sad fact was he knew it was the latter. Because that was what Jayson had needed. It's what he had always seemed to need.

The worst part was there was no point in thinking about any of this because it was too late. Four years too late. Now he was stuck here because of his job and a promise he'd made to a man who had been the only father he'd ever had.

It was going to destroy him.

He couldn't focus on the damn numbers on the damn page in front of him because of her! Always her.

Jayson flung the sheet off his desk in pure frustration.

What's too late?

Jayson growled at the idea that he was either hearing from a dead man or going crazy.

"Damn it, Duff! Stay out of my head!"

The knock on the door startled Jayson. It was partly open. He hadn't bothered to close it because there was a light crew at the stadium today.

Pete Wright, Minotaur Falls' one and only

sports reporter, was holding back just outside the door, probably not sure how to proceed given that Jayson had just admitted out loud he thought a dead man was talking to him.

"I want it officially on the record that I'm not crazy."

Pete smiled and held up his hands. "Didn't say you were. Can I come in? I'm hoping to get a few words about next week's tryout camp for tomorrow's edition."

"Sure." Jayson believed that a solid relationship between the manager and the local press made for a good relationship between the team and the town that supported them. And that helped to keep the seats filled, which was something Pete's wife, Minotaurs owner Jocelyn Wright, wanted very badly.

Beyond that, Jayson and Pete were friends. Jayson would never forget Pete's wedding to Jocelyn. Their wedding had been his first night with Scout and it felt as important to him as any other anniversary in his life.

The day he was drafted.

His Major League debut.

The day he woke up from the coma.

The day he took Scout's virginity.

How was he ever going to get over her

when the reality was she ranked above all that other stuff?

Pete came in and saw the spreadsheet Jayson had flung on the floor. Without a word he picked it up and handed it back to him.

"Wind blew it off," Jayson muttered, which was patently ridiculous in a windowless room, but what was that in comparison to shouting at a dead man?

"So, a week of tryouts...thinking you're going to find any gold in all that rock?" Pete took the chair on the other side of the desk from Jayson.

Jayson laughed. Pete wasn't far off base. These open camps were more about trolling for prospects rather than identifying real talent. The kids out there in high schools and colleges who had serious talent had already been picked up at this point.

Camps were about trying to find that one-in-a-million shot where someone who longed to play the game somehow got through unnoticed. Or sometimes it was about kids who had fallen off the radar because of injury and were trying to get some attention again.

And sometimes it was just about fluke talent and a hunch someone had.

Jayson gave his stock professional answer.

"Camps are a great way to find new talent. We're going to take very seriously anyone coming in for tryouts, give them a tough evaluation and hope we find some great ballplayers out there who have the potential to make the team."

Pete dutifully wrote the answer, then looked up at Jayson. "Off the record."

Jayson shrugged. "We'll see, but you know how it goes. Mostly just has-beens who still think they have a shot or the close-but-not-good-enough-to-be-a-pro players."

He wasn't sure why Evan popped into his head. Talk about a fluke. Jayson snorted. "Well, there is this one prospect. Totally out of left field. I mean that literally. The guy's not even a baseball player, but Scout…sees something."

Pete's attention seemed to immediately pick up.

"No," Jayson said, shaking his head. "Don't even go there. Scout's still reeling from Duff. She's not in her right mind."

"Hitter or pitcher?"

"Hitter. Pretty smooth swing," Jayson admitted grudgingly. "The guy is ancient, though. He's got too much ground to make up in too little time. Never going to cut it."

"What's ancient?"

"Twenty-seven." Which was only seven years younger than Jayson and he sure as hell didn't feel ancient.

"Why am I getting the impression you don't like this guy?"

Jayson shook his head. It had nothing to do with Evan personally. He barely knew him. It was that Scout was even willing to give this guy a second look. Something about that bothered him. Like somehow Evan was worthy of her attention.

Of course it didn't necessarily help that Evan was handsome, obviously super fit and only two years younger than Scout. Maybe that second look she was taking wasn't necessarily at his swing.

No, that couldn't be. She was nowhere near ready to form any kind of emotional connection to another person. Meaning someone not Jayson.

He tried to think back to that day at the high school. Had there been any flirting? Of course Scout's version of flirting was usually being balls-out honest. So no declaration that she thought he was hot to the guy's face. Jayson was going to take that as a positive sign.

"Not at all. You asked for interesting people who are going to be here this year, I'm telling you this guy is one of them. I just don't give it much of a chance."

"But if Scout sees something... I mean, you know her eye for talent."

"I do. Which is why she's employed with the Rebels."

"How's she doing?" Pete asked without needing to clarify.

Jayson shrugged. "She went to work the other day. I saw her eat something. I guess that's progress."

"And you? How are you doing?"

Jayson blinked at the question. "What do you mean? I didn't just lose my father."

Pete huffed softly. "Yes, you did. You know I get that you want to be there for her..."

"Not want to be...have to be there for her." He'd promised Duff.

"Just remember you're grieving, too. I know how Duff talked about you. You were the son he never had, and while he supported your move to Texas I think he was always a little heartbroken you and Scout never made it official."

Yeah, Jayson knew that, too.

What's too late again?

"No, I'm not going there." Jayson said it, but he wasn't sure to whom.

Pete nodded as if he understood. "Sorry, didn't mean to lay it on. Especially now. Sometimes I forget it doesn't end happily for everyone."

"And did it? For you and Jo?"

Pete smiled, not broadly, not bragging. Just a quiet lift of his lips. "That's the thing you realize when you cross over to the other side. There is no ending. It's up and down and happy and sad and good and ugly. But the love, that's always there."

"I kind of hate you right now." Jayson felt free to admit it.

"I know this is none of my business. Also I'm a guy and guys don't meddle in other guys' personal shit. But I knew you two back then and I have to say you were the real thing. I don't know if that ever really goes away."

Jayson didn't know if it did, either. He didn't know if he would always have Scout lodged somewhere in his heart taking up the space that might belong to some other woman who thought Jayson LeBec was worth the risk.

"I really can't go back there," Jayson muttered, picking up the spreadsheet as a way to indicate to Pete that the interview was over. He couldn't go back there because it hurt too much. The crazy part was it didn't seem to hurt any less now.

"Understood," Pete said as he stood up. "Remember what I said about Duff, though, and give yourself a break. You need time to heal just like everyone else does. We're all going to miss the old man, but I know what he was to you."

Savior. Mentor. Father. Duff was everything to him. Otherwise, Jayson wouldn't be here.

"Yeah," he said tightly. "Thanks, Pete."

Pete left the office and Jayson went back to staring at the numbers. Staring at numbers that he simply couldn't process because that question kept rolling around in his head.

What was too late?

CHAPTER SEVEN

CRACK!

Scout looked over at Jayson and smiled smugly. Tryouts were under way at the Minotaurs' stadium and they were sitting on the bleachers with a few other coaches taking in everything happening on the field.

Another pitch down the middle and another hit sailed out of the park.

"Billy is making it easy," Jayson muttered. "It's not freaking batting practice out there."

"He's just warming him up," Scout said, not commenting on the sour grapes Jayson was currently choking on. "Billy can't help it if he's pitching against someone who has such a natural swing."

"All I'm saying is I would like to see what he does against something other than a fastball down the shoot."

Roy Walker, former legendary pitcher and now pitching coach for the Minotaurs, came up the bleacher steps to join them. He sat next to Scout and bumped his shoulder—a shoulder still healing from career-ending rotator cuff surgery—gently against her own. It was his way of asking how she was, which was nice that he did it without the actual words so she wouldn't have to answer.

She nudged him back.

He was her brother-in-law so she supposed he had an official right to care. It was weird. He'd only been married to Lane for two months, a wedding they had planned in weeks so that Duff had been able to see it, and still he seemed like more of a brother to her than the whole time Lane had been married to her ex-husband, Danny Worthless.

Danny had just been some guy who'd married her sister.

Roy, even in the short time he'd been around, was family. He'd kept Lane sane during Duff's slow death. Scout wished he could have done the same for her, but he had to have his priorities.

Besides, she had Jay… Scout blocked the thought from her mind. She didn't have Jayson. She didn't have him or Duff or anyone as far as she was concerned.

What she did have was a spectacular eye for talent.

Crack.

"Billy's got his fastball a little too high, but he's clocking in at a solid ninety miles per hour. Who's that guy out there hitting them over the fences?"

"Here we go," Jayson grumbled from the seat on the other side of Scout.

"What's your problem with Evan?" she asked him rather than answering Roy.

"I don't have a problem with *Evan.* You know, you say his name like you've known him longer than ten minutes."

"Well, you're not counting the twenty minutes I talked to him when he showed up to camp today."

"Who is Evan?" Roy asked again.

"Evan Tanner is a twenty-seven-year-old high school baseball coach. We went to check out one of the kids from his team and found him taking batting practice. You ever see a more natural swing than that?"

"Yeah, on say, I don't know, Derek Jeter?" Jayson quipped. "Or maybe Albert Pujols?"

Scout made a face and turned back to Roy. "It's a stretch, I know. Played football growing up and when his college career ended he got into teaching and coaching. A baseball position was the only one open so he taught himself the game. Took his team to the state championship in his second year—"

"Because he's got a kid on the team named Ronny Wells who has actual pro potential. Geez, Scout, what is it with you and this guy? You should be focused on the kid, not the coach."

Scout heard anger in Jayson's voice and was stunned by it. Since he'd been back in the Falls, she'd heard pity in his voice, sorrow and gentleness. Even when he'd been yelling at her at a gas station on the side of the road it had been more frustration and pain.

This was actual anger. He was angry with her. It was odd but in a weird way it made her feel the most normal she had since losing Duff. Like now he thought she was strong enough to handle his being mad at her.

"There is no me and this guy," she reminded him. "There is a scout and a talent she's evaluating and if you would take the bug out of your butt long enough to focus your attention on his play, you would see I'm right about him."

"He's got a sweet swing," Roy said, backing her up. "But that's a long way to go from hitting a ball to making the pros."

"Yeah, but there is only one way to get

there and that's to actually see him play. Roy, tell Billy to throw him the curve."

Roy stood up and shouted from the stands to get Billy's attention. Without the seats being filled with people it was easy enough for the kid on the mound to hear his coach. Roy tapped his elbow, then pulled his ear, then held up two fingers.

"Really," Scout asked. "All that? When you could have just held up two fingers?"

"Hey, I don't want him to know what's coming."

The three of them watched Billy pitch a pretty decent-hooking curveball.

Crack!

Then they watched Evan Tanner go yard.

Scout rocked on her seat a little desperate to say something, but knowing she was making more of an impact by not saying anything. Jayson's silence certainly said it all. So instead she got up between the two men and started walking down the bleachers to the field.

"I'm going to switch him to the outfield. See how he handles defense."

"Sure. You do that," Jayson shouted at her back.

And for some crazy reason it made Scout

smile. Actually smile. She pressed her fingers against her mouth, to feel that her lips were indeed curving.

She was smiling, when she'd thought she never would again. A pang of guilt then hit her in the gut. As if she'd been disloyal to Duff. Her smile faded and she focused only on what was in front of her, and that was baseball.

She'd found a raw player with a boatload of potential talent. The fact that he also irritated Jayson…that was just gravy.

"HOW IS SHE DOING?" Roy asked him as soon as Scout was out of earshot.

Jayson, trying to remove the scowl from his face, turned to Roy. This was important stuff. This was family stuff.

"It's all anyone asks me." Jayson laughed mirthlessly. "I don't know why anyone thinks I have the inside track on Scout's emotional state. If anything I'm more on the outside looking in. Her choice."

He watched her walk down the bleachers and start talking to some of the position coaches. They would probably think she was crazy for the attention she was giving Evan. No coach, who spent their entire lives living and breathing the game of baseball, was going to want to take a chance on a twenty-seven-year-old who'd simply "taught himself" the game.

It was unheard of. Baseball had to be in the bones of a person if they had any shot at the majors.

The worst part was that it would hurt her with the guys upstairs. Greg was new to the organization. He wouldn't feel the same kind of loyalty toward Duff that his predecessor had. And Jayson worried that she didn't know sometimes how precarious her position was with the club. Duff had shielded her, and so had her gift for spotting talent. But at the end of the day baseball was still a man's game and not many men liked being told about it from a woman.

Especially not from a woman who knew more than they did.

As long as she was right, people tolerated her. Even liked her.

But that would change the moment she started to guess wrong. Not that he thought the club was looking for a way to get rid of her. Jayson didn't think it was that extreme. He just had a sense after talking to Greg at Duff's memorial service that he would tolerate her mistakes less than others. It was sexist and wrong, but it was the situation.

The thought was chilling. He tried to imagine anything more devastating to Scout. First losing Duff, then losing baseball. Jayson couldn't let it happen. He had to get her to start seeing things clearly again and fast.

Jayson turned and realized Roy was staring at him intently. "What?"

"You're serious about being on the outside?"

"Of course I am. Scout and I can barely stand to be in the same room anymore."

"Well, that's because of the elephant that's always sitting between the two of you. Hard to share all that space. Makes me wonder why you don't do something about it."

Jayson shook his head. "There's nothing to do. Scout and I were once a thing and now that thing is over. I'm here to coach a winning team. That's it."

Roy shook his head. "You know, I once fell in love with someone and it didn't work out. Actually, disastrous might be a more appropriate term. Train wreck. Shit show. She hated me. I could go on. I figured that was it. There was no going back and making it right.

I was never going to be with that person and I had to move on and accept it."

Jayson looked at Roy because he happened to know the punch line to this particular story.

"Five years later I married her. Because some things you just can't accept." Roy stood, obviously deciding he'd made his point. "Whatever you are, Jayson, you're not on the outside."

Jayson watched him walk down the bleachers and he had this sudden urge to pick a fight. What if he'd hurled some insult at Roy? What if he could get Roy pissed enough to want to hit him? How would that feel, to slam his fist into something solid? To have something solid hit him back. A way to release this anger building inside of him.

Of course Roy was still recovering from shoulder surgery. And Jayson's doctors long ago warned him about avoiding any more damage to his face lest he undo some of the fine work the plastic surgeons did in delicately putting all the bones back together.

Still, a man could fantasize.

He looked out over the crowd again and spotted Scout. She was talking to Evan, who was leaning down to listen to everything she was saying.

Yes, his evil self thought. *Now* that's *the guy I want to hit*.

"OKAY, IF YOU don't hear your name, then thank you for coming but we have no need to see any more from you. Doesn't mean we might not be giving you a call, but you don't need to come back to camp tomorrow."

Scout listened while Chuck, Jayson's assistant manager, started to read off names. Chuck was such a softy he never could say the truth outright—that if you didn't hear your name you were essentially done with the squad for this year. The people being called back again tomorrow would go through another evaluation. If they cleared all five days, it might mean more scouting reports of their fall ball appearances. If they performed well there, they would be considered for the draft.

Baseball players had to be looked at again and again because it was such a subtle game. Not like basketball or football, where size was such an obvious factor. Baseball players could be thin or fat. Tall or short. Fast or slow. It was all about how many tools they could bring to the game and if the tools they had superseded the ones they didn't.

A thousand times, you could look at a player. A thousand times, and still be wrong. The reality was that of the players drafted, only a handful each year would eventually make it up the through the ranks to the Major League.

"James Guess, Mike Senate…"

Scout tuned out Chuck, knowing it was going to take him a while to get through the list. More than a hundred and twenty players had shown up for the camp. Thirty-two had made the list.

"Hey, Scout."

She looked over her shoulder to see Lane approaching. Scout bobbed her chin in acknowledgment.

"How's it going?" Lane asked, nodding to the group of players standing around. "Any gold out there?"

"Maybe. What are you doing here?"

"Thought I could snag Roy for some lunch. I start my new job soon so this will be our last chance to hang out during the day for a while."

Scout's sister had left her job in Virginia to come home to Minotaur Falls. Or more accuratcly, she'd left her job because of a patient who had committed suicide. Something she hadn't been able to forgive herself for at the time. Which Scout thought was ridiculous. Lane was a physical therapist who worked with wounded vets. She wasn't a shrink or a mind reader.

In the end, the timing worked out because she'd been able to be a full-time caretaker for Duff, giving Scout the breaks she needed. Now there was no one to take care of. So it made sense she would find work again.

That made Scout want to cry and, consequently, she instantly found herself sniping at Lane for no reason.

"So that's how it works?"

Lane looked confused. "How what works?"

"You two want to spend time together always. I mean for Pete's sake you saw him this morning, and you'll see him tonight. Do you really have to come down here just to have lunch with him?"

Lane was ready to say something but she took a breath instead. "Yes, Scout. That's how it works. I love my husband and so I want to see him. Love is crazy like that."

"Makes you look a little ridiculous, I think.

Coming all the way down here just for some food and probably some lip action."

"What's your problem?"

Scout crossed her arms over her chest. "I don't have a problem. I'm just being honest. Besides, Roy's probably not going to appreciate all the heckling he'll get when the players realize his wife wants a little afternoon delight."

"You have no idea what you're talking about," Lane said. "And normally I might get angry and point out how wrong you are, but I understand that this is just you grieving. You need some place for your anger to go, so it might as well be toward me. I'm sure Mom and Samantha will be happy for the break."

Scout didn't know how to respond. Mostly because Lane was right and she found it galling to have to tell her so. There was no reason to snap at Lane because she was in love. Because she was happy with a man who loved her in return.

No reason at all.

"Or maybe this isn't about Duff. Sam said you got into a fight with Jayson the other day."

"Great, now you two are going to start ganging up on me. It's bad enough I think

my family likes my ex-boyfriend more than
they do me. I don't need you and Sam teaming up against me."

"We're not *teaming up* against you. We're
your sisters and we love you. We're trying to
support you. Jayson has been amazing. You
need him and you know it."

"I don't need anyone," Scout murmured.

It was odd but a weird memory of the day
Duff died came back to her. She'd watched
Lane put her hands on Duff's wrists, feeling for a pulse. There had been this rattle
and then there was only stillness. Lane took
her fingers off his wrist and said that he was
gone. Scout remembered falling but she didn't
remember anything after that.

"You're wrong. You need Jayson. I don't
know why you two can't just work out whatever it is you need to work out. It's obvious
you still have feelings for each other."

"There is nothing to work out," Scout said
tightly. "He left me. Do you remember that?
Do you remember what that did to me?"

Lane sighed. "I do. But I also know that in
four years you haven't been able to move on.
You must still care about him. If you do care
about him, and it's obvious he cares about you

or he wouldn't have come back, why can't you both try again?"

Scout felt as if her sister was stabbing a bunch of tiny needles into her skin. There was nothing obvious about anything Jayson did. Certainly not to Scout.

"He came back to be the manager of a Triple A baseball team. He didn't come back for me."

If he had come back for her he would have told her that already. He would have done something to let her know that he wanted a second chance. He wouldn't have pulled over into a gas station to rehash everything that had gone wrong. That would have been the last thing a man who wanted to restart a relationship would have done.

"Scout, that man spent the past three months basically keeping you upright. He forced food down your throat when you wouldn't eat and got you to take sleeping pills so that you would at least get some rest. He sat for hours with Duff mostly because he knew you wouldn't want to be in the same room with him, which would force you to go outside and get some fresh air. Why do all of that if not because he cares about you?"

"He did that for Duff. Not for me."

If he really loved her he wouldn't have left her. You didn't leave the people you loved.

The pain of that day came washing over Scout and it helped to remind her why there couldn't be any going back.

Lane nodded, her chin jutting out a little in a way Scout knew too well.

"Fine, so you say you're over Jayson."

"Yes. I'm. Over. Jayson." The words felt like straw in her mouth. *I'm over Jayson. I'm over Jayson.* She would practice it a hundred times a day if she needed to until it felt more natural. Because no one held on to a love gone wrong for four years. That was ridiculous.

Or very, very safe.

"Then you should start dating again," Lane said.

"Are you insane? Look at me—I'm a mess. I can't date anyone."

"Scout, I hate to say this but Duff is going to be dead forever. He's not coming back. I get the grief you're going through. I'm going through it, too, but you can't let it control your life. You say you're over Jayson, fine. I'll believe you. But you need to start doing the things that other women who are over their

ex-boyfriends do. And that is find someone
new."

"I don't want someone new," Scout said
stubbornly. She wanted someone old. But she
couldn't have him because he'd broken her.

I'm over Jayson. I'm over Jayson.

"So you're never going to get married.
Never going to have kids."

She was never going to marry Jayson. She
was never going to have Jayson's kids.

"I guess not."

"I don't buy it," Lane said righteously. "I
see the way you look at me and Roy when
we're together. I know this is something you
want. And you should want it. Because when
it works, it's beautiful. So convince me you're
over Jayson and start looking for someone
who can give you everything, Scout. Then
maybe you won't be in such a pissy mood all
the time."

Scout gave her the bird, which made Lane
laugh.

"Okay, well, I'm going to go find my husband, who I love, and we're going to have
lunch and I'm going to get some lip action.
Because that's how we roll now and he won't
even mind the heckling…because it will have
been worth it. And you can sit here and pre-

tend you're not filled with jealousy. I know better."

"You used to be the sister I liked," Scout said sadly.

"I still am," Lane said as she gave Scout an impromptu kiss on the cheek. Scout rubbed it off like the immature person she was and stared moodily at the field in front of her.

Go on a date. Find someone new. Lane might as well have asked her to fly a spaceship to the moon.

"Ryan Abrams, Seth Garner, Evan Tanner," Chuck announced. "And that's all, folks. For everyone whose name I called we'll expect to see you here by nine tomorrow. Everyone else, thanks again and good luck with your careers."

Scout looked up and saw Evan in the crowd of guys who were congratulating each other. A callback was a small victory in the scheme of things, but it was a victory. There were still four more days to go.

Go on a date. Find someone new. I'm over Jayson.

It's what a normal girl might have done. Scout never pretended to be normal. Maybe she should give it a shot.

Filled with a sudden purpose she got up and headed out to the field.

Evan Tanner was handsome. Evan Tanner was talented. But most important, Evan Tanner was not Jayson LeBec.

"Hey, Evan, do you have a second?"

Evan jogged over with a huge smile on his face. "Can you believe they want me back?"

"Yes, I can believe it. I'm the one who said you have talent," Scout snapped. Which, considering what she was about to do, was probably not the best approach.

"Right. Well, I don't know how to thank you. I thought my athletic career was over. The idea that I might have a second chance and it's baseball…it's mind-blowing. My dad…he's going to freak out."

"Yeah, yeah. Mind-blowing. So it's sort of like you owe me, right?"

"Uh, sure. Yeah. Anything you need, just ask."

"I want you to go out on a date with me." Scout waited as he took a moment to process the request. At first he looked shocked, then a little wary.

"Is that allowed? I mean…professionally speaking."

"Oh, good point," Scout said putting her

hands in her back pockets and thinking about potential consequences. "See, it's not like there is a protocol for scouts messing around with players, since usually they're the same sex. Unless, of course, the player and the scout were gay, I guess, but I don't know any gay baseball couples, so who knows. I think we're fine."

"Then…yeah…sure. A date with a pretty girl. Who would say no to that?"

"Excellent! We'll talk details tomorrow. In the meantime go home and rest. Tomorrow will be harder than today."

"I'm ready for it," he said with a broad smile.

He really was very handsome. Way more handsome than Jayson with his broken face.

Why that made her sad she didn't know.

CHAPTER EIGHT

Four and half years ago...

So THIS WAS IT, Scout thought. This was what love felt like. Waking up and seeing Jayson sleeping in the bed next to her, suddenly everything became clear. All her emotions solidified into a single point and she knew that this was the real thing.

It was crazy, too, because it wasn't just one emotion. It was fear and excitement and anticipation. For that moment when he would wake up and see her and smile.

When she would see that as much as she loved him, he loved her in return.

There was a time when Scout didn't think she would ever have something like this. After all, love was this huge, encompassing thing. What had she ever done in her life to make her worthy of it?

She didn't care. All she knew was that she was in her boyfriend's (she loved using that word) bed, she was happier than she ever thought she could be and when he woke up she was considering saying the words to him.

I love you.

That sounded way serious. Like maybe too serious. Like maybe they weren't quite ready for that step. It had only been four months. Granted it had been a pretty intense four months. They worked together all day; they spent almost every night together.

Duff had basically turned a blind eye to the fact that his daughter rarely slept in her own bed.

But still. Saying the words. The. Big. Serious. Words.

Scout didn't think she was ready for that kind of declaration.

Maybe I'll just whisper them.

"Jayson," she whispered. "I…"

His eyes blinked open. They were a normal blue, but to her they were the most fascinating eyes she had ever seen. She could look into them for hours, which sounded a little creepy, but there wasn't much about her reaction to him that wasn't over the top.

Or some might say batshit crazy. In some ways Scout didn't care for the feeling. She didn't like knowing that so much of her happiness was tied up in him. There was a loss of control she hadn't expected. When she thought about having a boyfriend, being in love, she imagined it as some pleasant pastime.

Someone to hang out with, have meals with, have sex with.

She did have all that with Jayson, but it was so much more. More consuming than she wanted it to be. There was no way to gently tap on the brakes. Instead she felt as if she was on a bike heading down a steep hill with absolutely no brakes to stop herself.

Except at the end of that hill was Jayson and of course he wouldn't ever let her get hurt.

Right?

"Morning," he muttered as he reached an arm out to pull her closer.

"Morning," she whispered back.

"Usually, you're gone when I wake up. This is nice."

It was true. On the nights she stayed over, she always woke at the crack of dawn. Then she would leave Jayson sleeping and sneak back into her place before Duff got out of bed. Pretending as if she'd gotten home late. To the point where she would actually muss the blankets and leave the door open so that Duff could plainly see she'd slept in her own bed.

She didn't think she was fooling him, but he was a little old-fashioned when it came to sex and dating and she adored her father enough to humor him.

"Duff's out of town," she reminded him. He'd gone to meet with the GM of the Rebels.

"Right. You know what I was thinking..."

Scout smiled and wiggled up against him, feeling his morning erection pressing through his cotton pajama bottoms. She found that adorable about him, that he liked to wear thin pajama bottoms to bed rather than go naked.

"Oh, I know what you're thinking," she said as she ran her hand over his naked chest, heading in a general southerly direction.

He caught her hand before she could land it where she wanted it, which made her pout.

That was correct. Scout Baker, tomboy extraordinaire, had learned how to pout. It worked almost every time, too. Unless Jayson was being really serious.

"I'm thinking that." He smiled and wiggled his eyebrows. "But I'm thinking something else, too. Something I've been chewing on, and seeing as how you decided to stay and grace me with your presence this morning I

think now is as good a time as ever. Scout,
I want to wake up to you every morning. I
think you should move in with me."

Immediately she sat up, the covers falling
away from her and leaving his bare chest ex-
posed. She realized how cold it was, which
made sense because it was the middle of
winter.

"Scout, now calm down," he said gently as
he sat up. "I see you're panicking and there
is no reason for it."

"Panicking!" she screeched. "I'm not panicking."

"Oh, no, we're heading to full-on howler
monkey," Jayson said, collapsing back in the
bed, his arm now shielding his eyes.

"I need… I need to brush my teeth." Scout
scrambled out of the bed and made her way
down the hall to the only bathroom in the
house. Jayson was renting the place, and although it had a lot of charm, it was still a
sixty-year-old house without a lot of ameni-
ties. Like one upstairs bathroom that you had
to walk to on cold wood floors on feet that
were now freezing, too.

Scout stood in front of the sink and even
she could see the wild panic in her eyes as
she scrubbed her teeth furiously.

Move in with him. Live with him. That was a big deal. That meant leaving her house, her room... Duff.

Not living with Duff and living with some other person. It was too weird.

Jayson followed her and she could see his reflection in the mirror. His nipples were hard from the cold and she felt bad for making him get out of a warm bed to follow her.

Just because she was crazy. She'd been about to tell him that she loved him. Of course she should want to live with him. After all, wasn't this where they were heading? To happily-ever-after land.

"Forget it, Scout," he said. And even though he was smiling gently she could see the disappointment in his eyes. "Forget I asked. You're not ready. I can see that."

Damn it. Now she was disappointed. Why couldn't she do anything normally? Why did everything have to scare her? Why couldn't she just accept that they were in love and the next natural step was moving in together? Where they could go to sleep every night and wake up together every morning.

It sounded wonderful to her. And horribly frightening.

"Jayson," she said around a mouth full of

toothpaste. She spit it out and then looked at him through the mirror because it felt easier this way.

"What?"

"Let me think about it. Okay? I mean, leaving Duff alone…it's a big step for me."

"You're right. It is. Take as long as you need. I'm not going anywhere."

"You promise?"

He wrapped his arms around her and kissed her neck, then her ear and he whispered into it.

"I promise."

She felt instantly relieved. The pressure gone from her chest. They had all the time in the world to decide if she would move in with him. Definitely something to worry about tomorrow and not today.

Because he wasn't going anywhere.

Present

JAYSON SURVEYED THE field and watched as the folks from yesterday who had been brought back for a second look fielded some balls. Most of these kids were junior college players, which made sense because scouts didn't always make it out to the junior colleges to check out the talent.

With the one very obvious exception.

Making his way over to Chuck, Jayson watched as his assistant coach jotted a bunch of numbers down. Sometimes erasing and re-doing, his eyes and his pencil were in constant motion, reacting to everything he was seeing.

"How's it looking?"

Chuck looked up from his score sheet of the various players. "They're young. Some of them have talent. Most of it raw."

"Any draft potential?"

"Maybe," he said. "I think you should take a look at this guy."

Jayson saw that Chuck was pointing to right field. Where he knew Evan Tanner was positioned.

"You're kidding."

"I know." Chuck sighed.

"He's, like, a hundred years old. By the time he spends a few years in the minors he'll be over the hill before he even has a shot at the majors."

"I get it," Chuck grumbled. "His age is a factor but he's got a bunch of tools in the belt.

Besides, Scout sees something in him and Scout's rarely wrong."

"Scout's still recovering from losing her father, okay? I don't know that we can trust her state of mind just yet."

Did he do that? Did he just sell out one of the team's best scouts to his assistant coach? It was one thing to say it to Pete as a friendly offhand comment. It was quite another to do it with a member of the Rebels organization. What was wrong with him?

Chuck was nodding. "I get that. I might have been skeptical, too. I mean the kid's never played the game at any level. He's a natural athlete, though. He's hitting everything we're throwing at him. He's got a cannon of an arm. And he's fast. Real fast."

Jayson looked out at the right field again. He watched as Evan ran under a pop fly ball, closing on it as fast as Chuck said. Then he watched him catch it and throw the ball to the shortstop, the cutoff man on the play.

"Good instincts, too. I'm telling you. We might be looking at some late-blooming baseball phenom in the making."

Jayson tried to stay open-minded about the guy and wasn't exactly sure why he was having a hard time doing it.

"Of course it doesn't help with him getting mixed up with Scout. I would have appreciated avoiding that drama."

"Huh?"

"Apparently it's all around the clubhouse. Scout asked him out on a date and the damn fool said yes. I gave him a deduction point for that, but I'm not going to lie—he's going to make the cut for tomorrow. Even though he's going out with her tonight."

Jayson blinked a few times, letting that information sink in. "Scout. Asked Evan Tanner. Out? On a date?"

"You sound funny, are you okay?"

No. Okay was the last thing he was. Instead there was apparently a hole inside his chest as wide as a tree trunk. He could hear buzzing in his ears and he knew rationally that this horrific burst of anger wasn't warranted.

Sadly, he was quite irrational at the moment.

"Call him off the field and send him to my office. I want to talk to this guy."

"You got it, Boss."

That's right. He was the boss.

He was manager of the Minotaurs and this camp exercise was about finding talent to fill the ranks of professional ball at all levels.

What it was not about was getting laid.

Evan Tanner was about to learn that the hard way.

JAYSON HAD GOTTEN back to his office in a hurry and made sure that he was seated behind his desk in a position of authority. Then he put his legs up on the desk. That's right. As the manager of the team, throwing his legs up on a desk was totally within his purview. He could do whatever he wanted around here. Because he was the boss.

He tried to imagine Duff doing the same.

Cleats are usually filled with dirt. Not much good on a desk.

"Oh, no," Jayson muttered. "Get out of my head, old man. This is my show. You brought me back here. You made me promise to look out for her. And this is what she does!"

Never said Scout was easy.

Easy? Scout was the opposite of easy. So much so that Jayson had this sudden urge to flip over the desk and put his fist through the wall.

The knock on the door startled him, which it shouldn't have, given that he was expecting the man. Evan Tanner poked his head around the door.

"Coach said you wanted to see me."

"Yes. Come in." Jayson stood and reached his hand out. It took everything he had in him not to form a fist. Evan shook his hand and then took the seat opposite the desk.

"Before you start, I just wanted to say how grateful I am to you and Scout for giving me this chance. I called my dad and told him what I was doing. He thought it was crazy, but he's excited. Something he hasn't been in a long time."

Jayson hated the man's smile. He hated his face, his teeth, and most especially he hated his perfect freaking nose. He couldn't help but wonder if this was the type of man who would run into a brick wall to catch a ball. Had Scout asked him that?

"Well, that's sort of what I wanted to talk to you about. Are you serious about giving up your career in teaching to pursue something that might very well amount to nothing? I mean, you can get a substitute to cover you for a few days at school, but if this continues you could be putting your job at stake."

Would anyone be that dumb? Of course, he had been so many years ago. Leaving college to follow the game instead of getting his degree. However, that was completely justified because he'd made it to The Show.

For a day. One damn day.

"I guess that depends."

"On what?" Jayson asked.

Evan shrugged. "I guess on you. And Chuck and Scout and all the other scouts who determine who can and can't play."

"And if we decide you can play?"

"Then, yes, I'm not going to let an opportunity like this slip by without at least trying to go for it."

Jayson could see the eagerness in the man's eyes. A chance to pit himself against others and win. A chance to prove he was among the elite. A natural athlete mentally as well as physically.

"Then why would you screw yourself right out of the gate by asking out Scout Baker?"

Evan jerked his head back. Jayson had delivered the accusation like a slap to the man's face.

"Whoa. I am not looking for trouble here. For the record, Scout asked me out. When she did I asked her if professionally that made sense. She didn't seem to think it was going to be a problem. Also, she seems like a nice girl. Obviously she loves baseball, so why wouldn't I say yes? But if there is some kind of rule or something that I need to know about…"

Make up a rule.

Jayson struggled to think of anything that would suggest avoiding fraternization between players and managers, but the hard truth was it had just never been an issue. So there was no rule.

Truly, maybe this was for the best. Maybe this was really why he had needed to come back: so he could see her move on with someone else. His dating other women hadn't helped him get over her, but if he saw her dating another man, falling for another guy, that might do the trick.

Or it might turn him into a murderous son of a bitch and Evan Tanner's days might be numbered. It was hard to know. Jayson considered himself an easygoing man. This violence was new to him and it came as no surprise that Scout had been the one to bring it out in him.

She was the source of all his strongest emotions.

"There's no rule," Jayson finally relented. "It just sends a signal that your focus isn't entirely on baseball. This is only your second day at camp. You're expected back at noon tomorrow for another look, yet you plan to be out all night on a date?"

"Whoa again. Nobody said anything about all night. We're talking about dinner. I can't be focused on baseball and go out for dinner?"

Is that what they were doing? Just dinner. Not dinner and a movie? Because when he and Scout used to go to the movies they very rarely saw much of the movie. Scout would practically be in his lap before they made it through the previews.

"All I'm saying is you might want to think about it. You've got a lot of ground to make up. You're competing against kids almost ten years younger than you. If an organization like ours is going to take a chance on a draft pick at your age you need to show them that you're willing to put everything you have into the game."

"I won't let you down. Mostly because I don't let myself down. Ever. Are we done?"

"For now."

Evan stood and walked to the door, and Jayson wasn't certain that he had accomplished anything by their little chat.

"You're still going to do it, aren't you? Go out with Scout," Jayson said.

Evan turned slowly, but he had a determined expression on his face. Jayson knew before the guy opened his mouth what he was going to say.

"I am. She asked me out and I said yes. I don't think it's appropriate to break a date with only a few hours' notice. I'm aware of what you need from me out on the field and I'll take your advice to heart. I also won't be a minute late tomorrow. But, all due respect, I'm a man, not a kid, and I'll do what I want when I want."

Jayson might have actually liked him if he didn't hate him so much.

"Well, then, good luck. Scout's not exactly like any other woman."

Evan nodded and closed the door behind him. Jayson picked up and threw a baseball magazine and watched as it sailed across the room, smacked the door and slid to the floor.

Since when did he become this guy? Since when did he throw things and bark at people?

Maybe he shouldn't be taking his anger out on Evan or the magazine. Maybe he should put the blame squarely where it belonged.

With Scout.

Jayson stood and suddenly he had a new purpose.

Duff, he thought, *I'm hoping you can't see this from where you are, but I'm about to go strangle your daughter.*

CHAPTER NINE

SCOUT LOOKED AT the two dresses she'd pulled out of her closet and couldn't decide between them, mostly because she hated both of them and figured that was the point of having a mother and a sister anyway. If they were going to be here, then they might as well make themselves useful.

She took both dresses downstairs to the living room where Samantha was talking on her phone, most likely to a client. She was using her smooth lawyer voice. Alice and Bob were sitting reading.

Scout walked over to her mother just as Sam was saying goodbye and disconnecting the call.

"So which one?"

Her mother looked up. "For?"

"A date. Tonight."

Her mother and Samantha exchanged knowing smiles. "A date, huh? Well, I would go with whatever color you think Jayson would like. I know it's old-fashioned but letting a man know you dressed especially for him is flattering. And men love to be flattered. Don't you, Bob?"

"Every day," he said without looking up from his book.

Scout rolled her eyes. Bob was the last man on the planet who looked as if he needed to be flattered.

"I'm not going out with Jayson. I'm going out with Evan."

She said the words, heard them leave her mouth, and it was as if they almost didn't seem real. Why was she going out on a date with Evan? She didn't even know if she liked Evan. Scout imagined that was the point of dating, to see if she might like him, but she certainly hadn't done anything like this before.

"Evan? Who's Evan?" Samantha asked, clearly upset by this new person's entrance into her sister's world.

"He's one of the players who came to camp. Remember the baseball coach I told you about?"

"Yes, but you didn't mention liking him that way."

Scout shrugged. "Well, I don't know if I do

like him *that* way. But the thing of it is, it's been four years and I'm over Jayson."

Those words felt even thicker in her mouth than the ones about her going out with Evan. She didn't want to think about Jayson because if she did that, then she would wonder about what he thought about her going on a date and then the whole thing would start to crumble.

If you were over someone, really over someone, you didn't care what he thought about you dating other men.

It seemed impossible that there was ever going to be a time she wouldn't wonder what Jayson was thinking about what she did. But it couldn't be that way. She couldn't think about him *forever.*

She had to get over him. She had to.

"Elizabeth, is now really the best time for you to be considering going out with some new man?"

Scout looked at her mother. "You mean because of Duff? Should I stay in mourning or something for a certain period of time? I think they ended that kind of formality at the turn of the century."

"You're in pain. And you're acting out because of that pain and I would hate to see someone get hurt because of it."

Scout was looking at her mother's face, listening to her voice, which sounded an awful lot like Sam's soothing lawyer voice, and trying to put together what she was saying. Normally she wouldn't have been so thickheaded—one of the side effects of her grief. As if she was in a constant state of hangover that meant her mind just wasn't as sharp as it had once been.

"You think I'm going to hurt Evan. With just one date?"

Her mother sighed. "I'm afraid you're going to hurt Jayson."

Hurt Jayson. But Jayson said he'd loved her in the past tense. That had to mean he was already over her. Even though he still wanted to fight with her.

"I broke up with Jayson four years ago. Four years. That's an Olympics."

Alice laughed humorlessly. She glanced over at Bob, and Scout could see some kind of mental exchange. "When it's love, time means nothing."

It felt as if a shard of glass had just been shoved under her skin. As if somehow she could recover from losing her father, *her father,* but never recover from losing Jayson.

That made her angry and her mother was always a convenient target.

Scout lashed out with the harshest thing she could think of.

"As if I'm going to take love advice from someone who cheated on her husband."

There, thought Scout. That had to have hurt. Her mother would finally have to admit to what she'd done. Everyone always thought it because of how soon she'd married Bob after her divorce from Duff was official, but Scout was the first to come out and say it out loud.

Alice looked as if she'd been sucker punched, which in all honesty she had. The words "I'm sorry" flew out of Scout's mouth before she could stop herself, even though she really shouldn't be sorry because it was true.

Bob stood and put his hand on Alice's shoulder while Samantha just glared at Scout as if she wanted to hit her.

Scout probably deserved it.

Still no one said anything.

"Look, I said I was sorry," Scout repeated. "But come on. It's not as if we didn't all know it."

Alice lifted her hand to her neck. "You think I cheated on your father with Bob."

"Mom, you married him like the day after the divorce was final. You're going to sit there and tell me you weren't involved while you were still married to Duff?"

"Yes. That's exactly what I'm going to tell you. Bob and I were friends. Maybe more than that if I'm being honest, but I would never have done something like that. All this time and you thought…no wonder you were always so angry at me. I thought it was just about the divorce, but you thought I hurt Duff. You thought I cheated on him."

"You did hurt Duff! He loved you." That's why her mother was a traitorous bitch.

Alice nodded. "You're right. He did. And I was sorry to hurt him, but I just couldn't be what he wanted me to be. And he couldn't be what I wanted, either. But listen to me—I would never lie about something like this… I never cheated on him."

Bob stepped in front of her as if shielding her from any more of Scout's fire.

"I told you your mother and I had history. I never stopped loving her. Not for one minute. The second she told me she was getting divorced I asked her to marry me. This wasn't some sleazy affair, Scout. This was two people who should have been together twenty-five years ago not wasting another minute being apart."

And just like that everything she thought she knew about her mother and Bob and the divorce was suddenly very different.

She dropped the dresses on the carpet and fell into what had been Duff's favorite chair.

Bob had always been very careful not to sit in it even though it was the most comfortable one in the house. In hindsight, Scout realized that was really very thoughtful of him.

"So it's true?" she asked. "You can just love someone and have it never go away?"

He nodded.

"So Bob loved you and you loved Bob. Then who loved Duff?" Scout's voice cracked on his name. It shouldn't be right that he didn't have a chance to be loved.

Alice shook her head and came over to stroke Scout's hair. "It's always so black-and-white with you, Elizabeth. I should have suspected what you thought, but it's not as if I could get you to talk to me. Certainly not back then. I did love Duff. And for a time we were happy. It wasn't as if Bob came back into my world and suddenly I wanted to leave your father. Our marriage was over long before that."

"And Duff wasn't perfect, Scout," Samantha said. "He made some mistakes. Big ones."

There was tension in the room. Scout could see Bob looking over at Alice, but neither said anything.

Normally Scout would have taken the opportunity to strike back at her sister for daring to say anything against Duff. But she didn't have the energy. It was as if all the anger had been sucked out of her, leaving her empty.

She looked at the dresses at her feet and realized she hated them both. The only dress she'd ever really liked was the red one she'd worn to Jocelyn and Pete's wedding, her first official date with Jayson.

Jayson was going to find out that she had asked out Evan Tanner. Scout wondered exactly how he was going to deal with that.

But first things were first. Scout stood and scooped up the dresses. She walked over to Bob, who was intent on resettling into his book after that disturbing squabble.

"I've sort of been a dick to you, Bob."

He raised his eyebrows. "Sort of?"

That actually made Scout smile. "You should sit in this chair," she said, pointing to Duff's. "It's the most comfortable in the house and you'll have the extra light from the lamp."

He held her gaze for a second and then nodded. "Thanks."

Scout wanted to head back to her room. It felt as if it was going to take hours if not days to process what she'd learned. Nothing some good hiding wouldn't fix.

Alice crossed her arms over her chest. "Aren't I going to get an apology, too?"

Scout shrugged. "You're my mother. I shouldn't have to apologize to you."

Alice huffed but didn't say anything else as Scout walked over to the stairs. Then Scout considered that she'd basically called her mother out for being a cheat. That she'd referred to her any number of times as a traitorous bitch. Something that in the end hadn't been true.

"I'm sorry, Mom." A whisper in the room, but heard so clearly. "For everything. I really am."

"Thank you, Elizabeth. Apology accepted."

"I still don't know if I'll forgive you for leaving him, though. It upset me to know how hurt he was when you left."

Alice nodded. "That's fair. But just so you know I'm still not going anywhere."

Scout looked at her mother, and for the first time she could see how similar they were. They both had the same stubborn chin.

No, her mother wasn't going anywhere because Scout still needed her. For the first time Scout took real comfort in that.

"Thanks, Mom."

Four years ago

JAYSON STARED AT Duff's door and considered what kind of news he was going to hear on the other side of it. That was always how it was when you were called to the manager's office. Sometimes the news was good and you were moving up from Single A ball to Double A. Or from Double A to Triple A.

Sometimes the news was the best and you were moving up to The Show.

And sometimes the news was the worst of your life. That the team was releasing you. That your career as a player was over.

Jayson remembered that day with brutal clarity. He knew it was coming. Hell, everyone knew it was coming. He'd been lucky the impact from his injuries weren't more serious. But they were career altering.

He couldn't run full speed without getting

dizzy. The headaches he experienced when he tried were debilitating. They had originally put him on injured reserve, but ultimately the truth was inescapable. He no longer had the physical health to be a professional ballplayer.

"Sorry, kid. You gave it your all. Don't think we'll ever forget that."

It was forgotten as soon as his locker was packed.

Jayson remembered staring at that locker and wondering who was being called into some manager's office somewhere else to replace him. Hearing the news that they were going to be called up, most likely that night, now that there was an official roster spot open.

He couldn't say why, but that feeling of loss was in some ways like losing his father all over again. He'd been nine when his momma had told him his father wasn't coming home anymore. Wasn't going to see him anymore.

Jayson remembered his mom smiling and trying to say how it was a good thing. How they were a team and were better off without his drunken father. Jayson had wanted to believe her. Even at nine he knew his father was a loser. But still there was that sense that he wasn't good enough for the old man to even visit. As if he was less of a son.

Then he grew up to be told he was less of a ballplayer.

Jayson didn't like to think about those days after he'd been released. He'd holed up in his apartment for weeks, drinking himself into a stupor, thinking how, baseball player or not, maybe he wasn't much better than his father after all.

Until a phone call from Duff Baker changed everything.

Now Jayson was wondering if he was about to be told that he was even less than that. If Duff, who had given him a second chance at a life in baseball, cut him loose… Jayson didn't know how he was going to handle that.

What would Scout say?

Scout. Just the thought of her made him happy and angry and crazy all at once.

They had been together for five months. Five months and she still wasn't even close to committing to moving in with him. Although any time the subject came up, she would always say that she was getting closer. Closer to what?

But worrying about what was behind the door had to take priority over worrying about Scout for now.

Jayson smiled at the thought of confiding in his boss about his girlfriend problems. As Scout's father, Duff would probably appreciate how difficult she could be. Then again, being her father he might not be thrilled with the idea of them living together outside of marriage.

But marriage would be an even bigger step for Scout, and Jayson knew with her it had to be baby steps.

Knocking, he waited until he heard a beckon before he opened the door. Duff was sitting down with a bunch of spreadsheets scattered over his desk and two open cans of soda that Jayson knew from experience would each be half-filled. Duff never could get through a full soda before he decided it was flat.

"You wanted to see me, Duff?"

"Yeah, Jayson. Have a seat."

Jayson couldn't detect anything in the older man's voice. He couldn't get a read on his expression, either, as Duff was focused on the spreadsheets in front of him.

Jayson sat and could feel his palms grow damp.

This was crazy. There was no reason to be this nervous. Yet that hollow feeling in the pit of his stomach couldn't be ignored.

Was this how it was always going to be?
Was he always going to be waiting for that
moment when he was told he was less than?

"Jayson, I'll get to the point."

He held his breath.

"I'm putting your name in for a coaching
position. There are a few spots opening up
in the organization and I want you as a candidate."

Jayson blinked. "But I've only been scouting for five months. Do you honestly think
I'm ready…"

"Wouldn't recommend you if I didn't.
I see how you are with the players around
here. The way they listen to everything you
tell them. You know how to spot talent now,
working with Scout, but that's not your future. You're a born manager. If we're going to
get you on that path, you need to start sooner
rather than later. It's a slow build, but you get
the right attention you might just find yourself back in The Show someday."

Jayson shook his head. He couldn't believe
his luck. An actual coaching position. And
then he had to question that luck.

"Why me?"

Duff raised his eyebrows. "Why do you

think? You're dating my daughter. I want to secure your future so I can secure hers."

Jayson's jaw dropped. Sure, he'd suspected something like that, but he didn't think Duff would actually come out and say it.

"Uh…Duff… I mean, I can't… That's just not right."

The old man shook his head and laughed. "You idiot! As if I would ever mess around with the game by putting someone in a job they didn't deserve. This is baseball! That would be like spitting in a church. Do I look like the type not to hold sacred the thing I care about most?"

"No, sir."

Then Duff's eyes narrowed. "What is it, Jayson? Why can't you see what everyone else sees? You made it to The Show. You did it on hard work, determination and having more baseball knowledge for your age than anyone I've ever met. You have a way about you that doesn't get too hot or too cold. People trust you. Respect you. Which makes you a natural leader. Yet I tell you this and it's like you don't see it. Like you're always looking over your shoulder."

Jayson opened his mouth, then shut it. He wanted to refute what Duff had said, but he also didn't want to lie to the man. "I made it to the majors for a day, Duff. Just one day."

"Which is something that most professional baseball players never do. Stop seeing what you didn't do. Start looking at what you did."

"I'll try. And I'll put in for that job."

"You do that. You'll be interviewing with the Rebels. They fill all the coaching positions. All you'll have is my recommendation. The rest is up to you."

"That it?"

"That's enough, isn't it?"

"It is." Jayson reached his hand across the desk and shook the older man's hand. He stood as a thought occurred to him. "Does it bother you that, as talented as she is, Scout's never going to have a chance at one of these jobs?"

Duff sighed. "Sometimes. Don't ever tell her I said that, though. I don't want her to think I expected her to be anything than what she was. A beautiful, talented woman."

"Amen to that." Jayson laughed.

Duff chuckled but then grew serious. "I like you, Jayson. I like you for Scout a lot. You're the type she can push against and push against but ultimately you won't budge."

"Thanks, Duff. That's important to me. I

doubt Scout would date anyone you didn't approve of."

"No, I doubt she would. But if you go down this path, to move up you need to move around. Jobs open up and you got to jump on them."

"I know it." Jayson paused for a second not sure how Duff would feel about his daughter moving away from home. But the reality was if he was going anywhere he would be asking Scout to go with him. "Scout does, too."

Duff nodded. "She does. She also doesn't like change very much. Once when she was a young girl her mother and I decided it was time to get her a new blanket for her bed. The one she had was barely threads held together by string. Of course she pitched a fit. Over a damn blanket. Probably because she did, we decided to dig our heels in. Made her throw away the blanket. Stood there while she put it in the trash. Then we made her put the new blanket on her bed. That night we checked on her and the new blanket was on the floor and she'd put on two sweaters instead to stay warm."

Jayson smiled, visualizing a stubborn little girl version of Scout. "That sounds like her."

Duff nodded. "Her mother didn't want

to give in. Said we would be setting a bad precedent if we did. I couldn't be as strong. Scout was always my weakest link. I fished the old blanket out of the trash and washed it. Handed it back to her the next day. In hindsight, I can see her mother was right and I was wrong. Scout needs to be forced into change. Kicking and screaming if need be, because a person who can't change stays stagnant. I don't want that for her."

"I'll keep that in mind."

"You're going to need to be stronger than I was," he said gravely. "And you're going to need to be more stubborn than Scout is. That's not something just any man can be."

Jayson smiled. "Don't worry, Duff. I know my girl."

He nodded. "I hope you do, son. I hope you do."

CHAPTER TEN

Present

JAYSON KNOCKED ON the door with a little more punch than was probably appropriate, but hitting something felt good even if it was just a door.

After a second he could hear Roy grumbling to knock it the hell off and then the door was open and Jayson could see he'd already pissed Roy off. Too bad. There was enough pissed off to go around.

"Is Lane here?" Jayson asked, annoyed that Roy was standing in his way.

"Yup."

Jayson waited until he realized Roy wasn't moving. "You going to let me in to see her?"

"Not with that attitude. You look like you're ready to take a player to town for not running hard down first. The only one who gets to yell at Lane is me. And I never yell at Lane because she wouldn't like that."

Jayson took a breath and calmed himself down. He didn't realize how much of his anger was on his face for anyone to see. His first plan had been to track Scout down and have it out with her directly. What the hell was she thinking asking out a potential draft pick?

What the hell was she thinking asking anyone out, for that matter?

But then he realized if he pushed her, that would only serve to make her dig in her heels. He needed to understand what was happening first before he got into it with her. Which meant tracking down the next closest thing to Scout and right now that was Lane.

"Look, sorry. I didn't mean to come across like a crazy man. But…well… I'm a little bit of a crazy man right now. I need to talk to Lane. Which I will do calmly. I promise."

That seemed to do the trick. Roy backed up and allowed Jayson inside. Jayson had been to their place a million times, it seemed. This was the escape house when the intensity of what was happening at Duff's place got to be too much.

This is where they could drink beers and talk about the old days with Duff without having to see Scout's face. This was where some of the tension fell away and everyone could breathe just a little easier.

Jayson had needed this house. Sometimes the sorrow just got to be too much. Losing Duff by inches. And maybe even worse, watching Scout lose Duff.

"Hey, Jayson, what's up?" Lane walked into the living room and for a second he was struck once again by how much she looked like Scout. Softer. Maybe even prettier, although he never would have admitted such a thing to Scout, but still very much alike. It was one of those crazy things in life, though, that he didn't feel a smidgen of attraction for her. She might as well have been *his* sister.

And it wasn't because she was married and it wasn't because he'd dated her sister; it was because she just wasn't Scout.

"She asked out Evan Tanner. On a date."

Lane winced.

"You knew!" Jayson accused her.

"Hey," Roy said. "Remember, no yelling."

Lane grimaced. "He might have the right to in this case. I think I did mess up. I was pushing her, Jayson, and… I think I pushed her right into the arms of someone else. I'm sorry."

Jayson shook his head. "What were you pushing her about?"

"Can I get you a beer?" she asked, clearly wanting to avoid the question.

Jayson just looked at her.

Lane sighed. "She said she was over you and I told her I didn't believe it. The next thing you know she was walking out into the middle of the field to Evan. I think she did the date thing as a way to prove me wrong."

"Over me? That's what she said." Jayson felt a hollowness in his gut.

Lane rushed forward. "I don't believe it. I don't believe it for a second. But you know her—she can just be so…"

"Scout," Jayson filled in.

"Yes. She can just be so her. You've been so amazing for her. She wouldn't have gotten through Duff's passing without you. We all know that, Jayson. I think we all just hoped…"

"What?" He laughed harshly. "That there would be some romantic ending? That Scout and I would find a way to fix everything that was broken? It's clearly not going to happen. She's over me."

"Okay," Roy announced. "This definitely sounds like it calls for a beer."

Jayson sat down heavily on the couch, his head between his hands.

"I'm sorry," Lane said again as she sat down next to him. "I thought it would help her to see what's right in front of her face."

Jayson looked at Lane. "What's right in front of her face?"

"That you love her. That even after all this time you still love her. That she loves you, too."

"No, Lane. What I know is that she's over me."

Roy walked back into the living room and handed Jayson a beer. He opened it and took a sip without really wanting it, but not knowing what else to do to stop this awful churning in his gut.

"So you knew?" Jayson asked. "This whole time that I wasn't...that I hadn't..."

Lane and Roy exchanged a look. It was one of those intimate looks between married people that made any single person who saw it feel lonely because he was on the outside looking in.

"You wouldn't leave her side the whole time Duff was sick. That's not exactly ex-boyfriend-who-is-not-still-feeling-something behavior," Roy said. "What I don't get is why you don't just tell her. You think it's been too long but you've heard our story. It's never too late."

"I told you it's complicated," Jayson said moodily. It was so easy for them to talk about love. Just blurt out what you're feeling and it will all be okay. That worked fine when things ended happily.

But he'd already blurted out his feelings to Scout once upon a time and that hadn't ended well. There was no reason to think doing it again would be any different. And even if it was different, it wasn't as if he could believe in it the way things were now.

Scout was in pain. If she turned to him to ease that pain, that wasn't love. That was just a way to stop the grieving for a time. Scout had made a choice.

No way to make the choice again because Duff was gone.

Lane sipped her beer and bumped into his shoulder good-naturedly. "I know complicated. Roy and I were complicated. Until we weren't. I have to ask, Jayson, if you didn't think there was any hope between you two, then why did you come back?"

"Duff called me back," Jayson admitted. "They offered me the job, the Rebels did, but I turned it down. I didn't see the point in coming back. The truth is I've been approached by a few other teams lately with some pretty high-profile positions. I didn't really need this job, but it was certainly the best offer with the most potential."

"Hold on. You turned down a Triple A managing job? At your age?" Roy asked incredulously. "Because you didn't think you could handle seeing Scout again?"

"I know. I mean seriously, I was going to let some girl from four years ago affect my career? What kind of idiot can't get over a woman who rejected him?"

Roy tentatively raised his hand, which should have made Jayson smile but it didn't.

"Yeah, well, I wasn't happy about it but I wasn't about to stir everything up again by coming back. Then Duff called. Told me what was happening. That old man…he could make me do anything."

Lane patted Jayson's leg. "That's how it was with Duff. When he loved you, you couldn't help but love him back. With that love came loyalty. It's why when he called I came home, too, and stayed even when I knew he'd brought me home for Roy."

"A man she hated," Roy reminded her with a smile.

"A man I hated," she agreed, smiling back at him. "Until I didn't."

Jayson took another swig of his beer. "I'm trapped. The old man has me trapped. I can't leave her, I can't have her and now I'm going to have to sit around and watch her date some other guy. You've got to be kidding me."

"Jayson, trust me," Lane said, her head resting on his shoulder. "Scout is working through a lot of stuff. Not the least of which is you. You're going to need to let this play out."

"Or you could do the opposite," Roy said.

Jayson looked up at him. "What's the opposite?"

"Fight for her."

Jayson glared at Roy. "Look, I told you this isn't some romantic comedy, okay? This is my life."

"I get that and I'm telling you, your problem with Scout is that you love her too much. You love her like Duff loved her. Which means you are always letting her do what she wants. You're pissed that she had a choice four years ago and you think she didn't pick you. This time don't give her a choice."

Jayson thought about how true that was. Definitely since he'd been back, whatever Scout needed, whatever Scout wanted, he'd tried to give it to her. She was hurting so much, how could he not try to give her everything she wanted?

"What are you saying? I tell her that she can't go out with this guy? Have you met Scout? She'll have a different date lined up every night."

Roy shrugged. "I'm just saying I wouldn't make it so easy for her. If you're not happy about her dating someone else, then let her know you're not happy," Roy told him.

"I'm not happy," Jayson said aloud. It felt good to admit. He didn't know what was going to happen with Scout. He didn't know what could happen. But he was not ready to accept the idea of something happening with her and Evan Tanner.

"Then do something about it," Roy told him as he clinked his beer bottle against Jayson's.

Lane did the same, completing the informal toast. "Yeah. Give my sister hell. I can't wait to watch."

THIS WAS A MISTAKE. Scout knew it the minute her doorbell rang. Her mother and Bob had said nothing as she allowed Evan inside her home and he introduced himself. Samantha had been upstairs working.

There really wasn't much else to say, so they left. Which was probably a good thing because the only thing Scout could think to say was "This is a mistake." Not the best way to start out the night.

The hard truth was she didn't want to date Evan Tanner. She didn't even know Evan Tanner. This didn't feel like moving on; it felt false.

But before she could admit her feelings, Evan was escorting her to his car, opening the door for her and then in almost no time at all they were entering The Cove, which was the only really nice restaurant in Minotaur Falls. Scout referred to it as the one with the tablecloths.

As she walked in she wondered if she would know anyone. Would people see her with someone other than Jayson and look at her as if she was somehow stepping out on her man?

Which of course she wasn't. They had broken up years ago, and although he'd been supportive of her during Duff's death, that didn't make them a couple.

A memory of the day Duff died washed over Scout. She remembered knowing that he was gone. Hearing Lane say the words. She remembered falling—she *had* fallen—and then everything after that was dark.

She couldn't even say why it was important that she remembered what happened after she fell. But every time she went back to that day, that moment, she thought there was something important she needed to remember.

Except she couldn't.

None of this stuff she should be thinking about on a date with someone. She looked at Evan and wondered what Duff would think of him.

And it made her sad all over again.

"Is everything all right?" Evan asked.

Scout plastered a smile on her face. "Yes, of course. Why wouldn't it be? I mean, we're at this nice restaurant. I'm sure the food is going to be delicious. Why? Aren't you having any fun?"

He looked startled and she could see he wasn't really sure how to answer that… because of course he wasn't having fun. Because of her. Because she was thinking of Jayson and Duff and being sad when she should have been flirting and making him laugh.

"I'm sorry," she said. "This is…uh…my

first date since my father passed away. I'm a little nervous."

The reality was this was her first date since Jayson had broken her heart, but she didn't want to share that with Evan. It might send the wrong message. What kind of woman took four years to get over a man and date again?

Scout Baker, that's who.

The worst part: here she was trying to get past it and right out of the gate she knew it was a mistake.

I'm still not ready.

She wanted to scream. Why couldn't she get over him? It was like being trapped. Unable to move on, unable to go back.

"I was sorry to hear about your father."

"Thank you." It was an instinctive reply, but she could see he was sincere and looking at her a little warily. As if he was worried that he was on a date with a piece of china that might shatter at any moment. He was.

"Look, if you want me to take you home... I know what grief feels like. Sometimes it sneaks up on you and takes your breath away."

Scout smiled sadly. Evan did understand. That's exactly how it felt. She was about to tell him that she did want to go home and apologize for being the worst date ever when she realized he was still talking.

"...not a great idea anyway. Certainly Coach LeBec didn't think so."

"What did you say?"

"I just got the impression that Coach LeBec didn't like the idea of any fraternization of players with the staff. Not that I'm a player yet or anything."

"You're going to be a player... I'm never wrong. But how did you know Jayson wasn't happy about it?"

Evan laughed. "Uh, he called me into his office today and told me."

Scout's jaw dropped. She hadn't even known Jayson knew about the date. Not only did he know about it, but he'd also had the audacity to say something to Evan. Where the heck did he get off?

Just then Scout could see the door to the restaurant open and four men walk through it. Four men she knew rather well because they were all players for the Minotaurs. She could see Randy, the first baseman, slip the maître d' some money and in less than a minute the four of them were sitting at the table adjacent to Scout and Evan.

Luis, the catcher, was smiling. Randy seemed to be chuckling, too. The other two were trying to pretend it was a normal thing for the four of them to decide to go to dinner together.

"Hi, Scout," Randy said as they sat down.

"Funny seeing you guys here," Scout said evenly, although inside she was seething. This wasn't a coincidence. Luis was wearing a tie. Scout would have doubted he even owned a tie. No, this was deliberate.

This was Jayson.

Scout looked at Evan. "Did you tell anyone where we were going tonight?"

Evan nodded. "I asked one of the position coaches to recommend a good place to take you. He said The Cove was the nicest restaurant in town."

Jayson had talked to Evan about not liking him going out with Scout. Now suspiciously four of his players were sitting next to her while she was on her date.

She wouldn't have thought Jayson would stoop to such juvenile behavior.

"You know, I changed my mind," Scout announced. "I don't want to go home. I'm famished. Let's order."

"Hey, Scout," Randy said loudly enough for her to hear. "Jayson said to say hi."

Scout's smile was practically evil. "Yep. I'll let him know I got the message."

"Why do I think I'm not Jayson LeBec's favorite person right now?" Evan said softly under his breath.

"Don't worry about him. I'll deal with it. You just worry about not proving me wrong. Because I am never wrong when it comes to baseball."

"Yes, ma'am," Evan said and picked up the menu.

Scout did the same and decided that it appeared this wasn't going to be the worst date ever. She even felt practically giddy about it.

Too bad that had more to do with Jayson than it did the man sitting across from her.

CHAPTER ELEVEN

EARLY THE NEXT morning Scout was heading downstairs on a mission to confront Jayson about his tricks when she saw Bob and Samantha talking at the bottom of the stairs. They weren't exactly whispering but it was just strange to see the relationship the two of them had formed. It wasn't as if Samantha had ever lived with them. She was already in college when Alice and Duff had gotten divorced. And, given her natural drive and ambition, Samantha hadn't needed a place to live after college.

It had been Stanford for her undergrad, then to Harvard for law school, then on to her very lucrative career as a sports agent. There never should have been a time for her and Bob to grow close, yet obviously they had.

Bob wasn't the enemy. Neither was Samantha. It seemed strange to be able to let that old resentment go so easily. As if she was somehow less herself because she didn't want to hold a grudge any longer.

As if Duff's death had made her weak.

Or maybe his death had just helped to gain some perspective. Scout had lost a lot of time with her mother and Bob, who did seem to genuinely love her mother. She needed to start thinking about ways to change that. Like maybe not asking them to leave every day.

Like maybe admitting that having them here, in their quiet way, really was helping her get through this.

She watched as Bob said something low that made Samantha laugh. When Scout started walking down the staircase again it wasn't lost on her that they both immediately stopped talking.

"Morning," she said.

"Morning," Samantha said. "Have fun last night?"

Bob gave her a nod and they all proceeded to the kitchen.

"I did, but not in the way you mean," Scout admitted. "Don't get me wrong, Evan was a nice guy and all. A really cool guy. Lesser men might have crumbled. But the fun part was knowing that I made Jayson crazy. And

I'm also going to enjoy making him pay dearly for that today."

"Come again?" Bob asked as he went about pulling down the coffee and filters out of the cabinet.

Scout took a seat on one of the kitchen chairs, happy to have someone else make the coffee, and smiled as she thought about how she was going to nail Jayson to the wall today.

"Do you know what he did? He had the audacity to spy on me. Spy. On. Me. He found out where I was going to be and sent a bunch of guys from the team to sit next to us at the restaurant. Can you imagine?"

Samantha and Bob shared a look that Scout easily picked up on. "Yeah, yeah, I get it. You guys are all on team Jayson, but you have to admit that was a pretty lousy thing to do. I mean, here I am trying to start over and he goes and throws up a roadblock like that. Not cool."

"Or maybe he's making a statement," Samantha said. "Something along the lines of him not wanting you to start over."

Scout squirmed in her chair. She didn't really want to think about the reasons Jayson had done what he'd done. Only the actions. Actions she could counter.

What did it mean if Jayson wasn't ready for her to move on? Hadn't they both decided that there was no going back? It was too late for them.

Scout hated to feel a little kernel of hope. She hated that the most exciting thing she was going to do today was confront Jayson.

See Jayson.

Because it would mean she hadn't moved on at all, and that made her feel trapped again.

"No, I think he's just messing with me. And no one messes with a Baker girl."

"Amen to that," Bob said.

"So what are you going to do?" Samantha asked.

"I'm going to go over to his house and let him know that his little stunt didn't work. That if I want to date someone I will and if he thinks he can intimidate me, I'll invite him along on my next date so he can watch up close how much he doesn't scare me."

"So there is going to be another date?" Samantha asked. "With this Evan person? Even though you just said you're not into him?"

Scout looked at Samantha and considered her question. Bob was putting coffee mugs in front of each of them, and again it wasn't lost on Scout that he knew Samantha liked extra cream and no sugar. With Scout he just passed both the creamer and sugar in her direction.

Evan was handsome. Evan was nice. Evan had a streak of stubbornness in him, as well. Evident by the fact that Jayson had tried to get him to back out and he hadn't.

Evan just didn't make her think of anything except to wonder if he could hit Roy's sinking fastball.

It shouldn't surprise Scout. She hadn't asked him out because of any lustful feelings she had for him. Heck, after so many weeks spent with sadness, grief and anger as her only emotions, she didn't imagine she would ever feel something as basic as lust again. No, Evan had just been there. A single man whose name she knew.

She was pretty certain it went both ways. While he bravely stuck it out with the Minotaur players not two feet away from them, all they really talked about was baseball and what his next steps were going to be if he was considered draftworthy.

No, there was definitely no romantic interest on his part. All he did was shake her hand when he dropped her off, which at the time had been a huge relief and told Scout everything she needed to know about a romance with Evan.

So it really didn't matter that Jayson didn't approve because she had no intentions of dating Evan again. It was the principle of the thing.

"No, but that doesn't mean that Jayson can get away with what he did."

Samantha shook her head and laughed. "You're ridiculous, you know that. I've never met someone who can take spite to an art form like you can."

Scout just shrugged. "What? This is news?"

"All I'll say is that I'm rooting for Jayson," Sam said, then sipped her coffee.

"Me, too," Bob agreed.

Scout stood and scowled at them. "Well, you are rooting for the losing side."

SCOUT HAD JUST left the house and Bob and her mother had gone to shop for food. As soon as everyone was out Sam was relieved by the silence.

It wasn't that she didn't love her family, but having lived on her own for five years she wasn't used to people always being about. Especially people as cantankerous as Scout could be.

Sam didn't know what was going to happen between Scout and Jayson, but she knew one thing for certain and that was Scout was going to survive. Sam had been so worried about what Duff's death would ultimately mean for her younger sister. Those first few weeks she'd been little better than a zombie. But finally there was some life in her.

Not a shock that it was Jayson's doing. Sam wanted to lock the two of them in a room and not let them come out until they'd figured their shit out. Not the most sympathetic approach, she knew, but then again Sam wasn't by nature a romantic.

She'd given romance a try once and it hadn't worked out so well.

Or, more accurately, she'd trusted a man with her heart and he'd hit her.

There were days when Sam could still feel the sting of pain across her cheek. The rush of pressure against her eye when his hand made contact. It had only happened once. No apology had worked. No pleading that it would never happen again could sway her.

She took some satisfaction in that. That she hadn't let herself fall into a pattern of abuse. As soon as the shock had worn off from what he'd done, she'd removed his ring from her finger, left the apartment they shared in Chicago and never looked back.

But what she had not let herself forget was the fact that it happened in the first place. That her judgment had been so poor that she'd allowed herself to get engaged to a man like that.

She was a sports agent. Assessing talent was important, but assessing people was even more so. Her client list was selective. She represented only those athletes she could be proud to call a client, and she worked as hard as anyone could for them.

So how could she have gotten it so wrong in her love life?

It was a question she'd asked herself many times in the past five years. So much that she'd never once considered dating again. She felt sanctimonious about that decision, too.

Lane married a cheater the first time around, Sam got engaged to an abusive bastard and Scout had her heart impaled by the man she loved when he left her.

Except now everything seemed to be changing. Being around Lane and her new husband, Sam was starting to see that there was something to be said for a happy marriage. Lane was content in a way Sam had never seen her. There was no question that Roy adored her.

Of course, Alice and Bob's relationship was a solid argument for love, as well. She could see that their love was a bond that couldn't be broken.

That kind of love she very much believed Scout and Jayson were about to discover for themselves.

Which left only one Baker girl.

The doorbell rang and Sam winced. She'd been hoping for a longer break from people. Not to mention there were a few calls she needed to make on behalf of her clients. One pro of being an agent was that she could do her work from anywhere but the downside was that there really was no such thing as time off. Deals could be made any day of the week, twenty-four hours a day.

Whatever it was, Sam hoped she could deal with it quickly and get back to enjoying her alone time.

She opened the door and was startled to see a remarkably handsome man on the other side of the door. Tall and broad-shouldered, he had the face of someone a person could trust. Which made her instantly suspicious because Sam didn't trust anyone right away.

"Wow," he said.

That was all he said.

"Um…can I help you?"

"Oh, right. Sorry. It's just that I've met Scout and I've seen Lane around the stadium and, well, you're just a very nice-looking family."

He smiled sheepishly, but Sam was not impressed. She used her standard ice-queen expression, hoping he understood she was not a woman to be bowled over by a little flattery.

"I'm sorry, who are you?"

"Uh, I'm Evan Tanner. I was hoping I could speak to Scout."

Sam squirmed a little. Scout had made it clear she wasn't interested in Evan but that didn't mean he wasn't interested in her. "She's not here. Look, Evan, you should probably know something about Scout…"

"You mean how she used to date Coach LeBec?"

"Heard that, did you?"

"Yeah," he said, his lips curving. "One of the coaches filled me in about their history. I just wanted to let her know that while I think she's great and all I don't think it's a good idea that we see each other anymore."

"Probably not," Sam agreed, her opinion

of Evan improving with his sound judgment. "Their history isn't totally…historical."

"Yeah, I figured that out when the team showed up at the restaurant. Okay, well, just let her know I stopped by. I wanted to talk in person to make sure there were no hard feelings. She kind of put this baseball bug in my head and I'm having a hard time shaking it. I don't want to do anything that might jeopardize that."

"I'll let her know," Sam told him.

Then he smiled and the open and trusting face was made even more attractive with a bit of mischief in his eyes.

"You don't happen to have history that's not history with any baseball players, do you?"

It was so startling to Sam she nearly gasped. She was still wearing her ice-queen expression and he was flirting with her? She bristled and he must have seen her reaction because he immediately backed down.

"Sorry, but I had to ask." He shrugged as if it was a normal event to flirt with a girl he thought was pretty. "You'll let Scout know I was here?"

"Y-yes," Sam stuttered. "Of course."

He turned and started to walk down the porch steps, and Sam had this crazy urge to call out his name. To make him turn around. To say something that might make him smile again.

She shut the door as quickly as she could.

SCOUT BANGED FURIOUSLY on Jayson's door. Camp wasn't starting until noon and Scout knew Jayson would take any opportunity to sleep in. The man was a chronic snoozer.

Or at least he had been. Maybe that had changed and now he was a new man who got up and out at the crack of dawn. No, it couldn't be.

He had to be home because she was ready for their big confrontation.

After a few more seconds without a response she was seriously beginning to doubt herself until finally the door was opened by a fairly irritated and half-naked Jayson.

The sight of his chest nearly made her lose her breath. She felt like an addict who, after years of denying herself her addiction, was being tempted again. She remembered what that chest felt like, what it tasted like, what his heart sounded like when she rested her cheek against it.

"What the hell, Scout? It's nine in the morning!"

So he hadn't changed and his outrage almost made her smile. Nine to him was what six was to most people. Good, that meant he'd be cranky. A cranky Jayson made for a better fight.

"Where do you get off?" Scout charged, pushing past him to his living room.

She had known where he lived since the moment he rented this place, but this was the first time she'd been inside. It was just a rental. Baseball people rarely bought a place until they knew their situation was going to be permanent…for a while. Or until they made it to the majors and had the money to do whatever they wanted.

So the furniture was nondescript, but among the bland and serviceable couch and recliner were a few things she recognized from their time together. His guitar, which he'd set on a stand like a piece of art but that rarely ever got played because he couldn't be as good at it as he wanted to be. His pictures. Most of them of him and his mom together.

The two of them were so tight, but when Scout was with him it never felt as if he was a momma's boy. He didn't jump at his mother's every command even though they talked nearly every day.

Scout used to take some comfort in his relationship with his mother. As close as he was
with her, she thought he would never resent
how close Scout was with Duff.

Seeing those pictures she was so familiar
with sitting on the mantel above the fireplace
took a little steam out of her fight. She wanted
to ask how Melody was and when he'd last
been home to see her. If Melody ever asked
about her.

"What do you want, Scout?"

She didn't turn around to look at him.
She figured she was better off not seeing his
chest. No doubt he had been getting out of the
shower. Probably just had enough time to put
on a pair of jeans. She bet if she looked he
wouldn't have the top button done. She might
see that smattering of hair on his stomach
that led directly to... Nope. Not going there.

"I want to know who the hell you think
you are messing around with my love life?"

His eyebrows shot up. "Love life? Really."

Scout squirmed. "Whatever. The point
is you knew I was going out on a date and
you sent the players there on purpose. Then
I find out from Evan you actually talked to
him about it."

"Yup."

Scout's jaw dropped. "Yup? That's all you have to say for yourself?"

"Yup."

Now she had to turn around. Jayson was standing there still shirtless and, yes, the top button of his jeans was undone. His arms were crossed over his chest and he looked... pissed!

"Wait a minute, you're pissed at me?"

"Yes, I'm pissed at you. What were you thinking?"

"I'm trying to move on with my life, or did you think I was supposed to kick it Miss Havisham style and mourn you forever?"

"So after four years you decide your first date is going to be with a potential draft prospect? A draft prospect, by the way, that presents a huge risk to your career."

Scout was genuinely shocked by that statement. "My career? Seriously? Because I might be taking a flyer on someone. Aren't you exaggerating just a little?"

If it was possible Jayson looked angrier. "No, Scout, I'm not. You don't get it, do you? If this guy makes it through a few more days, which seems likely because everyone is taking your lead on this, I don't know what happens. Because if he was like any other player you would be putting together a prospect sheet and presenting it to your boss at the Rebels. Your putting forward as a legitimate candidate for the draft a player who is twenty-seven years old is going to make both Greg and Reuben raise their eyebrows. Once that happens Greg is going to look at you more closely and he's going to remember you're a woman."

Scout crossed her arms over her stomach. "I've been working for the Rebels for six years. They know me, they know my skill set. For Pete's sake, my track record with prospects is nearly flawless."

Jayson nodded. "Yeah, Scout. I get that and you get it, but they don't like it! I could see it in Greg's face when we talked. They tolerate you because you know your stuff. And you were always, always protected by Duff. That protection is gone now, Scout. You get that, right? I don't have anywhere near the clout he had."

Scout felt as if he had just punched her in the gut. No, she hadn't thought about that. She'd always felt secure within the organization.

"So what are you saying? I should deny Evan a chance at a professional career just to save my own ass?"

"That's not what I'm saying. But think of the visual, Scout. What if you do present this guy to Greg and Reuben and it comes out that you've been going out with him? How do you think that will look?"

Scout couldn't answer because it was too obvious. Recommending a player to her boss, a player she happened to be dating, would look horrible. For both her and Evan. Just by going out with him, she had hurt his already infinitesimal chances.

She was ready to bow her head and admit her mistake when she remembered what had brought her here in the first place. "What you're saying is true. Fine. It wasn't like I was going to go out with him again anyway, but you didn't send Luis and the guys to that restaurant last night because you were trying to save my career. Admit it."

He looked away and his jaw tightened. "Yeah, so what?"

"So what?" she repeated, exasperated. "What if I really liked him?"

Jayson crossed his arms over his chest and looked smug. "You just said you're not going out with him again, so you must not have."

"Yes, but what's going to happen with the next guy?"

"Geez, you're thinking about asking out someone else already. Is any single man in this town safe?"

"I'm allowed to date!" she squeaked, seeing stars form in front of her eyes.

"I don't know if that's a good idea in your current frame of mind. I mean really, Scout, do you think now would be a good time for you to start a new relationship?"

Of course it wasn't a good time. Intellectually she knew that, but she also wasn't going to stand by and let him tell her what she could and couldn't do.

"I want to move on with my life, Jayson. I want to date again, kiss someone again. I want to have sex with someone again. You can't stop me from doing that!"

She knew she was in full shriek mode at this point but she didn't care. What he was doing was wrong. He had to see how removed from the world she had become since he'd left her. A grown woman in perpetual hiding from everyone.

Then his head tilted and the look in his eyes changed. She knew that look all too well.

"I'm sorry, did you say something about sex?"

"Jayson... I didn't... I only meant..."

"No, you said you want to have sex," he said, walking toward her like a man who had a plan when he reached her. He looked around his house. "You're here. I'm a man. We have history. I'll have sex with you if you want."

The fact that her whole body shivered in delight was probably not a good thing.

"We can't have sex," she said rationally. "We broke up."

"Right." He snorted. "As if you've never heard of ex-sex."

Ex-sex.

No, she'd never heard of ex-sex. Because the only sex she'd ever had was with Jayson and he was the only ex she had ever had.

"Ex-sex, sweetheart. Everybody is doing it."

The thought was too tempting. "But do you really think that's a good idea? I mean with our history…"

"That's the thing about ex-sex. There is no history. There is no future. It's just sex with someone you used to like to do it with. No strings attached."

Scout couldn't see how there could be no strings attached. She saw nothing but strings with Jayson. Then again, maybe this was the way out. Maybe she had to do this casual meaningless physical act to break free of him. To once and for all break the spell.

Maybe they would have sex and she would think that it wasn't as hot as she remembered. That absolutely might do the trick.

"Okay, Jayson. If you're up for it, I'm up for it. Ex-sex with no strings attached."

He held out his arms as if to show her he was devoid of strings. When he did that she got a better, clearer vision of his chest.

She reached out with her right hand, thinking to place it over his heart like she used to so she could feel it beating beneath her fingers, but then changed her mind because that was too sentimental. So she touched him instead just above the open button of his jeans. She felt the flex of his stomach underneath her fingers.

She met his eyes. "Game on."

He smiled back, looking like a wolf that had just been gifted with a lamb.

"Game on."

CHAPTER TWELVE

HE DIDN'T KNOW how this had happened. Couldn't fathom that in one breath she'd been screeching at him that he needed to let her date other men, have sex with other men, and in the next moment she was touching him again.

Jayson did not hesitate, sensing that if she had five seconds to think about what she was doing she would put a stop to it. He even felt mildly guilty for taking advantage of her in this state. A fully functioning, nongrieving Scout would probably have never fallen for such a ridiculous ploy.

Ex-sex.

No strings attached.

Of course they couldn't have that. They were nothing but strings and had been for the past four years, even though they hadn't communicated in all that time.

But this was what it meant to fight for her. He had to at least see if they had a chance.

He owed them both that. He could see the future so clearly now. Neither one of them was strong enough to walk away. But they were too damned stubborn to walk toward each other at the same time. Someone had to make the first move.

Jayson reached out and wrapped his hand around her neck, pulling her inexorably closer.

Maybe she wouldn't feel like a live wire in his arms. Maybe she wouldn't taste as good. Maybe her lips wouldn't be as soft as he remembered. Maybe she wouldn't kiss him back as if she could never have enough of him.

Her mouth when he touched it was soft. When he thrust his tongue inside she tasted so good, and when her arms came around him he knew he was home. He wanted to sob, it felt so right.

She couldn't know that, though. For her this just had to be about sex.

He pulled away and she followed him with her mouth, not ready to give up the taste of him. It seemed as if she was a starving woman and he was a raw slab of meat. Normally he would have been more than content to let her feast on him, but not this time.

This time he needed to be in control. For both of them. So they didn't get too carried away with each other, because again, this just had to be about sex.

"You're delicious," he whispered into her mouth. "So hot and wet."

"Hmmm," was all she managed to get out even as she continued to seek out his lips as her hands roamed up and down his back and his butt. She was squeezing his ass and pulling him toward her and Jayson doubted she even realized what she was doing.

He cupped her cheek and held her face in place so he could see her eyes. Her pupils were dilated, her lips were already a little puffy.

"How are we going to do this, Scout? The easy way or the hard way?"

"Easy. Hard. Both."

He smiled at how incoherent she was and then again a little guilt and sadness crept in. He'd left her and she'd shut herself off from all men. He couldn't be proud of that, but still it felt primitively satisfying that she hadn't let anyone touch her. That she couldn't.

Only him.

"Well, since this is just sex I think we should keep it simple," Jayson told her as he pushed her toward the wall that divided the kitchen from the living room. He took a quick glance around at the windows. The shutters provided all the privacy they needed.

"Here. Now. Take off your jeans and your panties for me, Scout."

His order startled her. This wasn't how they used to do it. Back then it was always soft words, in a soft bed, with soft kisses that went on for hours. But now this was just sex, or at least she needed to believe that.

So he would give her what she expected.

"Shouldn't we... I mean the bedroom..."

"The bedroom is for lovers. We're not that. You're going to take off your jeans."

Her eyes widened and her breathing grew shallow. He backed away from her but didn't lose eye contact. "Now, Scout, you have about two seconds for me to get a condom."

Jayson turned then, trusting that she would do as he said. That she wouldn't run out of his house screaming. That he hadn't scared her.

He knew he was Scout's only sexual experience. He knew everything he'd ever done to her and shown her how to do to him. But this rawness, this blunt talk, this had never been part of their repertoire.

He'd always treated her as if she was the

most precious thing on earth. As if she was spun sugar that might fracture at the slightest rough touch. Maybe it was because she had been a virgin. Maybe it was because he always felt as if he had to protect her innocence.

Well, she wasn't a virgin anymore.

He made it to his bathroom, found the string of condoms he'd bought shortly after he moved back here in case he might need them and ripped one off.

When he came back to the living room Scout was standing there, not naked but with her jeans and panties down around her ankles.

"Faster. Kick them off."

She did. Then she reached for the bottom of her shirt.

"No," he said, not really sure where these instincts were coming from but deciding to just ride them out. "Leave that on. I want to feel you up under your bra. Like I'm stealing second base."

He came back to stand in front of her and did exactly as he'd said. He slipped his hand up under the soft cotton T-shirt and at first he cupped her over her silky bra. Nothing fancy for his Scout. No lace or crazy push-up inserts. Just her small, soft, sweet breast in his hand. With her nipple already hard and ruched before he'd even touched it or pinched it.

He did it now, harder than he might have in the past, and she emitted a soft gasp and swayed toward him as if she was at his mercy. He pushed the straps down her shoulders then ran his hands down her front, teasing her nipples with his palms until his fingers found her. He pinched them both again. Harder this time and she whimpered.

"Jayson…" She sighed.

"Good?"

"Yes. But different."

"That's because this is different." He bent down and sucked on her neck, then he nipped her earlobe. He wanted to take off her shirt so he could suck those hard nipples into this mouth, but there would be time later. Right now it was about the sex.

He reached his hand down between them and touched her. He was pleased to discover his words had been enough to get her to this point pretty quickly.

"Jayson, I'm going to come," she groaned, her head falling against his shoulder.

Immediately he took away his hand until she was whimpering again, but this time not from pleasure but from frustration.

"Wait for me."

"I don't know…"

"Wait for me, Scout," he growled into her ear. "Now unbutton my jeans and put this condom on me."

An act he'd never once had her do in all the time they had been dating.

"Why?" she asked, clearly confused by his direction.

"It will feel good. And that's all this is about. Feeling good together."

And she was there, reaching down with her hand, undoing his buttons. Next her hand was inside his briefs and she was touching him, then stroking him.

"Harder," he whispered.

Instantly, Scout tightened her grip, pulling up from the base to the tip and all the way down again, the way she knew he liked it. He reveled in the moment, enjoying the sheer mind-melting pleasure of having Scout stroke him off until he suddenly wanted more. And because this was just sex, he could have that.

"The condom. Now."

It took her a few seconds to open it, then fit it to the tip of his penis. He was tempted to help her but that wasn't her direction. She was doing this for him because he liked watching her do it. Once she rolled it down over his erection, she looked up at him with a shy smile that almost brought him to his knees

This was his girl standing in front of him again. Scout, who could curse like a man and spit like a man and talk baseball like a man. But when it came to the heart of her, the gooey center of her, she was all woman. Soft and sweet and his.

He lifted her right leg high around his waist, then he fitted himself to her entrance, pushing a little to get a sense of her tightness.

"This is going to be hard and fast, Scout Can you handle that?"

She nodded, then let her head fall back against the wall even as her hips angled to give him more access. If he could have stayed in that moment for his lifetime he might have considered it. Seeing her like this, so completely open to him. Letting him have her any way he wanted.

His body, however, had other demands. With one smooth thrust he was deep inside her and together they moaned their pleasure.

"It's like you were made just for me."

Jayson bent his knees for a better angle, withdrew and thrust deep again.

This time Scout screamed and it stopped him in his tracks.

"Scout, look at me."

"No," she said stubbornly, her eyes squeezed shut.

"Am I hurting you?" She was moving with him so effortlessly he didn't think so but he had to know he wasn't being too rough with her.

"No."

Another statement but her eyes were still closed and he thought that was okay. She didn't want to look at him. Didn't want to know that it was him and despite what he promised her there were sure to be massive ramifications when it was over. For now she just wanted to feel and Jayson wanted to give her every feeling he could. So much pleasure as a surcease from all the pain she'd been suffering from for months.

He reached his hand down between them, his finger barely pressing on her. He kept it just there, not applying the pressure she needed but offering just a hint of what was to come.

"Jayson!"

She was poised on the edge, needing to come undone, but waiting…for him.

"Now, Scout." He pressed his finger down harder and he could feel her whole body tighten in response. Inside she squeezed him and it was all it took to send him over the edge.

"Jayson!" she wailed, her hands, which had been pressed back against the wall, were now on his shoulders, digging in as her climax washed over her.

With one last deep thrust he was coming, too, and it didn't matter how many times he'd done it between the last time he'd been with Scout and now; it was as if he'd forgotten what it meant and how it was supposed to feel.

"So good with you," he muttered. He couldn't stop the words. "Always so good with you."

For a long moment they stayed there against the wall, both of them breathing hard waiting for their bodies to come back to themselves. Reluctantly Jayson pulled away from her and took a step back, her leg now sliding off his hip. For a second he feared she would slide right down the wall into a puddle on the floor, but she seemed to catch herself, both legs underneath her now.

He turned and went to the bathroom. He purposefully avoided looking at himself in the mirror above the sink. This had been his idea. A way to change their dynamic. To unstick them from the places they'd been glued to. Now he wasn't sure what came next.

When he came back to the living room she was sliding her jeans up her legs and the memory of her thigh in his hand wrapped around his waist made him hard all over again.

"You okay?" he asked. Which probably broke some sex-only etiquette. Of course she was okay. Why wouldn't she be? He'd given her a fabulous orgasm and he'd had one, too. That was no-strings sex.

But this was Scout and she would never be just sex to him.

She nodded, still without really looking at him.

And he thought he would pay any amount of money, sacrifice anything, just to have five seconds in her head and know what she was thinking.

He struggled for something to say. For a way to make the sudden awkwardness between them go away. Something witty, something cavalier, something that didn't communicate that his insides were buzzing and that the only word swirling around his brain was *again*.

Again.

Like a caveman he could hear the chant over and over.

Finally Scout broke through the chant with her typical bluntness. "So what's the deal with this? Is it a one and done or do we get to do this again?"

Yes!

Outwardly, Jayson kept his cool but inside he felt as if he'd just hit a grand slam. He shrugged. "That's the best part about ex-sex, Scout. It can be whatever we want. You want to do it again, we can. You don't, well, that's fine, too."

It wasn't even remotely fine, but he needed to do this in a way that didn't spook her.

"No strings. Remember?"

"No strings," she repeated, but she was looking at him in a way that was uniquely Scout. As if he was a magician and she was just waiting to see how he accomplished his next trick.

"See you at the camp?" he asked. Again as if it didn't matter even a little bit.

"Yup."

"You'll let Evan know you won't be seeing him again."

It might have been pushing it to remind her of how all this had started in the first place, but he wasn't going to be truly satisfied until he knew Evan was out of the picture.

"Hey, I'm only thinking about your career."

"Right," Scout said, although again with a side-glance that let him know she didn't trust him, which he was all right with, considering he was lying to her. "My career. I'll let him know."

Jayson said nothing else.

"I guess I'll see you later."

"Yup."

He could tell she wasn't sure how to leave. Did she kiss him, shake his hand, turn and go like nothing happened? He made it easy for her. He walked over, dropped a kiss on her head and gave her a light slap on the bottom.

"Off with you. I've got stuff I need to get done before I head over to the stadium."

"Right. Me, too. Stuff."

As Jayson watched her go he had the strongest urge to whistle. Which was strange because he really wasn't a very good whistler.

SCOUT OPENED THE door to her house and had the strangest feeling the past hour had been nothing more than a dream. She remembered waking up. Remembered having a mission to tell off Jayson. Remembered walking over to his house with a full head of steam and fury. Now she was opening the door to her place without any recollection of what just happened.

Then a memory flashed of Jayson telling her to take off her pants. Jayson making her wait to orgasm. Jayson pushing her against the wall and filling her so deeply it was as if they had connected in a way that would never allow them to separate again.

Ex-sex.

Was that something she could handle? With Jayson? Probably not, she realized, but it wasn't going to stop her from doing it again because she flat-out needed to do that again.

Walking inside she saw Sam on the phone pacing in the living room.

"It's an insult and you know it," Sam said into the phone. "I'm not even going to present him with the offer. Regroup, think about what you're doing and then get back to me."

Scout smiled. That was Sam's ice tone. She never sounded angry or upset or even really insulted. Just calm iciness, which made most lesser people tremble in her wake.

"So did you win?" Sam asked her as soon as she turned off the phone.

Did Scout win? Now that was an interesting question.

"Yes and no. Jayson made a few points that were…legitimate."

Scout tried not to blush.

"If I end up recommending Evan as a potential draft pick it wouldn't be to either of our advantages if people thought there was romantic interest between us. The guy has got enough strikes against him."

"Well, you won't have to worry about breaking his heart. He came over after you left to say the same thing. Doesn't want to take any chances."

"Yeah, I figured that. So you met him. What do you think?"

Sam bristled at that. "What do you mean, what do I think? I don't think anything. I mean, he was just here for a couple of minutes. That's all. Certainly not long enough to form an opinion of him."

"Hey, relax. I was just curious."

Sam settled down and Scout might have considered what her overreaction meant but she was too focused on other things.

Stop thinking about the sex.

Yeah, like that was going to happen. And it wasn't just that she'd had sex for the first time in four years or that she had it with Jayson. It was that it had been so flipping hot. Her experience with Jayson before was always soft, long kisses and gentle caresses and him doing anything he could to give her pleasure.

This morning it felt as if he was the one taking his pleasure, and for some reason that was a huge turn-on. As if maybe he'd always sheltered her when it came to sex. And now he was done with that. Maybe it should have made her sad, that he wasn't as protective of her as he used to be, but strangely it just made her feel stronger.

Strength was a good thing right now. Strength was what she was going to need to get on with the rest of her life without Duff. Then she thought about what Jayson had said before the mind-blowing sex.

"Jayson also said that if I do recommend Evan I might be taking a chance with my career."

"How so?"

"Evan is such a high-risk candidate it might make the higher-ups think I'm not competent at my job. The new guy, Greg, doesn't seem to be a fan. At least that's the impression Jayson got from him. Plus, he said I don't have Duff around anymore to protect me."

Sam frowned. "That's ridiculous. You're excellent at your job."

Scout sat on the couch and sighed as the truth of what Jayson said hit her in full force.

"Yes, but I'm a woman, Sam. A female baseball scout. You and I both know I've always been on a precarious ledge in that role."

"Oh, don't be so dramatic. You make it sound like you're the only woman working for the Rebels organization."

Scout shook her head. "They're all front-office jobs. Publicity, marketing, administration. That kind of thing. There aren't any women on the baseball side. No, he's right. I always had Duff to protect me, but now I'm on my own out here. A woman doing a man's job."

Samantha crossed her arms over her chest. "They can't fire you for being a woman. Let them try it and I'll sue them for discrimination so fast it will make MLB's head spin."

She would, too. "You know the game, Sam. They're not going to fire me because I'm a woman. They're just going to wait me out. Wait for that single mistake they can use. If

I don't do my job better than everyone else all the time…"

"Don't even think it," Sam said, sitting next to her and patting her knee.

"I can't live without baseball. I can't live without Duff and baseball." And Jayson, she thought. Jayson, Duff and baseball. Her own personal trifecta.

Sam put her arm around Scout's shoulder and tugged her close. Scout accepted the gesture of comfort and rested her head on Sam's shoulder.

"You won't," Sam assured her, making Scout feel marginally better until after a pause Sam added, "Just make sure you do the job better than anyone."

"Right."

CHAPTER THIRTEEN

Four years ago...

THIS WAS THE best feeling in the world, Scout thought. This was what true happiness was. She was drunk on it, high on it, completely and totally saturated with it.

"Oh, Jayson, that feels so good."

"That's it, baby, tell me what you like. Tell me what feels good for you."

Scout couldn't imagine feeling any better. Jayson was rocking slowly against her. Easing his body in and out of hers so perfectly, so effortlessly. She couldn't imagine a more considerate lover.

"You. All of you."

She was running her hands down his back, around to his chest to prove it. He was so perfect. So perfectly lean and muscular. She was all softness to his hardness.

Making love with him was always amazing, but in this moment she couldn't imagine anything being better. She imagined that some girls might be upset that they would only ever have one lover in their lifetime. But it didn't bother Scout even a little bit that Jayson would be her one and only. That he was going to be her first and her last. Because there was no question he was going to be her last. She was going to marry him and have his babies and they were going to play baseball. The boys and the girls.

He bent down to kiss her lips. "Are you close?"

"Yes," she whispered. Just one more thing to love about him. He always made sure she came before he did. He would tease her and say ladies first, but deep down she just knew Jayson had this intense need to satisfy her. To make her happy always.

Then he did some trick with his fingers below even while he continued to slide into her and she was up and over, feeling that wonderful exotic pleasure flow through her.

"Jayson. Jayson, I love you so much."

There, she thought. The words just sprang from her. She'd wanted to say them for so long but had always been so afraid. Now she felt fearless. They were lovers, they were in love, there was no reason not to say it.

She heard him groan deep and long and she wrapped herself more tightly around him while the pleasure overtook him, too. He collapsed against her for a moment until he rolled away from her. Not quite ready to leave the bed just yet to deal with the condom.

"Did I just hear what I think I heard?"

Scout smiled. Of course he would tease her about it. He had to know she'd been trying to say it for so long. "You know you did."

"Say it again, please."

This time it was harder, but in a way it was also easier. "I love you," she whispered.

He turned his head toward her but she couldn't look at him yet. It was still too raw. She'd never known this kind of vulnerability.

"You know I love you, too," he said.

"I do." She reached out and clasped his hand in hers. "I feel it, Jayson. Every day. And I never thought... I never thought it would be this big."

"Ditto."

"Ditto is not very romantic," she chided him.

"Sorry, babe. It's all I got." He rolled out of bed and headed off to the bathroom and she shamelessly watched his naked butt the whole time.

"Oh, hey, even more good news," he called from the bathroom.

"What?"

"Duff gave my name to the front office for a possible managing position. He thinks I'm ready for more responsibility."

"That's awesome!" Scout shouted. "And you're welcome."

Jayson came back into his bedroom and this time she shamelessly took in his naked front half, as well. "That's right. Thank you. I owe everything to Duff and you. You taught me so much."

And she had loved every minute of it. "You're going places I can't go, Jayson. But if you take with you all the things that I taught you, then it's like I'm there, too."

He reached out to stroke her cheek. "Move over."

Immediately, Scout complied and the two of them settled into each other's arms.

"I mean, if I can do this, really do this... well... Duff said I could go back. This time I could really prove myself."

She rubbed her hand over his chest. "You don't have to prove anything to anyone, Jayson. You're perfect."

He lifted her hand off his chest and kissed it. "You're biased.

"It will be interesting to see," Jayson said and Scout could hear the sleep in his voice as he was drifting off. Nothing like amazing sex to send both of them off into sleep.

"Hmm."

"Where the job will be?"

Scout didn't really hear that last part. She was just happy and content knowing she was here with Jayson and that someday he was actually going to be a coach for the Minotaurs.

Present

"HOW'S HE DOING, CHUCK?" Scout asked as she came up behind the man who was furiously taking notes on his clipboard as he studied the players on the field.

Chuck shook his head. "The guy is a natural talent. He can hit, he can throw. He's making these kids out there look as if they are just that...kids. But here's the deal, Scout..."

"I know," she said. "I know. He's twenty-seven."

"There is no getting around that number."

No, there wasn't. Maybe the smart thing was to cut him now. It was day four of the

camp with one more day to go. The group
was whittled down to about eighteen players.
Right now they were playing an actual game.
By tomorrow the scouts and coaches would
be expected to write up prospect sheets on
any candidates they thought might be draft
potential. Not only if they should be drafted,
but also what round they might be considered for. All that information just kept getting compiled and sorted out until the draft
in the summer.

Could she really write up a prospect sheet
on a twenty-seven-year-old player who had
never played baseball before?

It would be the easiest thing in the world
for Scout to just say she was wrong. That,
although Evan was a natural athlete, he had
too much to overcome to make it to the pros.
Would anyone really question that call?

Chuck wouldn't.

Jayson certainly wouldn't.

The only problem was, it was the wrong
call. Evan did have what it took and every
day he was proving that.

"Just keep an eye on him, Chuck. Let's
pretend he's seventeen and just evaluate him
based on that."

"Will do."

"What about the others? Any one to watch out for?" Scout asked him.

"You might want to keep your eye on the kid playing third base. Watch him swing the next time he comes up to bat."

Scout nodded as she went to take her seat in the bleachers. She watched the pitcher strike out the batter, and then as casually as she could she turned around and scanned the rows of seats behind her. Not really looking for Jayson. But maybe a little.

She'd seen him yesterday around the stadium but hadn't spoken to him at all. Mostly because she didn't know what to say to him, but also because she feared she would stutter and blush if she did say anything.

Ex-sex was a confusing thing. On the one hand, she liked it. More than liked it. On the other hand, it could mean sliding back into old patterns that she had already convinced herself she didn't want to return to.

Right?

Jayson had left her. Jayson had hurt her. What if the sex turned into something more? What if she started feeling connected to him again? What if she started loving him again?

Loving him again?

Okay, fine, so she probably had never

stopped loving him, but keeping all that inside was vastly different from sharing it with him. She needed to protect herself. She needed to remember the hurt.

Only that was super hard to do when she knew how much pleasure he could give her.

Just sex. No strings attached. So if he walked away from her again she couldn't be hurt.

Right.

"Who are you looking for?"

Startled, Scout turned around to see Lane and Sam walking down the steps toward her. Lane was carrying a tray of what appeared to be hot dogs and French fries and Sam was carrying a tray of sodas.

"What are you two doing here?" Scout snapped. She didn't want to get caught looking for Jayson when she certainly shouldn't be looking for Jayson. You didn't look for somebody when you were just screwing around. You didn't seek out the person.

It had to just happen naturally. Casually. Like, oh, hey, I didn't notice you standing there and since we both happen to be here let's do it again.

"Nice to see you, too," Lane said as she took a seat on one side of Scout while Sam sat on the other. "We thought it would be nice to bring you lunch. From the Dog Shack, your favorite."

"The Dog Shack is your favorite," Scout reminded her.

"Oh, that's right."

Lane handed out hotdogs, giving Scout the one with onions and spicy mustard, just the way she liked it. When she took her first bite she realized she was famished. She really needed to remember to start eating more.

The three sat in companionable silence as the game rolled on in front of them.

The three Baker sisters sitting together watching a baseball game. Duff would have loved to see that. The thought brought tears to Scout's eyes but she quickly brushed them away.

She had to get used to the idea that it was okay to think about him. It was okay to miss him.

"So who's the old guy everyone is talking about?" Lane asked as she munched on her fries.

"He's out in right field," Sam answered, pointing in the general direction.

Scout turned to Sam and raised an eyebrow.

"What?" Sam asked defensively. "It's not

like he's hard to pick out. He's the only grown
man out there."

"And does he still show promise?" Lane
asked.

The shortstop caught the third out, and the
outfield headed in to take their turn at bat.

"Yep," Scout said grimly.

"Scout, I know the predicament you're in,
but at some point you have to trust yourself.
You can't always be looking over your shoulder," Sam told her.

"What are we talking about?" Lane wanted
to know.

"Scout's afraid with Duff gone she might
lose her job."

"That's crazy!" Lane railed. "You've got
one of the best eyes in baseball. Everyone
knows that."

"Everyone here knows that," Scout corrected her. "The Minotaur coaches, sure. You
guys, definitely. But we're talking about me
writing up a prospect sheet on an over-the-
hill former football player and sending it to
the team's GM."

"Oh, I didn't know he played football,"
Sam muttered. "Explains the shoulders."

"Focus, Sam. This is about me, remember? Anyway, Jayson thinks it might put some

attention on me and maybe that isn't a good thing. Greg's new to the Rebels and he obviously doesn't know about the legendary Bakers of Baseball. He probably sees me listed on his scouting team and wonders what the hell I'm doing there."

"He should only be concerned with your work. Your track record," Lane grumbled. "It shouldn't matter that you're a woman."

"It shouldn't. But it probably does."

"It's so unfair. This is the twenty-first century!" Sam ranted.

"The woman thing might not be the only issue," Scout said, trying to think objectively. "There is something else to consider. I mean I've been out of it for several months."

"Yes, taking care of your dying father," Lane reminded her.

"Still, business is business. The organization can't stop because I'm sad. Now that I'm back, do I really want Evan to be the first person I'm recommending out of the gate?"

The three sisters turned their heads in the direction of the batter's box. Evan was stepping up to the plate. He didn't fidget or go through a pre-bat routine like so many of the other hitters did. It was probably one of the advantages of not playing all his life—he didn't have the opportunity to develop any silly habits. He just stood there in the box, looking down the pitcher, waiting for the ball to come his way.

And when it did he swung at it in perfect time and hit it out of the park.

"Oh, my," Sam said.

"Holy shit," Lane muttered.

"Yep. That's the guy I'm potentially putting my career at risk for."

Neither Sam nor Lane had anything to add. After all, what was there to say?

THE GAME FINISHED and Sam and Lane headed home. Evan had played the game at a very high level. He went two for four, including the home run. He was a solid base runner as well and put more effort into running down first than any of the other kids trying out.

No doubt the coach in him.

It was getting to the point where she just couldn't ignore the facts. Forgetting his age and lack of experience, Evan Tanner was a solid baseball prospect. And given his overall athleticism and maturity, she could actually see him progressing through the minors at a fast pace.

At the end of the day it was about whether

he had big-league potential. There was no point in sending a guy through the minors just for the chance to play Double A ball for the rest of his life, which is sometimes how it went down for players.

So the question to Scout was going to be, did Evan Tanner have what it took to make it to the majors?

Scout wasn't sure she was ready to answer that question. But she very much wanted to talk about it with someone. Someone who not only understood her love of the game and her commitment to finding the best players, but also knew what putting her job at risk would mean to her.

Hmm…where could she find that person now that Duff was gone?

She wasn't actually looking for Jayson per se. It was just that she needed someone to run some of this stuff by. A person who understood her, a person who understood baseball.

There was nothing clingy or wrong about that, was there? Nothing that suggested just because they'd had sex she was craving spending more time with him. That whenever she came down to the stadium she looked for his car and when she saw it something inside

her seized up. Like some snick of satisfaction
that he was in the same place she was.

That she had the potential to see him.

This is messed up.

It was messed up on both sides. He could
tell her all he wanted that he didn't want her
going out with Evan because of fear for her
job, but she would never buy it. And she knew
that ex-sex couldn't be some simple act between them.

But if they both wanted to pretend for a
time, couldn't they at least do that?

Scout made her way down to Jayson's office, which she tried not to think about as
Duff's old office. With that thought in mind
she knocked on the outer door first but
opened it, assuming he would be in his office. The space was very much as she'd left
it and it occurred to her that eventually when
the season started up again he would probably
need some admin support. He'd done without
while finishing the season this past year, but
really there should be someone to help with
the day-to-day logistics.

Someone else who would sit at what had
been her desk while Jayson ran the team her
father had run for so long.

A sob bubbled up and overcame her. This

had been her life. Her world for years and now it was over. And she was never going to have it back.

Jayson's door opened as if he'd been startled by the sound she'd made. He stopped when he saw her.

Right after Duff's death Jayson had been the one person she couldn't touch. The one person who she wouldn't let touch her. She always believed that if she did, if they had that contact with each other, then any remaining strength she had would be lost and she would crumple to the ground.

Yet Jayson had touched her yesterday. And by touching her…hard…he'd actually made her feel stronger.

She wanted to feel strong again. She wanted not to think about how this life that she'd loved so much would never be hers again. She wanted Jayson.

Without thinking about what she was doing she moved toward him, forcing him back into his office and shutting the door behind her. She locked it just in case but she doubted there was anyone left around the stadium.

She took off her shirt and pressed herself against him. Her mouth found his in one smooth, elegant motion.

Jayson didn't blink. Instead his hands were on her back, then sliding up her stomach. He took off her bra letting it fall to the floor between them and dipped his head so that he could suck her already hard nipple into his mouth. When she thought she couldn't stand it anymore, he moved on to the other one and treated it just as ruthlessly.

Then his mouth was gone but he was kissing her again so that was okay. It was as if he were feeding her all of his power.

She pushed back from him, reached for his shirt and pulled it over his head; when it got stuck he took over, which allowed her free access to his chest. This time she was the one who got to touch and kiss. Finding all the spots she remembered where he was particularly sensitive and making her way down until she found that trail of hair that was leading her to the place she wanted to go.

Oblivion.

Then she was on her knees in front of him. Her fingers were on his jeans and she was undoing his buttons and taking him into her mouth before he had a chance to tell her that's what he wanted.

She might have liked that, she thought. She

might have liked hearing him tell her what he wanted.

Of course, Jayson had taught her how to do this. But anything they had done was usually something she initiated.

She particularly enjoyed oral sex with him. It made him absolutely crazy and when it did, she felt like a sex queen.

Like now, when he was making those funny noises in the back of his throat as she ran her tongue around the crown of his penis. She was destroying him and she loved it.

Pulling back, she put her hand on his erection. Stroking him, she watched his face while she did it. The last time she hadn't been able to look at him for fear of falling into his eyes, but now she wanted to see his face wracked with the pleasure she was giving him.

She could see it there in his expression. His intent. His desire. But he was holding back. She squeezed him but didn't move to take him into her mouth again. This time she did want him to say it.

It was as if he knew what she wanted, as if he knew she wouldn't do anything more than stroke him unless he specifically told her to do it. He threw back his head and made some type of growling noise.

An image ran through her mind, scandalous, a little kinky, something she'd never done before, which made her act before she could think of how he might react. She pulled away from him, taking his erection in her hand and guiding it along her collarbone, then down until the crown of it touched her nipple.

"Ah!"

He was like a man on the rack tortured in the most delicious way.

This time he was the one pushing her away with his hands on her shoulders.

"Stand up."

Slowly she stood, not sure what to expect next. His hands went to her jean buttons, He undid them, then slid her pants and panties down her legs. She kicked them off. Then he turned them so that she was facing the desk. Putting her hands where he wanted them, he moved her legs apart.

"Stay there." He walked around his desk and opened a drawer. He took out his wallet, where he'd apparently slipped a single condom. Hoping for a moment like this between them?

He showed it to her with an evil smile, something she'd never seen on Jayson's face before. "This is what happens when you start having ex-sex. You need to be prepared that it can happen anytime. Anywhere."

He came around to stand behind her. She heard the tear of the foil, saw him toss the remains of it on the desk in front of her. Knew that this time he was rolling it over his shaft and any second he was going to be inside her.

They must have done it like this at some point in their past. With him behind her, but Scout couldn't recall a single memory. So maybe not. Mostly because they liked to look at each other when it was happening. So this not seeing him, now knowing what he was doing or where he was looking was making her slightly crazy.

Then his hand was rubbing over her bottom and she had a pretty good idea where he was looking.

She could feel his chest along her back, his thighs pressing in between her spread ones. His hands were cupping her breasts while his finger and thumb pinched her nipples.

When was he going to do it? When was he going to come inside…

"Jayson!"

The impact of his thrust nearly made her faint and this time there was no waiting for him as her orgasm exploded through her body.

He stilled his motions until she came down from the high, and just feeling him there, so deep and still inside of her, was like nothing she could remember.

How had she lost this? How had she let this go?

"You didn't wait for me," he said, his mouth on her neck sucking her there, ending with another nip on her earlobe.

"I...I couldn't..."

"Well, you'll just have to do it again because I'm not stopping until you do. Put your elbows on the desk, Scout. Yes, like that."

He pushed into her hard and she pushed back against him the same way. They weren't moving together in some beautiful melodic dance. Instead they were like two desperate animals slamming themselves against each other.

She could hear the creaking of the desk as each thrust pushed her against it, making it move ever so little. She could hear his grunting behind her and the sound of his hips slapping against her. Her own squeaks each time he found his way home. Had they ever sounded like this before? Had they ever been this raw?

She was writhing against him. The pressure building and building.

"Jayson!" she wailed, needing him to end it.

"Now," he barked and just that word, that single command, was enough to bring her to completion even as he pumped three heavy strokes inside her while she did.

She fell flat on the desk, her arms spread out beside her, her cheek against his blotter. She felt his hand on her lower back, and he was still inside her as if he was unwilling to break the connection.

"Jayson?" she asked tentatively.

"Yeah, Scout."

"What the hell was that?"

She could feel him chuckle.

"Damned if I know…but I like it," he said. "Ex-sex. Who knew?"

CHAPTER FOURTEEN

JAYSON REALLY NEEDED to get a grip. It was just sex. He'd had sex. Sex before Scout, sex after Scout.

But nothing had ever felt like that.

To avoid her, he bent down and scooped up her clothes. Then he took care of the condom and put his own shirt back on. He sat down behind his desk thinking that might put some distance between them, but how could there be any distance between them after that?

Yesterday had been hot. Today had been earth-shattering. He'd never felt so completely raw with another human being. Like all he would ever be able to do from this moment on would be to thrust his body into hers without ever stopping. Keeping them continually connected.

"Well, I'll say one thing, we sure have come a long way from that first time."

She was trying to make light of it. Trying to talk her way around the intensity of it. He should probably let her. The whole point of convincing her that they could do this with no strings attached was to make her think there was nothing to be afraid of with him.

Except now he was very much convinced that he had something to be afraid of with her.

It was a huge risk already on his part. After all, how was he ever going to know if he could handle the fact that he would always be second place in her life? Second to Duff. But he must have decided at some point that it didn't matter because he'd taken them this far.

He had.

He'd told her not to date Evan. He'd told her they could have sex. He'd screwed her in a way he'd never dreamed of doing and now it felt as if she'd infected him with some disease that would make it hard for him to be more than ten feet away from her.

"I want to be inside you again," he said, the words coming from a place he didn't understand.

She was still putting her shirt on from the last tussle and already he was getting hard.

"Uh… I don't know if that's a good idea… I'm still a little…"

He shook his head, trying to gain some control over himself. He was supposed to be handling her. Not the other way around. "No, you're right. We're in my freaking office, for Pete's sake. Anybody could have knocked."

That made Scout pause. "Uh-oh, does that make me creepy that I just had sex in my father's old office?"

"Were you thinking about him or me?"

"Jayson! Of course I was thinking about you. All I could think about was you."

"Then it's not creepy. And it's my office now."

She was looking at him, studying him. "You're angry?"

"No, not with you." Himself, yes. He was furious at himself for bringing them both to this point.

Because what if it didn't work?

What if he couldn't get her past her grief? What if she could never find a way to forgive him for leaving her? What if she never wanted to risk being in love with him again?

What if all this happened and he was left devastated again?

She was fully dressed now and standing on the other side of the desk. He struggled to find a way to take some of the tension out of the room but absolutely nothing came to him.

When she was gone she would have time to

think about what had happened, time to shore
up her walls. She would be worried, just as
he was worried, that things were getting serious between them again and what that meant.

She would realize that ex-sex was not
something the two of them could never have.
Considering the fact that it had been four
years and they still weren't over each other.

What had he done?

What if this didn't work?

"So we got a little sidetracked…" Jayson
said, the words coming from somewhere.

Scout smiled. "Sidetracked…that's a word
for it."

"You came down here for a reason?"

"Uh, yeah. Actually." She pulled up one
of the guest chairs and sat across from him.
"This is business. Okay?"

"Business. Got it."

Had he kissed her too hard? Her lips
seemed red and puffy.

Do not go there. Business. Scout. Baseball.

"You know it's day four of the tryouts and
Evan is still here."

"Yup."

"He made it through to tomorrow. Chuck
and I both agreed."

He didn't want to even hear Evan's name.

Didn't want the thought of her with any man polluting what had just happened between them. But she said this was business and she'd agreed to never go out with Evan again. He had to take some comfort from that.

"Seriously, I need to know the risk I'm taking."

Jayson looked at her and thought of how much she'd been through. First he came back into her world, then her father left it. Her mother was essentially forcing a reconciliation between them, and now some new guy in the front office appeared not to appreciate the talents a young female scout could bring to the table.

Add crazy sex to all that and he wondered how she was still standing.

But she was Scout so of course she was still standing. They had all been so worried about her. Her family. Him. The truth was she was stronger than anyone gave her credit for.

"I'm sorry, Scout. I hate that I did that. That I made you look over your shoulder." It had been the truth, but he'd said it out of jealousy and that wasn't fair.

Scout shrugged. "I needed to know. Someone needed to tell me. I've been a part of this team for so long, and here working with Duff these past few years, it was easy to think…I was one of them. That I was baseball people."

"You are baseball people!" he charged, hating that he even needed to tell her this. "You know more about the game than seventy-five percent of the people currently managing it. You can spot raw talent a mile away, and I looked at your damn track record. Your matriculation rate for those recommended by you who make it to The Show is nearly unmatched."

"Because I don't take risks," she admitted, throwing his words back in his face. "Which is why I need to know how far on the ledge this puts me if I hand in a scouting report on Evan."

Jayson leaned back in his chair. It was hard to know how he felt. On the one hand, he was pleased that Scout was even considering putting herself out there. It meant change. It meant progress. It meant she was growing and that could be nothing but good for them.

On the other hand, he hated that it was Evan she was taking the risk on.

"You're that certain."

"Jayson, if he was ten years younger I would be suggesting to the Rebels organization that he be considered as first-round draft potential."

Jayson sighed. "You're that certain."

"I'm that certain. I just… I mean you know what baseball means to me. If I lose it because of this… But at the same time, this is my job. This is what I do. This is everything Duff gave to me that he wanted me to share. He was one of the best there ever was. I'm his legacy. If I can't stand up for someone I believe in, then what am I doing?"

Jayson looked at her and he could see the determination in her eyes. "Write up the prospect sheet exactly the way you want to. I've got your back."

She smiled and he felt as if he'd been given gold. "I'm not wrong."

"You better not be."

She stood and seemed to not know what to do with her hands. "So do we need to talk about…"

"No," he said quickly. He didn't want to talk about what they had done, couldn't really even process it right now. "You don't talk about it. You just do it."

She nodded. "Okay." She turned to leave and made it to the door of his office when she stopped.

"Jayson... I'm glad you came back."

With that she opened the door and practically ran through it. He heard the outer door close and dropped his head into his hands.

He was playing with fire. What was he going to do if this didn't work?

You've got to make it work.

Jayson groaned. "Damn it, old man, stay out of my head!"

SCOUT WALKED THROUGH her back kitchen door and saw the gang assembled. Alice was standing over the stove making something that smelled delicious and Sam was studiously reading something on her phone while Bob sat with a book in his hands.

She considered how only a few weeks ago this sight might have been maddening to her.

Now she could see how wrong she'd been. How an empty house might have damaged her psyche. She'd told Jayson she was glad he had come back because she knew now those months before Duff's death and these past few weeks since it would have been unbearable without him.

The same was true of her family.

"Thank you all for being here."

They all stopped what they were doing and

turned toward her. It made her squirm a bit but they deserved this after putting up with her behavior.

"You were right. I needed you. Here with me. Even you, Bob."

He smiled. "I feel honored."

Alice walked over to her. "We do love you, you know. Nothing you could ever say or do would change that."

"Really? Because I accused you of cheating on Duff," Scout reminded her. Pretty awful stuff.

"You were wrong and you apologized and now that's over. And I still love you."

Scout looked at her mother, this woman who she'd kept at bay for so many years. All that animosity and for what? Because Scout had felt as if she owed it to Duff. Like someone needed to be on his side. To Duff's credit, he'd always discouraged that kind of thinking. He'd wanted Scout to be closer to her mother. To not hold her second marriage against her.

But Scout had been too damned stubborn.

What would it have been like if Scout could have gone to her mother after Jayson broke her heart? Because as wonderful as Duff was it had been clear back then that he'd been at a loss to handle Scout.

"I'm having ex-sex with Jayson and I don't know what to do about it," Scout blurted out.

"And I'll take that as my queue to leave," Bob announced. He stood with his book and walked by Alice, giving her a kiss on the cheek. "Let me know when dinner is ready and when it's safe to come back."

"Will do."

Scout slumped into one of the kitchen chairs and Sam was already up and getting a beer from the fridge. She set it down in front of Scout with a clunk.

"Talk. Now," Sam told her.

"I don't know how it happened. I went over there to yell at him for messing up my date with Evan and the next thing you know he's saying we can have no-strings-attached ex-sex."

"So this was Jayson's idea," Alice said. She and Sam exchanged a look and Scout pounced on it.

"Don't do that. Don't look at each other like you all know what's going on and I'm the only one who doesn't."

Alice sat across from Scout and took her hands. "Honey, sometimes things don't have to be as complicated as you make them."

Scout pulled her hands back. "That's all you got? You're supposed to be better at this kind of stuff than Duff was. Right now you're batting zero."

"All I'm saying is that you have to ask yourself how you feel about him."

"About Jayson? I feel ten thousand things about Jayson. That I want to be over him. That I don't want to see his face ever again. That I want to pretend I haven't been letting him affect me for the past four years."

"That you want to have sex with him again," Sam added.

"Like a million more times!" Scout put her hands over her face. "What have I done?"

"Do you want to be free of Jayson?" her mother asked.

It was a hard question to answer. For years she'd wanted nothing more than that. She thought she could will herself into being over him by simply dating someone else. Now she couldn't say what she wanted anymore.

"I'm so afraid of him. Of how he makes me feel. If we do this again and I get hurt again..."

"Then you get hurt again," Alice said.

"You know, Mom, you are really not good at this at all."

"Yeah, I think I'm with Scout on this. Sometimes it makes sense to avoid the pain," Sam added.

Alice shook her head. "My two daughters… you are both completely wrong. And you should talk to Lane. She took a risk with someone who hurt her. And look how that turned out."

"Dumb luck," Scout muttered.

"Not dumb luck at all. Lane just let love guide her. You need to consider doing the same. Take a risk on Jayson. Try loving him again and see where that takes you."

"But what if it ends?"

"Elizabeth." Alice sighed. "I know I set a horrible example with your father. I understand how that affected you. But I'm here to tell you not everything ends."

"Well, it did with him the last time and it nearly killed me."

"Yet here you are still standing," Alice reminded her. "You're a strong woman, Scout. I wouldn't have raised my daughters any other way. If you take a chance with Jayson and it doesn't work out, you will survive it. Just like you've survived every other loss you've suffered. Starting with me when you were just fourteen."

Scout felt the impact of those words in the back of her skull. "I chose to leave. To live with Duff."

"I know you did, but the result was the same. You still weren't living with me at an age when a girl needs her mother. Plus you carried all that animosity because I married Bob. I was practically dead to you and that had to have hurt."

Scout could feel tears in her eyes but she wasn't sure where they had come from. Then they were sliding down her cheeks and suddenly she was bawling, just like she'd been about to when Jayson had opened the door. She could feel her mother's arms around her. Could hear her telling her to hush and that everything was going to be all right.

Finally Scout tried to take deep breaths to stop the shuddering. Then she stood and wiped away the tears.

"I hate to cry in public," she muttered.

"We know," Sam said.

"Go upstairs and lay down for a while. A cold washcloth on your eyes might help. I'll let you know when dinner is ready."

"Thanks," Scout said. "Thanks for everything."

SAM WAITED UNTIL Scout was gone and it was just her and her mother. "She's been such a bitch to you for so many years. It's really kind of amazing you can just forgive her like that."

"Don't call your sister a bitch," Alice scolded. "And, no, it's not amazing at all. I'm her mother. Of course I love her. And you weren't around when things got bad between Duff and me. Can you imagine what it must have been like for her? Constant fighting. Knowing that separation was imminent. When I look back I have so much regret for not doing a better job with her. For letting my anger toward Duff show all the time. I didn't even consider what she would think about me marrying Bob so quickly. What conclusion she might have reached. It was thoughtless and selfish. And it certainly didn't win me any mother of the year awards."

"Yes, but she doesn't even know what all the fighting was about. Maybe if you told her and she could see that Duff was in the wrong she might understand better."

"No," Alice said sharply. "It's too soon for her to hear anything that might be upsetting about her father. And the truth doesn't change anything. The fighting was real, the divorce was real. That's what hurt her, and that's what she has to recover from."

"I just don't like keeping secrets from her," Sam said. "It doesn't seem right."

"Someday we'll tell her. For now we leave things as is. She's recovering. Slowly but surely. I don't know if that's because of us or Jayson or what, but in another few weeks I feel confident she'll be able to stand on her own."

Sam laughed. "Well, I'm not leaving until I see how the whole ex-sex thing works out with Jayson."

"You know, you might want to spend less time worrying about your sister's love life and more time worried about your own."

"I don't have a love life." And why an image of Evan Tanner's face should pop into her head she didn't know. Sam immediately squashed it.

"That's exactly my point. You can't let one bad experience affect the rest of your life."

Sam shook her head, rejecting what sounded like such simple advice. "Mom, I hate to tell you, you are a little naive."

"No, sweetheart, I hate to tell you, you are dead wrong. You have to put what that man did to you aside and move on with your life.

Or else he wins. And as a Baker girl you cannot let that happen."

Sam smiled sadly. "But I'm not really a Baker girl, am I?" She stood and kissed her mother on the cheek.

CHAPTER FIFTEEN

IT WAS FRIDAY and the last day of the tryout camp. A few of the locals came out to watch the game. The stadium gates were open and, because there were no concessions, people felt free to bring in their own box lunches and coolers.

"This town will take any excuse to watch a baseball game."

Scout turned at the voice behind her, not really all that surprised to see Sam had come back to take in another game. Her sister sat next to her in the bleachers looking suspiciously hot in a pair of skinny jeans, high-heeled boots and an obviously expensive peach sweater, which showed off her complexion to its best advantage.

"A free one on top of that," Scout said. "I'm sure Jocelyn's already thinking about a way to make money off this camp next year."

"Jocelyn Taft," Sam repeated. "I used to read about her all the time. I still can't believe she gave most of her money away and settled on this. She's married to the reporter guy?"

"Yep, she's something. Former billionaire turned baseball chick. And I have to say a pretty good boss to work for, at least when I was working for her. She knew what was happening with Duff, knew how much I was covering for him. She could have said something to Reuben, but she didn't. She just let me do my own thing and it worked. Until it didn't."

"Unlike your new boss, it would seem."

Scout didn't want to talk about Greg. She thought about what she'd done last night and fidgeted in her seat. To distract herself she eyed up what her sister was wearing.

"A little decked out for a baseball game, aren't you?" Scout asked. "Hmm, I wonder why?"

"I don't know what you're talking about," Sam said with her nose in the air.

"Right." Scout laughed. "You being here two days in a row to watch a simulated game has nothing to do with the fact that Evan Tanner is once again playing as part of the starting lineup. They've got him batting in the cleanup spot, if you're curious."

"I'm not," Sam insisted, her tone full-on ice queen.

"You know, technically speaking, I did date him," Scout reminded her. "It would be breaking the sister rule entirely for you to go after someone I was once involved with."

"First of all, I'm not going *after* anyone. Second of all, you went out on one bad date in which you were followed by your ex-boyfriend's players in an attempt to thwart said date. Seems to me that night was more about you and Jayson than it was about you and Evan."

Of course she was right but that didn't mean Scout wasn't going to give Sam a hard time about her interest in Evan.

"Said date," Scout repeated. "I love it when you get all lawyery on me."

"My point is, even if I were interested, which I'm not, it still wouldn't be any type of sisterly violation."

"Says the authority on sisterly violations. Hey, look, he's about to start batting practice. Why don't we go over and check it out."

Sam tensed. "There is nothing I need to check out."

"Dude, do I need to remind you that you are, in fact, a sports agent? And that he is potentially a candidate to be a professional ballplayer? Someone that a lot of other agents might overlook given his circumstances."

"He's only twenty-seven. You talk about him like he's already got one foot in the grave."

"Right. So much younger than say…thirty-three."

Sam's eyes narrowed. "I think I was a much happier person when you weren't speaking to me."

Scout laughed. "Come on. I'm serious. This guy is the real thing. At least come watch him swing a bat. You might not have my particular talents, but you still know a sweet swing when you see it, don't you?"

Sam scowled again. "Duff raised me the same way he raised you. I know baseball, too."

"Then you're going to want to check this guy out. What was Mom saying yesterday… that sometimes you have to take a chance?"

"Oh, sure." Sam tossed her arms in the air. "Now you decide to listen to Mom. Fine, I'll go, but only to shut you up."

The two made their way onto the field. As a scout, Scout had complete access to all the facilities and the field itself. There were times when she was looking at a player she wanted some distance so she could see how he handled himself in the field of play. But other times it paid to get in close.

"Hey, Evan," she greeted him.

"Scout," he acknowledged as he started swinging his bat around his shoulder.

"You remember my sister Sam."

"Sure do." He smiled. "Hi again, Sam."

Sam offered up a little wave.

"She wants to see you swing your big bat," Scout said. She could feel Sam's finger jab sharply into her back. It hurt but it was totally worth it.

Evan laughed, taking it all in good fun. "Sure. I would love to show Sam how I swing my big bat."

For that Scout took another jab to the back. "Quit it."

"I'm a sports agent," Sam said, as if he'd offended her somehow. "I take my job very seriously…Mister Tanner."

"It's just Evan."

"Well, Evan, I take my job very seriously."

"Yes, you said that."

"My sister seems to think you have talent."

"I don't think it, I know it," Scout interjected.

"Anyway, I would consider it very unprofessional of me if I didn't at least take a look at what you can do."

"Wait a minute," Evan said. "Are you talking about representing me? As my agent."

"Of course not. Don't be ridiculous," Sam huffed. "You're not even drafted. But if you were drafted and did move through the ranks as far as the majors, I potentially could or could not consider offering you my services. I have a very select client list."

"Yeah, Evan, she's uber exclusive but she's landed a bunch of sweet deals for some players. So show her what you can do."

Scout was pretty sure Evan's intent to show Sam something had more to do with impressing her than it did potentially landing her as an agent. Either way he stepped into the batter's box with a gleam in his eye.

Scout figured they were both in store for a show.

And he didn't disappoint. Pitch after pitch he hit the ball. Never missing when the ball was solidly in the strike zone and, just as important, never swinging when it was out of it. The kid pitching to him wasn't a stud like Roy Walker might have been, but the likelihood was he would also be recommended for the draft so it wasn't as if he was batting against a pitching coach.

After about twenty or so balls he finally backed out of the box and turned to see the sisters' reaction.

Scout smiled and just nodded. "I'm not wrong about baseball, Evan. I never am."

Except Evan clearly didn't care so much about what Scout thought. He was obviously waiting on Sam's reaction.

"Well?"

"Not bad," Sam said casually. "Good luck today."

"Thanks. I'll take all the luck I can."

They left as he returned to the dugout. A few other guys came up to take batting practice and Scout and Sam returned to their seats to get ready for the start of the game.

"So come on," Scout said. "Tell me what you really think."

"You want my opinion? I thought I didn't have your baseball talents."

"Sam, don't give me crap right now. You know I'm taking a huge risk on this guy. Tell me what you think."

"Do you really think that? I mean I know that's what Jayson said, but are you seriously suggesting that if you recommend Evan for the draft it might cost you your job?"

"He doesn't look good on paper," Scout said honestly. "And sometimes paper is all they have to go by."

Sam scrunched up her face. "Then don't do it. Let Jayson or one of the other coaches submit the information. Can't that be done?"

"No, Sam. I'm a scout. It's my job to assess talent and my job to report on that. If I can't put my name on something, that just makes me a coward."

"So you're seriously willing to put your career on the line for this guy?"

Scout could hear the incredulity in Sam's voice. "My job is to judge baseball talent. This guy's got it. If I back down from him, what's the next thing I'm going to back down from? Now tell me what you think."

Sam nodded. "I think he's got a really sweet swing. I think Duff would take one look at him and identify him as a player. You're not wrong."

It was grim satisfaction, but it still was good to hear.

JAYSON LOOKED OUT over the stadium and took pleasure in the sight of a baseball game in progress. He made his way through the stands, taking in the families who had come out on a beautiful late fall day to watch a meaningless simulated game.

This was what baseball was all about, he thought.

People could come to a game and watch events unfold. Or they could sit and talk amid the backdrop of a fairly low-paced game with a few moments of excitement interspersed.

Easy. Baseball was always easy. At least for the people watching it. Not so much for those who played it.

He glanced at the heads in the stadium and found the one he was looking for her. In her preferred spot on the first base line. Her blond ponytail and baseball cap immediately drew his attention.

Or maybe it was just her. Maybe she was always going to pull him toward her. His inexorable moon. He thought about what had happened in his office yesterday and wondered what would happen if he went down and sat next to her. How long would he hold out before he asked her to go with him to his office, or his car, or heck, maybe a broom closet somewhere in the standing-room-only section?

That way lay danger.

He knew that. Instinctively he knew it, but he didn't care. His feet were moving and he was heading down the steps and weaving his way in and out through rows of seats to get to her.

He took the open seat next to her. "Hey."

She started and he wasn't sure if it was because he legitimately took her by surprise or it was just the fact that she was seeing him again.

"Hey," she said back with a smile.

"This seat taken?"

Cheesy, awful line. Could he be any lamer?

"Uh, actually yes."

Okay, so not only was he lame but he was also being shot down. Not sure what he should do he was about to get up and spare himself any more agony when she just hit him on the shoulder.

"Sam went to the bathroom so you should be good for the next hour or so."

"Sam came to watch a simulated game?"

"No," Scout corrected him. "Sam came to watch Evan. Who just happens to be playing in a simulated game."

"What the hell is it with that guy?"

"Well, he's handsome. And he's an amazing athlete. Plus, he's a nice guy…"

"You don't stop talking about him soon, I can't account for what my next actions will be."

Scout smiled, clearly unafraid of his threat.

"I'm serious," he said, leaning into her to whisper into her ear. "It might involve spanking. How would you feel about a little spanking, Scout?"

Her whole body wiggle told its own story.

"Yes, I think you might like that. So by all means go on and keep talking about Evan Tanner."

She blushed and Jayson felt as if he was some kind of sex god. He'd never spanked a woman in his life but if just the words were enough to make Scout blush, then he was all for it.

"How come it's like this now?"

"Like what now?"

"Between us. The sex I mean. I always thought we had really good sex before."

Jayson shifted in his seat. It was crazy but it made him feel uncomfortable to talk about what they used to be before. He didn't want to go back there; he only wanted to think about them going forward.

"We did have really good sex."

"But it wasn't... I mean it wasn't as..."

Hot. Dirty. Neither of those words really worked. "Intense."

"Yes, intense. Is it because it's ex-sex? Is that really how it's supposed to be?"

It was questions like that that reminded him she'd been a virgin when he'd first had her. A virgin until him, then nothing since him. There were still so many things about sex that she didn't know unless he told her.

Which was fine by him because the alternative was her with other men and that was not something he wanted to imagine.

He thought of a hundred lies he could tell her. Things he could say that would allow them to go on pretending for a little while longer. But she had to know that what was happening between them was more than just meaningless sex.

"No, Scout. I think it is what it is because it's us. And maybe we're different people than we were back then and that's reflected in the sex."

"You were always so careful with me in the past. I felt cherished."

Jayson winced at that. He certainly hadn't made her feel cherished the last two times together, but he wouldn't take back a single moment because although it was different, it was still them.

"Now you make me feel…"

Scout let her words trail off and Jayson winced again. Maybe she hadn't been feeling what he'd been feeling. Maybe she hadn't liked the way he spoke to her. Or maybe she did while it was happening but upon reflection it made her feel used. He would hate for that to be the case.

"Strong."

Jayson blinked. Then released his breath. Strong wasn't a bad thing. Strong was a good thing.

"Powerful," she added with a shy smile.

Powerful was even better than strong.

"Keep going," he told her.

"I feel like we're equals now. And maybe instead of you always trying to please me and make me feel good you're taking something for yourself. Something that you trust me to give to you. And that makes me feel strong."

Jayson closed his eyes, growing hard. "Come with me now."

"I should be watching the game. I'm supposed to be evaluating the talent."

He leaned down again so he could whisper in her ear. "The only talent you're going to be evaluating in the next thirty minutes or so is my sexual talent. Specifically my oral skills. Do you remember those, Scout?"

"Yes. You always were a complete five tool player," she said as she blushed even harder.

"Come with me now," he repeated, reaching over the seat to take her hand. "I'm going to lay you out on top of my desk and do wicked things with your body."

Their eyes met and the desire and the need were so clear in hers. As clear as it must be in his. He took her hand in his and brought it over to his side of the seat, subtly placing it on his erection so she knew exactly where he stood.

"Yes, I think I've seen all I need to see of those players."

They stood and started to move up the steps with him just behind her using her body in many ways to shield what was pretty evident in his jeans.

"Oh, wait!" Scout said, turning to face him. "What about Samantha?"

"You can text her later. Say business came up."

"Yeah, she's probably going to know what that business is. I sort of let it slip about the ex-sex."

"Do you care?"

Please say no.

She waited a beat before she said, "No."

He smiled and climbed the step so he was just taller than she was. He meant only to brush her lips with his as a silent thank you, but as soon as he felt her mouth beneath hers he became ravenous.

"Hey, get a room, pal! My kid's with me."

Scout jerked away and Jayson immediately stepped back with a mumbled sorry to the immediate vicinity. Before they realized what was happening they were running up the steps through the mezzanine area to the elevator that would take them up a level to the stadium offices.

As soon as the elevator closed behind them Jayson was reaching for Scout. Not that he had to reach very far; she was already moving into his arms. Jayson cupped her cheek so he could feel the soft skin there and tilted her head just the way he liked it so that she was at the perfect angle.

She was delicious to him. The sweetest nectar, the tastiest wine.

"Four years," he whispered against her open mouth, loving the feel of her hot breath blending with his. "How did I go without this for four years?"

"Jayson…"

The elevator doors opened and they sprang apart.

Jayson checked to make sure the coast was clear and grabbed Scout's hand. He all but pulled her to his office. Locking the outer door behind him.

"I want you naked and on my desk in like three seconds, Scout."

She was already lifting up her shirt when Jayson felt his cell phone buzzing in his back pocket. He pulled it out with the intent to toss it on the desk and forget about it when the number on the display caught his attention.

Scout was unhooking her bra. "Scout, wait. I have to take this."

He wasn't sure why he had such a gut reaction to the number. It probably meant nothing. But it wasn't as if he got calls from the GM of the New England Rebels every day.

"Hey, Reuben, what's up?"

Jayson listened to the conversation and

came to understand what it meant when people said white as a ghost. As he hung up, he didn't feel like there was any blood left in his face.

Scout slowly refastened her bra and put her shirt back on.

He waited until her shirt was in place before he said anything. He didn't want any part of her naked when she heard what he had to tell her.

"You sent the prospect sheets in already," he said softly.

Her chin jutted out. "Last night. I didn't want to chicken out. It wouldn't be fair to Evan. He deserves a shot and shouldn't lose that because of me."

"Greg spoke to Reuben about you and they would like you to head to Boston. They want to see you at headquarters tomorrow afternoon."

CHAPTER SIXTEEN

"I'M GOING WITH YOU," Jayson told her. "We'll drive. First thing in the morning. It's about a five-hour trip so we should have no problem getting there around one or two in the afternoon."

"No, you're not." Scout's head felt cloudy. Like it had when she woke up the morning after Duff had died. As if she was on some different plane of existence. Not part of the world. Not away from it.

Again the memory of the day Duff died came back to her as this kind of other-worldly event. She remembered Lane saying Duff was gone. She remembered feeling as if she was floating…falling…and then nothing. That moment right after felt like a total blank. Gone.

That didn't matter now.

She'd sent in a prospect sheet with a strong recommendation to draft a highly unlikely can-

STEPHANIE DOYLE 285

didate. She'd done it because it was important to her, only now she might lose everything.

"You certainly are not going alone."

"You don't even know what this means," she said, trying to maintain a modicum of hope. "So they want to talk to me? Maybe they just want to talk directly to me about Evan."

"If that's the case, then what is the problem with me coming with you?" Jayson argued.

"Because you're doing it to protect me!" She was furious. Out-of-control furious except she couldn't say why or at whom. Maybe fate in general. Sadly Jayson was the only person in the room she could take that out on.

"What's so wrong with that?" he snapped. "Why can't I do that?"

"Because you're not my boyfriend! You're my ex-boyfriend. Ex. Over. I'm not your responsibility. You didn't have to come back here because Duff asked you to. When he realized he was dying. He was the reason you did it. He would have asked you to come for me. Did you think I couldn't figure that out?"

Jayson ran a hand through his hair and she could see he was contemplating lying but he didn't have it in him to lie to her about something so big.

"Okay, maybe he did ask me, but you also know deep inside that I came back for you."

Scout shook her head, rejecting what wasn't reality. "No. How can I? A request like that from Duff, when he was sick? You would have done anything for him."

"He knew you were going to need me and he was right. Well, I'm here, Scout. I've been here for months and you have needed me. This thing that's happening between us is real."

"Is it? Or am I just so desperate and alone right now that I'm grabbing on to the only comfort that's out there for me now?"

She could see the hurt in his face. The way he absorbed her blow…it was so stalwart of him. It made her want to keep firing.

He took a deep breath, as if he'd actually been punched in the gut and was trying to shake it off. "You're scared and you're acting out right now. We're both going to calm down, take some breaths and come up with a plan for tomorrow."

"No. *We* are not. Because we're not a *we* anymore. You left me, or I didn't follow you, whichever way it went we couldn't make it work. And hot sex isn't going to change that. Admit it. You'll always wonder if I had it to do all over again if I would chose any differently. If I would pick you over Duff and my life here."

"I'm willing to let the past go," he said through clenched teeth. "We could have a new start."

"Really?" Scout asked, hating that she couldn't believe what he was saying. What he was saying sounded so hopeful. "I know you, Jayson. What it meant when your father left you. I understand what it meant for to you to be rejected like that. The second I told you I wasn't going with you, it was over in your mind. No second chances for me. You didn't call me one time, not one time after you left."

"Are you serious?" he shouted. "You're seriously going to say the problem was I didn't try hard enough. When your feet were buried in three feet of cement keeping you at Duff's side."

"See," she said, making her point. "You're never going to get past that. You're never going to believe I would pick you first over anyone. And I'm never going to know if you would have ever come back for me. Not because Duff was dying. Not because you pitied me but because you loved me."

"Of course I love you!"

The words nearly reverberated off the walls. Scout felt them in her head and her body, in her bones and her blood. She wanted to believe them. She wanted to so badly but she couldn't.

She felt like a cornered animal, not sure which way to turn but only that she had to escape. Fast.

"I can't do this right now." She could feel she was starting to shake.

Jayson sighed but said nothing at first. Clearly uncertain of what to do with her in this state. "Let me take you back to my place. We can talk there."

"No. There is nothing to talk about anymore. I told you once that all you ever do is hurt me but the truth is all we ever do is hurt each other. We couldn't make it work. What we felt wasn't enough to keep us together. So it ended. Four years ago. We both should have moved on by now. Just because my life is coming apart doesn't mean you have to step in and play the hero. It was wrong of Duff to even put you in that position."

"You don't understand," he growled. "It wasn't like that."

"No, Jayson, you don't understand. I have to be my own hero. I'm releasing you from your promise to Duff. I'm not yours or anyone else's responsibility. I'll handle Boston and whatever comes next on my own."

Scout stepped around him toward the outer office door. She turned the doorknob and realized it was locked. Locked because they were two twisted people who apparently couldn't keep their hands off each other.

"Maybe the pleasure, the physical pleasure was just a way to try and make up for the pain," she whispered as she undid the lock. "But it will never be enough. Goodbye, Jayson."

She hoped he heard her.

She shut the door behind her and didn't look back.

SCOUT PULLED THE single skirt she had out of her closet and stared at it. It was blue. That was about the most she could say for it. She knew there was a matching suit jacket buried somewhere and figured she needed to find it.

It's not as if she could show up to a meeting with her boss and the team's GM topless. No, that probably wouldn't go over very well at all.

But as she continued to stare at the closet it took her a moment to remember what she was supposed to be looking for.

A top. No, a blouse. And a jacket. So she would look professional. A person should look professional if she was about to be fired.

Fired from baseball.

A knock on the door startled her. Who could possibly be knocking on her door? Then she remembered she had her family staying with her. Her mother and her sister and Bob. They were all here because Duff was dead.

She opened the door and saw Bob's face. The face of the enemy for so long and now he was just Bob.

"What's up, Bob?"

"Jayson called. Said you've got a meeting in Boston tomorrow."

"Yep."

There he goes again. Trying to protect you. Trying to get you help. Letting your family know what was about to happen so they could support you. Eventually it would stop. His caring. Eventually that would end.

Besides, she didn't need anyone's support. No, that wasn't true. She didn't want it. She wanted to be strong enough on her own, but she probably wasn't. At least she could admit that now.

"What are your plans?"

"I booked a flight out of Albany. Should be back by dinnertime if all goes well. Maybe Mom can make one of my favorites for dinner. I really like her pea soup. But she also does a mean pot roast. Do you like pot roast, Bob?"

Bob just stared at her for a moment. Scout couldn't fathom what her expression must look like right now.

Did she look dead? Because she felt dead on the inside.

Goodbye, Jayson.

Had she really said those words again? Because there was a time when she would have sworn she never would say those words again. That if she ever got a second chance she would take it.

Not that his being back here was that second chance. No, his being back here was for Duff.

She could have almost forgotten that. If she'd laid down on his desk today and made love to him, she could have almost forgotten that he wasn't really here for her.

"I'll take you to the airport. Then call me when you land and I'll pick you up."

"I can drive myself."

"I know you can, but I'll take you."

"Okay. Thanks."

Bob turned to leave but then stopped himself. "You're going to think this is crazy and maybe it is, but when I came back from my military assignment and your mom was married to someone else I never felt heartbreak like that in my life. I mean I had just been through some pretty bad shit and none of it seemed to compare. So if you need someone to talk to about anything...well...I've been there."

He was truly a sweet man. She'd been awful to him for years and in her hour of need he was offering whatever help he could. There was just one problem. In the end it all worked out for him. He got his true love after all.

So, no, he didn't know exactly what Scout was going through.

Still. "Thanks, Bob. I really appreciate it."

He nodded and left her alone. Everyone left her alone for the rest of the night. They didn't ask her to come down for dinner. Or fuss with her at breakfast the next morning.

No one said anything about the skirt and the blue pumps that pinched her feet. They didn't comment that her hair had been blown out and left to hang down her shoulders without being pulled back into a ponytail.

Bob didn't say much during the drive to the airport, either. They'd had to get a very early start to be there in time and Bob had only gotten to drink one cup of coffee. He was very clearly a two-cup man.

They arrived at the airport and Bob pulled up to the curb. "You'll call me when you land?"

"Yep."

"Scout..."

"I'm okay, Bob. Really. This is nothing more than a business meeting. Everyone needs to chill out."

She hoped that sounded convincing.

"Right. Okay. Then call me as you're leaving and I'll be waiting here for you when you land."

"Got it. Thanks again."

She could see it in his face. The worry. But she could also see the helplessness. Because there was nothing he could do. Nothing anyone could do.

After all baseball was a game, but it was business, too.

IT ALL WENT rather smoothly. Without any luggage it was easy to navigate through the airport. The plane took off as scheduled. Scout got to Boston with time to spare. She wandered around the city to kill a few hours before the scheduled meeting at two o'clock.

Reuben and Greg had only kept her waiting five minutes before they called her inside. They showed her Evan's prospect sheet and mentioned that they had some concerns.

Actually those concerns had started long before the prospect sheet arrived. Apparently what Scout had done to cover up Duff's failing condition had become common knowledge.

Although both men understood why she had done it, to protect her father's vaulted legacy, they did have to point out that she hadn't acted in the best interest of the organization. After all, the Minotaurs were the Rebels' Triple A team, a vital stepping-stone for players hoping to move to the next level. Without proper management, had those players been getting the direction they needed?

And of course now she was recommending such an unqualified candidate they didn't feel they could continue to trust her in her current role.

However, out of respect and loyalty to Duff, they were willing to find her another position within the organization. Something maybe in administration or the travel arrangements department?

Scout smiled but regretfully felt that it would probably be best to part ways. She didn't see much of a future in that type of role.

A cab was waiting for her outside the building. She made her flight and landed on time back in Albany.

All things considered, the day had gone rather predictably.

However, she didn't think she would call Bob. No, it probably made sense to take a different approach.

Four years ago

"HEY, SCOUT, I'M HOME."

She heard Jayson's front door open and then close behind him. Scout looked at the pot on the stove in front of her and winced. This was supposed to have been her attempt at cooking.

Stupid idea actually. It's not as if Jayson needed proof that she was capable of doing other things. But she wanted to show him she wasn't all work all the time. All baseball all the time.

That she had other interests and other hob-
bies. Things like cooking. Except the pot in
front her proved to be a hot mess of what was
supposed to be chili.

Maybe cooking wasn't her thing. Maybe
she should try gardening.

"Hey…oh, my…what is that smell?"

Jayson came up behind her and glanced
over her shoulder.

It was brown and muddy looking. Did it
smell bad enough to permeate the whole
house? Obviously it did. All she knew was
that when she tried to smell it, it burned her
nostrils.

"What are you doing?" he asked.

"Well, it was supposed to be cooking. Only
it didn't go so well."

"Scout, you don't cook."

"Technically that's not true. I haven't
cooked in the past, but it doesn't mean I
couldn't learn to cook in the future. I mean,
I'm not completely without domestic skills."

Actually, apparently she was. At least when
it came to homemade chili.

"Do you want me to try it?" He was sweet
enough to ask the question, but it was clear
he did so with a great deal of hesitation.

"No," she said, afraid of what the mountains upon mountains of chili powder would do to his insides. If it could burn nostrils just smelling it, she didn't imagine eating it could be a healthy decision. "Next time I'll try to be less creative and just follow some instructions. I mean, how hard can it be to cook?"

"Whatever. Besides I wanted to take you out tonight. We're celebrating!"

She turned around and she could see his excitement. It made her instantly excited, too. Because she'd learned that's what love was. What he felt, she felt and vice versa.

"Lay it on me."

"I got a job offer as a manager. Assistant, and it's Double A, but still it's a foot in the door."

Scout needed a second to process that. He got a job. He was going to be an assistant manager. But the Rebels' Double A team was in the Texas League. That couldn't be right.

"But isn't that Texas?"

"Houston. I know it will be a real change from the northeast. But the northeast was a real change from Louisiana so I guess I'm just going to have to get used to it."

Scout didn't know what to say. She didn't

know what to think. The only thing that kept going through her mind was Texas.

Texas was very far away from Minotaur Falls.

He must have seen her expression.

"Scout, wait a minute. You don't think… I mean I'm not leaving…"

"Oh, thank you, God!" She wrapped her arms around him and held tight. He wasn't leaving. He was simply excited that he got offered the job.

"…without you."

She took a step back from him. "What do you mean?"

He was smiling and he looked so sure of himself. So sure of his future.

"I mean I want you to go with me. I want us to live together. Ask the Rebels for a transfer and if they don't give you one, then you'll find another team to scout for down there. You're Duff Baker's daughter, so it's not like you're going to have a hard time finding a job."

Right. She was Duff Baker's daughter.

"You want me to leave Minotaur Falls. You want me to leave my dad?"

"Not leave him. No, he's still your dad. You'll do what my mom and I do. I'll hook you up so you can Skype with him every night if you want."

"Duff isn't going to Skype," Scout snapped. "You know he hates anything resembling technology."

"Fine, you'll call him every day. But this is a huge opportunity for me, Scout. And you know this is how it works in baseball. I've got to go to the job. I can't wait for the job to come to Minotaur Falls."

"Why not? Eventually Duff's going to want to retire. Why wouldn't you just wait…"

"Because I'm not waiting for Duff to retire! And then, what, just step into his shoes? How is that proving anything to anyone? I need to do this on my own. Show them that I can do this job at a high level. I do that and we both know what comes next. We're talking The Show."

Scout shook her head, unwilling to accept that this was his only option. "I hear what you're saying. I just don't see why you have to go to Texas to get there."

He looked hard at her then. It was always the same look when he was trying to figure out what was going on inside her head. Something he'd really never been able to do. Scout used to think that was a good thing. That she would always be something of a mystery to him. A puzzle he could never solve exactly so he would always keep trying.

Now she wasn't so sure. Now she wanted him to know how scary the prospect of uprooting her life and following him to Texas was.

"I thought you would be excited for me. For us. Living together is the next step. You get that, right?"

"I do, but I want to do that here."

Jayson scowled. "Really? I thought we couldn't live together here because you thought Duff would disapprove."

Scout winced. That had been her excuse. "Eventually, he'll come around. He's just old-fashioned. I need to ease him into these kinds of things."

"Or you could tell him that you're a grown woman and you're capable of making your own decisions."

This was an old fight. One she didn't want to have again. She just needed him to say that he wasn't going to take the job. That he was going to stay here in Minotaur Falls and wait for a coaching position to open up on the team.

She wrapped her arms around his waist and snuggled against him. His body was stiff but eventually he would soften. Jayson loved her. There was nothing he wouldn't do for her.

"You don't want to go to Texas," she said against his neck. "It's hot and dusty."

"Scout," he said, pushing her back, "I'm not joking about this. I came home tonight and I thought this was going to be a slam dunk. I know you're really close with Duff. I get that. I love my mother the same way. But at some point you have to move on. We have to move on together."

"Right. But why can't we move on together here?"

"Because the job is in Texas," he said flatly.

There was so much finality in his tone. As if her opinion on this didn't matter at all. As if he'd already decided and what she wanted meant nothing. That wasn't how love was supposed to work.

"Then you just need to wait until the job is in Minotaur Falls." There, she thought. That sounded final, too.

Jayson shook his head. "You don't get it, Scout."

"What?" she asked, although she didn't really want the answer. Because she could feel in her gut that she wasn't going to like it.

"I already accepted the position. I'm leaving in two weeks. Now, are you coming with me or not?"

CHAPTER SEVENTEEN

Present

"I'LL HAVE ANOTHER, CHRIS." Scout pushed her empty glass forward on the bar. Maybe a little too hard because she knocked it over.

She could see him looking at her with a frown.

Really, she thought. Should a bartender be so judgmental?

"You sure that's a good idea, Scout?"

Apparently this one was.

"I'm not driving, if that's what you're worried about. Took a cab."

"I'm more worried about you being able to walk out of here."

"You have a clue how much cabs cost from the airport?" Scout asked, ignoring his concern in favor of the continued pursuit of oblivion. "A shit ton of money, that's how much. I guess I should be worried about that now that I don't have a job."

"Look, I'll give you another drink but you've got to promise me you're going to call someone to come get you."

She studied the earnest bartender, a person she knew in passing. Someone she knew by name but not really someone she would call a friend. He didn't know anything about her life or her situation. There was just this assumption that there was someone she could call. Someone who would come pick her up.

"Who?"

He seemed confused by her question.

"Who am I supposed to call?" she repeated.

"I don't know. A friend. One of your sisters."

So he was aware she had sisters. The three Baker girls were sort of infamous in this town. But he didn't get what had happened to her today. He had no idea she couldn't just call them.

"I don't want to call them," she mumbled sulkily. "Then I would have to tell them. And then they would be all 'poor me.' And I would hate that. You know who I really want to call…"

Wow, Scout thought. She thought she wanted Duff. She thought he would be her natural first choice. Of course, he was dead so that was impossible, but just because he was dead didn't mean she couldn't still want him to come get her. Want him to fix everything and make it better.

But instead of his name, the first person that actually popped into her head was Jayson.

Jayson had seen her at her worst. Jayson knew her greatest flaws. Jayson was the only person she would even consider letting see her like this.

And he was the last person she could call because she had said goodbye.

She had said she didn't need to be rescued. She had said she didn't need a hero.

What an idiot!

Chris put the drink in front of her. A double shot of whiskey on the rocks. Her third one. However, he didn't take his hand off the glass.

"You promise me you'll call someone. I don't care who it is."

"Why can't I just get a cab like the other drunks?"

"Because you're not like the other drunks and it seems like you need someone looking out for you. I get it. Everyone around town knows about you and your dad and how tight you were. Now you just lost your job."

"Did I tell you that?" Scout asked, shocked that she should be so forthcoming with a bartender she barely knew when she couldn't even face telling her family.

"After drink two," Chris said. "That's a lot for anyone to handle. So you want to come to a bar and get drunk, that's your right. But you're not leaving here unless I know you're in good hands. Everyone here loved Duff. He would have wanted to make sure you were looked after."

"How very gallant of you," Scout said. Swell, another hero. Except totally not the one she wanted. She would call a cab when she was ready and the earnest bartender could go screw himself.

"Can I have my drink now?"

He pushed the glass toward her and walked away.

Good, she thought, happy to be left with her drinks and her slurred thoughts. She didn't want to talk anyway. Her phone, which had been blowing up since her plane landed, still sat unanswered in her purse. She knew that was a dick move. Everyone was probably worried about her. But what was she supposed to say? That she got fired and she wanted to get drunk and everyone needed to back off and leave her alone?

They wouldn't do it. They would want to come to her rescue and take care of her in her fragile state. Hell, between Duff dying and now this, no doubt Alice, Bob and Sam were going to be permanent residents in her house.

She wondered if Jayson knew already. Would Reuben have called him to give him a heads-up? Probably.

Maybe he was looking for her… No…she needed to stop thinking that way. Jayson was gone. If not physically, then he had to be gone emotionally. There had to be some way, some magical way, to make herself get over him.

Some potion she could take.

"Or maybe just this drink will do it. Maybe this one is the one that's going to make me forget everything," she muttered into the glass as she took another sip.

It was like liquid fire in her mouth and it offered sweet relief from her thoughts. By the time she finished this drink she'd be unlikely to remember her name, let alone the name of someone she could call.

"There you are! She's here, Lane."

The voice sounded vaguely familiar but Scout didn't have the energy to turn around.

Instead she just lifted her hand in the air and gave a half wave.

"S'up."

Instantly she was flanked by her sisters, who were both probably glaring at her. Not that she would confirm that because she wasn't going to look at them. No, she was going to stare down at her drink because right now her drink was the only thing that mattered.

Her drink was going to offer her forgetfulness and oblivion. Her sisters were not.

"We're going to fight this," Sam said first. "I'm going to draft a complaint. We'll sue for sexual discrimination. We'll file tomorrow..."

"You're not drafting anything," Scout said. "They didn't fire me because I'm a woman. They fired me because I lied to everyone for the year Duff was sick. They said I wasn't acting in the best interest of the organization, and they were right. And then I did something colossally stupid by recommending a highly unlikely candidate."

"Who is more than qualified to play professional baseball," Sam insisted.

"Yes, but they don't know that. All they have are the numbers and the only one that counts to them is the number twenty-seven."

Lane took the stool next to Scout and Samantha sat on her other side.

"What are you drinking?" Lane asked.

"Whiskey. Feels like a whiskey kind of night."

Lane must have caught the bartender's eye. Because the next thing Scout saw was Chris pushing two more glasses on the bar. One in front of Sam and other in front of Lane.

"How did you know where to find me?"

"When you didn't call Bob we just assumed...things didn't go well. You being you, you would want to hide somewhere rather than come home to your family. There are four bars in Minotaur Falls. This was the third one we tried," Sam explained as she sipped her drink.

"Scout..." Lane started but then stopped. Scout looked at her and she could see she had no idea what to say.

"I know, right. It's like the worst thing ever." So why Scout was laughing she had no idea. Laughing wasn't quite accurate. The sound she was making was more like cackling.

"It's not the worst thing ever," Lane said as she rubbed her back.

"Nope. Duff dying. That was the worst

thing ever. Me ending it with Jayson. Again. Pretty damn sucky. But I'm going to say being fired from baseball...this sort of ranks."

"What do you mean ending it with Jayson again? I thought you were having ex-sex," Sam said.

"Ex-sex? That's a thing?" Lane asked.

"Apparently it is for Jayson," Sam said, talking over Scout's head.

"I don't know if that's the best idea," Lane suggested. "I mean she's pretty raw right now..."

"Oh, for heaven's sake, Lane, that was his way back in," Samantha said. "Clearly he wanted to get her in bed again, hoping she would come around and finally see reason."

"What reason?" Lane fired back. "He left her and, granted, we all agree she should have gone with him, but he still hurt her pretty bad. He never called or emailed. Because she didn't do what he wanted, suddenly he was completely out of the picture?"

"Yeah!" Scout cheered as she listened to her sisters battle it out over her head.

Sam frowned. "Maybe that was wrong back then, but it's obvious he still loves her now. If she would just get her head out of her ass and see that, she might have a chance to be happy."

"Scout, what do you want?"

Scout looked at Lane and then at Sam. "Oh, I'm sorry, was I involved in this conversation? It sounded like you two were figuring out my life without me. Which, given its present condition, I'm sort of okay with."

"We just want to help you," Lane said. "We love you."

"You can't help me."

Sam sighed as she sipped her drink. "Why do you always have to be so difficult? Why can't you just acknowledge you need us and let us be here for you?"

"Because I don't need you! I'm fine. Or I will be fine. I mean, seriously, what am I supposed to do—tuck myself into a ball and cry on your lap? You think that's going to help?"

"No, I think drinking too much whiskey in a dive bar is a much better answer," Sam huffed. "How are you drinking this stuff by the way? It's foul."

"Sorry, we can't all drink the fancy stuff, Samantha. Some of us don't have a job."

"You'll find another job. You're too good at what you do and you have enough contacts in the baseball world to help you out. Not to mention…"

"I'm Duff Baker's daughter," Scout said and raised her glass in salute. "Or at least I was."

"Sam's right, Scout," Lane said, obviously playing the role of good cop tonight. "You're going to have other opportunities."

"I'm sorry. Did another Triple A team move into town when I wasn't looking?"

Scout could practically see Sam and Lane exchanging looks behind her back.

"Oh," Scout concluded from their silence. "I get it. I'm supposed to leave town. Find another job, another life someplace else."

"It has been done before," Sam said. "And honestly, Scout, it might be good for you. To get away from this place for a while. Give yourself some separation from your memories with Duff."

Scout looked at her sister and wondered how the two of them could resemble each other, yet be so totally different. "Those memories are all I have left of him and you want me to get further away from them."

"If you're going to move on with your life, you're going to have to. You can't just erect a shrine to him and decide you're going to worship at its feet day and night. You need to get a grip and start living again."

"Sam," Lane snapped. "A little harsh maybe."

"No, Lane, please," Scout said, cutting her off. "I got this. See, you have to remember Sam never really liked Duff…"

"That's not true," Sam interjected. "I loved him. As much as you do, whether you believe it or not. But he wasn't perfect, Scout. By any means."

"He was to me," Scout insisted.

"Because you never saw anything you didn't want to see. He was just a man, not a saint, and he screwed up big-time."

"What are you talking about?" Lane asked.

Sam squirmed on her stool. "Nothing. Forget about it. This whiskey must have gone to my head."

Scout had a lot of whiskey in her head right now, too, but that didn't mean she couldn't tell when Sam was hiding something.

"You have a secret. You always sucked at keeping secrets."

"Scout's right," Lane concurred. "What was it, Sam? I mean we all knew that you and Duff had a falling-out over something. He would certainly never talk about it. And all that time you spent whispering with him when he was dying. What was that all about? I didn't understand it at the time, but it seemed… It felt like he wanted you to forgive him for something."

"Duff made me promise I would never tell you. Mom…well…she said it would be my decision now that he was gone. I mean I have no idea how important it is, but it just seems like too big a thing for you both not to know. Like, how can you be my sisters and not know this really big thing about me?"

Scout had no idea what she was about to say next but the sense of impending doom was descending on her again. She took another sip and braced herself.

After all, how much worse could things get?

"Duff was not my biological father. Bob is."

Scout couldn't hear past the buzzing in her ears. "What did you just say?"

"You heard his story. He was a navy SEAL and he was being sent on a long-term, apparently very dangerous assignment. He didn't want Mom to have to live like that, wondering if he was going to come back or not. What neither of them knew was that she was pregnant at the time."

"Holy shit," Lane muttered. "I'm going to need another drink."

"Mom was pregnant. When she married Duff." The words felt thick in Scout's mouth.

"Duff had always had a thing for her, even when she was dating Bob. When he realized she was in trouble he stepped in and married her. I think Duff always thought Mom would grow to love him as much as she did Bob."

"Holy shit," Lane repeated. "And you've known. All this time?"

"No," Sam said, her mouth getting tight. "Apparently Duff never wanted it to come out. I was his daughter and that was it. But when Bob and Mom met again, she couldn't not tell Bob. And so she couldn't not tell me. That's what Duff and I fought about. The fact that he would have kept that secret from me forever. It wasn't fair to Bob or me. In the end, I think it was the last straw for their marriage."

"Bob is your dad. And you've known this since you were…" Scout let Sam fill in the numbers.

"Eighteen."

"And you kept this secret…"

"Again, that was Duff. He made me promise never to tell you. Not until after he was gone. I think he was afraid… I think he was afraid if you knew, somehow we would be lesser sisters. Which is ridiculous, of course. But that's how messed up his thinking was. It was why he never wanted me to know. As if somehow he would be less my father if I knew the truth, when he was the man who'd raised me. The man I would always call… well…the man we called Duff."

"Sam, this is… I have no idea what to say," Lane muttered, still clearly shocked.

"It doesn't change anything," Sam insisted. "It's just a biological fact. Although Bob and I probably have grown closer as a result."

The looks they shared, the private conversations between them. It all made sense now. She'd called her sister a traitor for accepting Bob as part of her mother's life. But she wasn't just accepting him. She was embracing him.

Her biological father.

Scout felt filled with a cold fury. Once again not really directed at anyone. It was fate. Fate was her enemy. Because, while fate took Duff from her, it left Sam with a back-up father.

Scout had to lose everything but Sam got to keep Bob. How was that fair?

"You bitch," Scout slurred as she took her last gulp of whiskey.

"What did you call me?"

"Right. Sorry. You uppity bitch!"

"Scout, calm down," Lane told her.

Scout was done listening to both of them. "Duff's gone. Baseball is gone. Jayson—" Scout swallowed around the rush of nausea "—is gone. But you get to have Bob. Of course you do. You get to have your dad!"

"He's not my dad. Duff was my father and I lost him the same as you did. You're not the only one hurting. The only one grieving. Not everything is all about you, Scout," Sam said coldly.

Scout got off her stool. She wanted away from Sam. Away from Lane. She wanted away from everyone. She stumbled and both Sam and Lane tried to steady her.

"Get off me!" Scout shouted, shaking them both away.

They were standing now, too, and Lane was trying to maneuver Scout in the direction she wanted her to go, which was toward the bar's front door. "Come on, we're going to take you home and put you to bed. We'll talk about this in the morning."

"We're not talking about anything! I want you gone," Scout shouted at Sam. "I want you and *your dad* gone tomorrow from my house."

"You're drunk and acting like a child," Sam stated.

The fact that Sam's freaking hair was perfectly styled and unruffled for whatever reason infuriated Scout.

"You want to see drunk, I'll give you drunk."

Scout pumped all her anger and all her rage into that moment and when her fingers closed into a fist she knew in which direction she wanted to send it. Right into Samantha's perfect face.

The impact was satisfying. Scout could hear her sister yelp and it was a delightful sound.

Sadly the momentum of that punch on unsteady legs filled to the knees with whiskey sent her down on top of Sam. Needless to say Sam was not at all pleased to find herself laid out on the floor of the bar. Scout knew this because Sam immediately began kicking and hitting Scout with what felt like a fair amount of rage.

Scout thought she could feel Lane grabbing her blue suit jacket by the neck, but her sister was going to need a heck of a lot more help if she thought she was going to get Scout to her feet. Scout was pretty sure she was spending the rest of the night on the floor.

Which was disgusting when she thought about it.

That was until two large men entered into the fray and lifted Scout to her feet, separating her from a still hissing Samantha.

"Get off me," Scout shrieked, not enjoying being wrangled as if she was some kind of animal. In another burst of anger, she turned and managed to take another swing at the man who had been helpful enough to pick her up.

In hindsight, that was a very bad idea because he happened to be a cop.

"That's it," the officer said. "You're coming with me."

Scout had barely processed what was happening to her when she felt the snick of something holding her wrists together. The next thing she knew she was in the back of a stinky police car.

"Officer, I'm very sorry."

"Tell it to the judge. I'm writing you up for drunk and disorderly."

"No, not about that. I don't care about that."

"Then what are you sorry for?"

"I'm about to get sick in your car."

And with that three doubles of whiskey and what was left of her lunch came spewing out of her mouth and onto the backseat of the already smelly police car.

It was the perfect end to this horrible day, Scout thought.

CHAPTER EIGHTEEN

"YOUR BAIL HAS been posted."

Scout looked up at the police officer who was unlocking the door to the holding cell. She'd been placed there a few hours ago, along with another drunk who was passed out on the bench and a woman Scout believed to be a hooker, given that her shorts revealed more ass than most of Scout's thongs did.

She stood up on unsteady legs and waited a minute before she took her first step. Not that she was still drunk. Hurling all the alcohol seemed to take care of that problem. No, it was just the shock of everything that had happened that day.

"Do you know what time it is?"

"Just after one a.m.," the officer answered.

Good, at least the day was over.

Now it was a new day. A new day where she no longer worked for the Rebels, her dad was still gone, but apparently her sister's dad was not and…what was that other thing?

Scout followed the officer to a door that opened into the main area of the police station. Minotaur Falls had a low crime rate and it was after one in the morning, so the station was quiet.

Scout had been expecting Sam. As crazy as it seemed, even though Scout had decked her, if anyone were going to get her out of jail it would have been Sam. She was the lawyer in the family.

Of course that didn't mean she still wasn't going to be extremely pissed, which was going to make for a hell of drive home.

But it wasn't Sam waiting for her. Or Lane or, thank God, her mother.

No, there was Jayson with his special, imperfect face, looking at her as if she was a hot mess. Because she must look like a hot mess.

Yes, once again it was Jayson to the rescue. She should have railed at him. She should have told him to leave and that she would find a way to save herself.

But she was so tired.

She walked over to him, trying to keep her chin up. "They fired me."

"I know."

"Duff isn't Samantha's dad. Bob is."

"I know that, too. Lane told me everything

when she called. It would seem your sister Sam is sporting a fairly prominent black eye and refused to come down here to bail you out. Your mother thought it might be better if I came and got you instead. I'll take you home with me tonight."

Her mother thought she should be with Jayson. Her mother didn't know that Scout had essentially kicked him out of her life yesterday. For wanting to do the very thing he was doing now.

Saving her.

"I'm supposed to tell you I can take care of myself," she said, looking at him, willing him to know that she simply wasn't capable of it right now.

"Yeah, and how is that working out for you?"

"I hit my sister, and I almost hit a cop. I have a hearing for a drunk and disorderly charge in six weeks. The fine can be as high as a thousand dollars, which really sucks when you don't have a job."

Jayson just nodded and put his arm around her. "So I think we'll go with my plan for now. A hot shower, a cup of chamomile tea and a soft bed."

"With you in it?" she asked. She didn't

have the right to ask him. Not after what she'd said. Which was mostly goodbye. But it was too late. She'd already done it.

He looked down at her, his expression solemn. "If you want me to be."

"I do. Tonight... I really do."

If it made her weak, she didn't care. If it made saying goodbye to him again that much harder, she didn't care. She was done. At the end of her rope and she had nowhere to fall. The only thing that was under her was a giant, gaping pit of despair.

She needed to be saved, and for some reason she kept wanting him to do it.

Jayson did exactly as promised. He got her home. Shoved her gently into the shower and had tea ready for her when she came out. He offered her one of his T-shirts to wear and she deliberately picked what had always been her favorite one. And when she climbed into bed he was waiting on the other side of it.

She rolled to him and he tucked her up into his arms and it was like those four years had never happened and he had never gone away. This was simply them.

She listened to him breathing, allowed herself to put her hand over his chest where she used to always put it so she could feel the beating of his heart. Once it was there he placed his hand on top of hers as if he would hold her hand in place there forever.

It felt like the sweetest homecoming.

Scout had no idea what tomorrow was going to bring. She only knew that for tonight this is exactly where she needed to be and who she needed to be with.

THE SUN WAS rising and Jayson, surprisingly, was up with it. He looked down at the sleeping Scout, snoring, and wondered why it was they just couldn't seem to make what was so clear and so obvious work. What trick were they missing? Was there some special magic that the fairy-tale couples got that they just didn't have access to?

Jayson remembered what Roy had told him. About not being able to get over Lane for years and thinking he was never going to have a chance with her until he did. And it was working.

This should be their opportunity, shouldn't it? Duff brought him back here to keep her upright, but surely this was supposed to be their second chance.

It is. Just don't let her shake you loose.

"I'm not a damn bull rider," Jayson muttered, not caring anymore where those strange thoughts were coming from. He just wanted this to be easy. Or easier. And now it wasn't going to be. Not even a little bit.

Especially once he told her what had happened after Reuben called him to tell him they had let Scout go.

He looked at Scout again and he thought how she had never been easy.

Actually, that wasn't true. Liking her had been easy, but love…

When the love came it sunk in so deeply and so completely he hadn't been able to get it out of his system.

He remembered their first date at Jocelyn and Pete's wedding when she'd undone her hair and kicked off her shoes and told him that she liked him. Asked him flat out if he liked her. No flirting, no batting her eyes. Just straight up. That's who she was.

She was the girl who didn't tell him she was a virgin because she thought it might be a turnoff. She was the girl who'd never been in a relationship, so she just jumped in with both feet and gave him everything. Handed it to him on a platter, really. Her whole heart. What was that if not a risk?

It was only in the end when he'd asked her to take the biggest risk that she'd balked.

Maybe she was right. Maybe if he'd continued to call her, text her, email her...she might have realized how wrong it was for them to be apart. She might have made trips to visit him and those trips would have gotten longer and longer.

If he hadn't been so damn stubborn. That was the real truth. Everyone said it about Scout, but he'd gotten rejected and he turned that into every rejection he'd ever gotten in his life.

Maybe if he'd done things differently, he could have made it easier on both of them.

But he hadn't. And now here they were and she was in his bed. Because she loved him or because she needed him—he wasn't sure that he cared. For now, for this brief time, she was his girl.

He got back in bed and turned toward her.

"Scout," he whispered as he leaned in close. He kissed her nose like he used to when she stayed over, and when he backed away he watched her scrunch up her face.

Exactly like she used to do.

Soon she was going to wake up and realize that the Rebels had fired her, that her sister had kept this huge secret from her and that Duff was never coming back. But he was also going to be the first thing she saw, and deep down Jayson knew it would make her happy.

Her eyes fluttered open. He could almost watch it happen. Watch as the memories started to flood back, watch as she realized all those things she knew to be true about her life. Then her eyes met his and he could see that she'd just figured out he was the one who kissed her nose and she hated it when he did that.

And she smiled.

Maybe this time, he thought. Maybe this time was going to be different for them. This kind of love, it didn't just happen. He was sure of it.

"I want you to know before you say anything that I would run face-first into a brick wall for you," he said quietly as he stroked her cheek with his finger.

"Dude, you ran face-first into a brick wall to catch a fly ball. That's not saying much."

He laughed as they fell into another former dance.

"Thank you for coming to get me last night. Especially after…"

"I don't want to talk about that. None of that here in this bed, this morning."

She blinked a few times. "What do you want to do?"

"I want to make out with you, Scout."

She instantly covered her mouth. "Uh…no. Morning breath," she said it as if he was the stupidest person in the world.

"Well, go do your thing. I was already up and brushed my teeth."

It was her first rule. No kissing until they had brushed their teeth. He thought it ridiculous but he respected her boundaries. He thought the fact that she was scrambling as fast as she could to the bathroom was a good sign.

"There's a spare toothbrush in the closet," he called. He'd bought it when he came back to town with the crazy idea that something like this might happen and she might need one. Because her other rule was forbidding the use of each other's toothbrushes.

"Oh, and Scout?" he shouted over the running water. "When you come back bring a condom. They're in the cabinet over the sink."

The running water stopped. There was silence for a minute and then he heard the distinct sound of the cabinet opening and closing again. Just that sound made him hard. She was going to come back to bed, they were going to make out and then they were going to make love.

She stood in the doorway in her favorite T-shirt and he could see most of her long pretty legs. He loved her long pretty legs, especially when they were wrapped around his waist.

The foiled package dangled from her fingers. "We're not going to have ex-sex. Are we?"

"No, we're not. We're going to make love like we have been doing this whole time because that's really all it ever is between us. And we both know it."

"Are you still going to tell me to do stuff… because I have to say I kind of like it."

"You're not a virgin anymore, Scout. So maybe it's time I stop treating you like one. Before, when I was with you, every time we made love the first thing I always thought about was trying to make it better than the first time."

She smiled. "Every time was."

"Yeah, well, now I don't think about that. Now I just think about how badly I want you." He got up on his elbow and threw off the covers, shameless in his naked desire for her.

"What do you want me to do?" It was barely a whisper.

"I want you to take off that shirt so I can see you naked."

She lifted it off. And did he think that maybe she was doing it a little slower than she could have? Definitely. Dragging it out so he could see her panties first, then her bare belly and finally her breasts, which were perfection. When the shirt fell and she pushed her panties down her legs, she waited for his next command.

Except he was done telling her what to do. For now.

"This is your show, Scout. What do you want me to do?"

She blushed and he could see it spread from her neck all the way up to her cheeks. She glanced down at her hand and saw the condom as if just realizing it was there. Then she came over to the bed and climbed on top of him, her hair falling down over her shoulders. He reached for a lock of it and rubbed it over her tightening nipples.

She bumped against his erection and he thought he had figured out her intention.

"Do you want to ride me, Scout? You once told me you didn't like being on top."

"It always used to remind me of the first time, which hurt so much. But you're right—I'm not a virgin anymore."

"No, you are not. And I would love to lie back and let you do all the work. But you have to do one thing for me first. You have to kiss me."

"I did brush my teeth." She smiled, bending down and nipping at first his lower lip. Then his upper lip. Her breasts were pushed into his chest, his hands were cupping her beautiful ass and her tongue was in his mouth. She was tasting him, tempting him to taste her.

"I love your mouth. Your flavor."

"It's your toothpaste," she teased him.

"It's not. It's you and it's a taste that hasn't left me in four years. God, I missed you. Have I told you that yet? This whole time I've been back did you know how much it hurt to be away from you? To hear your voice, to see this pointy little chin of yours." He kissed that lovely chin for good measure.

Scout cupped his cheek, her eyes not leaving his even to blink. "Every day, I missed you. Every day, I thought about you."

With a new fierceness she bent down and took his mouth again. Then she spread herself out completely on top of him, so her thighs were on top of his, her center was pressed against his, her soft belly on his hairy one, her breasts with her nipples now rock hard pressed against his own. It was as if she wanted to connect them completely.

Jayson wanted to roll her over onto her back; he wanted to come inside her now and finish the process of their union.

Except she was rising up above him again, the condom still between her fingers. She ripped the foil open and scooted down his body until she was resting on his thighs, his erection like a prize in her hand.

"I've wanted to do this for you," she said stroking him before she covered him. "Now that I know you like it."

"I do." What wasn't to like? Getting to watch the woman he loved touch him this intimately. She slid the sheath down over him and then raised up, using her hand to guide him. He wanted her to take her time so that she had no qualms whatsoever about this position again, but she was already easing him inside her body and there was no resistance. Just one sweet long stroke right to her core.

He watched her face when she realized he was in her to the hilt. She looked down at him and smiled. "That didn't hurt. Not even a little bit."

Jayson pressed his hips up into her. "What about this?"

She gasped. "Yes, please."

He thrust up again and again and she gasped with each one. With his hands on her hips he eased her up and then down, showing her how the motion should work, guiding her so that she was coming down when he was pressing up. When she picked up the dance and used her hands to press against his chest, he knew the pleasure of it had taken over.

She was enthralled, with her back arched, pressing ever harder, sending him even deeper. He cupped her ass to still her for a moment.

"Stop. Too much," he muttered. "Don't want to come yet."

"No, don't come," she breathed. "I want you to wait for me."

But then she resisted his hold and starting moving again, this time twisting her hips in a way that made him crazy. It was as if she couldn't stop. As if her whole body was on this ride and he couldn't slow her down even if he wanted to. She started panting and he could see the flush all along her skin, her breasts gently bouncing in a way that was driving him insane.

"Please tell me you're close, sweetheart."

She cupped his face again and it forced him to open his eyes. He hadn't realized he'd closed them, but it had been his only way to hold back. But when he saw her eyes, saw what was reflected in them, he knew he was done.

The pleasure slammed into him and his hips jerked. She cried out and pressed so hard against him he didn't think anything would ever be able to separate them again. The two of them rocked back and forth, letting their orgasms take them over. Letting their bodies do what they needed to do.

When it was over she collapsed against him. "Jayson," she whispered into his ear and it was the sweetest sound he ever remembered hearing.

Eventually they were going to have to get up. They were going to have to leave this bed and face the world and the reality that waited for them, but for now this was bliss.

She kissed his neck and eventually moved so that they slipped apart. He realized how much he hated that. The disconnection part. It probably never bothered him so much in the past because he always knew there was going to be another time.

This time he couldn't be so certain. He thought he should tell her now and get it over with. But he just wasn't ready to let the beauty of this moment go.

Neither was she. Instead of moving she snuggled closer into his chest.

"Give me a second, sweetheart."

"You'll come back, though? We don't have to wake up yet?"

Jayson looked at the clock. It was nearly eight now. He had no doubt her family would still be worried about her, except for Sam, who might still want to throttle her.

But he had nowhere to go and another hour wasn't going to kill anyone. "I'll come back. We don't have to wake up yet."

She smiled but then her smile grew a little sad because she knew that all he could give her was another hour, two at most.

Then Scout Baker was going to have to face the music. Jayson couldn't spare her that. And for the second time in her life she was going to have to decide whether or not she was willing to take a risk.

CHAPTER NINETEEN

"I'M GOING IN with you," Jayson announced. "And I don't want to hear no, okay?"

"Oh, trust me, you're not going to get any argument from me. If I ever needed a hero now is the time. It's entirely possible that if I walk in there, Sam might kill me."

They were sitting in Jayson's car just outside her house. Her house, which was filled with people who no doubt were all very angry with her. Unless of course they had listened to her drunken rants and had left already.

She wouldn't blame them if they had. But given that the driveway was filled with cars, she was fairly certain they were all here. Which meant she was going to have to make this apology in person.

"You ready?"

Scout took a deep breath. "As ready as I'll ever be."

Together they got out of the car and Scout followed behind Jayson up the driveway like the coward she was, but when he opened the door that led into the kitchen, he stepped back so she could walk in first.

The scene was much like she imagined. Sam sat at the table brooding with a cup of coffee in front of her and a bag of frozen peas over half her face. Alice and Bob looked at Scout, one slightly wary, the other sorely disappointed.

"I'm sorry," Scout said, leading off with that directly.

Sam dropped the bag of peas, practically snarling. "Look at what you did to my face."

Scout winced. She'd never seen a purple quite that shade before. "I didn't even know I could hit so hard."

"I'm going to carry this for weeks. People are going to think…"

Alice moved to put her hand on her daughter's arm. "We talked about this, Samantha."

Sam took a deep breath. "You were drunk. You didn't know what you were doing," she said as if she'd had to practice that line over and over.

"Oh, I knew what I was doing. I just was out of my head when I did it. And I'm sorry. I don't know why finding out you still had your dad rocked me like that. But hitting you was wrong and I'm really sorry about the shiner. I get why you're sensitive about it."

"For the last time, Duff was my dad. Just because there is Bob doesn't change what Duff was to me."

Scout nodded but she didn't necessarily agree. Right now Bob was looking at Sam as if his whole world was wrapped up in her, and if that wasn't being a father, then she didn't know what was.

"I'm sorry you had to find out that way," Alice said. "I'm sure it came as a great shock."

"It was sort of a multiple-hit day. I don't know why I thought whiskey was going to fix anything."

"It always seems like such a good idea," Bob said with a smile. "Sadly it never seems to end that way."

"You took good care of my girl, Jayson," her mother said. "I appreciate that."

Jayson just shrugged. Scout was having a hard time reading him this morning. In some ways she felt closer to him than ever, but it also was as if he was hiding behind a wall he'd built.

Not being able to handle another shoe dropping at the moment, Scout decided they could all safely stay here in her kitchen for a while.

"Coffee?" Scout asked him.

"Sure," Jayson replied, taking a seat at the table.

"We have bagels, too," Samantha said. "I'll toast."

She got up from the table as Scout poured two large cups of coffee.

"I really am sorry," she said again when Sam was next to her. "You know I would never seriously want to hurt you. I was half-crazy. I was just so…"

"Angry. And hurt. And you'd just lost your job. I shouldn't have told you like that. Not in that situation. I get it. But you called me an uppity bitch," Sam whispered back. "That was really mean."

"You're right. I'm sorry. I mean, sure, you're a little uppity, but that doesn't mean you're a bitch. You know, until you go all ice queen on someone."

"Scout!"

"Sorry, but it's true. Doesn't mean I don't love you, though."

Sam split the precut bagel and put it in the toaster oven. "I have absolutely no idea why I still love you."

Scout bumped her shoulder against Sam's. "Sisters?"

Sam sighed. "Fine. Sisters."

"Well, really half sisters."

"Scout!"

Scout smiled. "Too soon?"

"Too flipping soon," Sam said.

Just then the doorbell rang and Scout wondered what could possibly come next.

"Why do I have the feeling Armageddon is standing on the other side of that door?" Scout asked the room with a sense of dread.

"I'll get it," Jayson said, standing. "If it's Armageddon, I'll let him know you're not home."

He walked past her, and again Scout didn't know how to read him.

"It occurs to me that you made it sound last night like you two were over...but, funny, he had no problem coming to your rescue," Sam pointed out.

"That's because he's Jayson. He'll always come to my rescue."

And he would. It didn't matter if they were over or together. She was starting to realize Jayson was always going to be this *person* in her life. No matter what their circumstances.

It was beautiful in a way. But also sad, if they couldn't find a way to make things work between them. Something they hadn't been able to do before.

"Not Armageddon," Jayson announced. "But someone just as powerful."

"I can't be called powerful when I'm wearing tennis shoes," Jocelyn Taft Wright announced as she walked into the kitchen.

It was true, in her jeans and light cardigan, she looked more like a woman about to go play a casual match of tennis than a business mogul and owner of the Minotaurs. But it didn't make her any less formidable.

"Hey, Jo," Scout said. "I take it you heard."

"I heard and I'm furious. Everyone knows what kind of talent you are. What could they possibly be thinking?"

"They weren't really happy about all the lying I did to cover for Duff. Something about not acting in the best interest of the club. Added to that my very high-risk prospect, they felt I wasn't suited to that particular role any longer."

Jo crossed her arms over her chest and huffed. "Well, they can't do it. The Rebels may control the coaching staff, but it's still my team and my stadium. You're a part of that, Scout. We'll find a role for you. You can work with Jerry, running the place. Gosh knows he needs all the help he can get. I mean no one knows more about the town and that team than you do. I know it's not the baseball side of things, but it could be a new challenge for you."

Scout considered that offer. It wasn't the worst deal. And besides, she would still get to work with Jayson in some capacity.

She turned to him. "What do you think?" Scout didn't question that she was asking him his opinion. Something had changed between them this morning and she decided she liked them better this way than when she was pushing him away.

Who said having a hero had to be such a bad thing anyway? Maybe she could lean on him every once in a while. And when he needed rescuing, she could be there for him.

"I think it's a great opportunity," he said with a sad smile. "If that's what you want to do."

"You think maybe I should try and get another job scouting? You know that wouldn't be easy."

"No, it wouldn't be," he admitted.

"Plus, it would most likely mean leaving Minotaur Falls. I just don't know if I could do that yet. I mean, everything is still so raw.

Plus, if I did take a job at the stadium at least we would be working together."

He shook his head. "No, we wouldn't be."

There it was, she thought. That thing that he'd been holding back all morning. The thing that was probably going to destroy her. Again.

"When Reuben called to let me know they had fired you, I resigned."

Scout gasped. "Jayson, you didn't."

"I don't believe them, Scout. I don't believe it was about you covering for Duff or sending in that prospect sheet on Evan. I wasn't going to work for people like that."

"Jayson, you have to call them back. You have to apologize. This was your chance. A couple of years in Triple A and you were most likely going to The Show. The Show! You can't give all that up because you're defending my honor."

"There is another job," Jayson said slowly. "One I was offered before Duff called me to come back here. Third base coach on a Triple A team in the Arizona league. They're affiliated with the San Francisco Miners. It's a step down from this but the kicker is that there will be a spot opening up next season with the Miners. One of their base coaches is retiring. I could be back in The Show sooner than you think. And it will give me an opportunity to see the game managed at that level, which I think could prove to be a good experience."

Everyone else seemed to be nodding, but all Scout heard was Arizona and San Francisco.

Two places that were very far away from Minotaur Falls.

"You're leaving," Scout whispered.

The room got quiet as they all looked at Jayson.

He only had eyes for Scout. "Yeah. I am."

Scout's jaw dropped as she felt as if the past four years of her life hadn't happened. That she was right back there in the worst sort of déjà vu.

Only she wasn't. Those four years had happened. And there was one thing significantly different about this time. This time he wasn't asking her to go with him. She waited, but he didn't say anything else.

The pressure of the moment got to be too much. The words he wasn't saying that she couldn't not hear.

"I'm going to my room," Scout announced and she started moving at a pace that would get her there sooner rather than later. The floor had just fallen out from underneath her again and she needed to be in the safest place she could be.

Hadn't that been with Jayson? This morning.

She rounded the stairs and was halfway up when she heard Jayson say something to her family.

"It's probably best this way."

Best what way? That they both suffer the heartbreak all over again? She'd been so close, so close to real happiness and now he was taking it away again. How could he?

Once inside her room she closed the door. Felt the power of being able to lock it against the world.

But as she stood in the center of her room there was no comfort for her.

Just the excruciating knowledge that if he left her again, the loneliness might crush her.

SAM SAT ON the couch and decided she was done with the frozen peas. They had mostly thawed and any healing effect she had been getting from them was now gone.

She got up to return the bag to the freezer but stopped in the kitchen, wondering whether that was okay to do. If frozen peas thawed, should they be frozen again?

Sam felt like a woman of thirty-three years should know something so basic about food. But because her single culinary skill consisted of toasting, she was at a loss. Better to be safe than sorry, she dumped the peas in the trash and headed back to the couch, where she felt she was entitled to stay for the reminder of the day feeling sorry for herself.

She wished she could have stayed angry with Scout longer. Her little sister deserved it, but the truth was Scout was currently being put through enough stress to last a person a lifetime.

Jayson leaving? Did he really think that was the best thing for them? She could clearly see the way he looked at Scout. Donald had never looked at her like that. Not really.

He'd been possessive and controlling, which at the time had made her feel incredibly sexy. As if he was the only man powerful enough to challenge her. To take her on as the woman he wanted in his life.

He was brilliant and successful and he exuded confidence in every facet of his life. The challenge of him had been addictive. Holding her own with him, while still knowing that he was her true alpha.

They had dated for only six months when

he proposed. Not that it had really been a proposal. He'd simply told her they should marry and she believed it. Until one night three months later they got into a fight over the wedding plans.

Over the guest list. Sam had wanted to invite Steven Mallory, who had been a friend from law school and now had his own practice. They had never been romantic during their years in law school, but they had always maintained a close personal friendship. The hours of studying together in the library at Harvard Law had bonded them.

Don had lost it. He was convinced Steven and she had been lovers. He raged that she was disrespecting him by inviting her former lover to their wedding.

Sam often tried to recall every minute of that fight. At the time it had all been too shocking. Yes, he'd been drinking but not to the point that it would have changed his behavior so drastically.

Now she could look back and see the patterns she'd missed. The things she'd overlooked because she'd been so infatuated with him. She'd thought the way he'd always kept his hand on her lower back any time they went anywhere together was just his way of letting her know he was always there.

When really it was just his way of announcing to anyone who saw them that she was his.

His property.

At the time when he ordered for her, or told her what she thought she might like, she considered it to be old-fashioned. Now she knew he had never seen it as a joke when she suggested that she might not eat what he'd chosen for her.

So when she recalled every detail of that night, it was like peeling an onion. Every layer of the man she'd thought he'd been had fallen to the floor with each horrible word he shouted at her.

Until finally she started to become so angry herself that she shouted back and he backhanded her across the face. When Sam recalled that moment it was in slow motion.

She could see him raising his hand to her but still the whole time doubting it would actually happen. That she, Samantha Baker, beloved daughter of Duff Baker—beloved biological daughter of Bob Sullivan—was actually going to be hit by a man who was supposed to love her.

It was unfathomable. Right up until the moment it happened.

Maybe it was a good thing Scout clocked her, Sam thought. Now maybe she would remember this black eye as the last time she ever got hit in the face.

The doorbell rang and she started. Bob and Alice had gone out to run errands. Scout was still upstairs in her room hiding from reality. Lane or Roy wouldn't have bothered to ring the doorbell, which meant it had to be someone else.

Someone who was going to see Samantha with a massive shiner.

"Damn it," she muttered, but the doorbell rang again and she had no choice.

She tried to push her sleek hair over half her face to cover it, but her haircut was specifically designed to shape to her face, so it kept falling back into place.

That's what you get for a two hundred dollar haircut in a top Chicago salon.

Cautiously she opened the door and wanted to groan when she saw who was on the other side.

Of course it was Evan Tanner. Of course it was.

"Hey, can I come in? I just heard some rumors and I need to talk to Scout."

Rumors of Scout's baseball demise were no doubt all over town by now. Evan had probably already put the pieces together and was feeling some responsibility for what had happened. Which was ridiculous as all he'd done was be an outstanding prospect.

But as soon as he was inside standing in the living room, he took in Sam's face.

"Who did that to you?"

She could hear the anger in his voice. Despite only having met her a handful of times and having a few conversations, he seemed ready to defend her.

"It's not what you think."

"Then tell me what it is."

His tone caught her attention. It wasn't a question anymore. It was a demand said in a way that he expected her to answer him. Immediately.

Sam didn't do demands. Not anymore. But she refused to leave him with the idea that she would tolerate such rough treatment from anyone.

Well, anyone besides her drunk little sister.

"Scout did it. We were fighting and she

was drunk. She swung and my eye sort of got in the way."

Instantly his expression changed. As she knew it would. Now it was okay that she had a purple ring around her eye the size of a baseball because it wasn't a man who'd done it.

His lips trailed up at the corners. "I have two sisters so I know a little something about how out of control it gets when they start fighting. Although that's a whole new level you got on your face right now." He paused for a second, then cursed under his breath. "She was drinking because she got fired, wasn't she?"

"She was drinking for a lot of reasons, but, yes, that's what started her off."

"It's my fault," Evan said, rubbing his hand over his head as if he was trying to figure out a way to fix it.

Except he couldn't and it wasn't his fault. Scout, were she willing to come out of her bedroom, would tell him the same thing.

"It's not your fault. You're a prospect. She's a scout. She did the right thing. And I have no doubt that there were a lot of other factors involved in her termination, not the least of which is her being a woman. But that might just be my inner Gloria Steinem coming out."

"I didn't realize… I mean… I just wanted to play. Just to see if I had what it took. I don't think I ever understood what a risk she was taking."

Sam considered that. It was true. Scout had taken a risk and it wasn't like her. "Evan, you may not realize it but you might be the best thing that ever happened to Scout. Maybe she had to take that risk and have the worst thing happen only to realize it wasn't the actual end of the world."

"Isn't it for her, though? She got fired."

"There are other jobs in baseball. Heck, she just got offered a pretty sweet job by the owner of the Minotaurs. Not that I'm hoping she takes it. Scout needs to do her thing. But she's going to have to take another risk to see if someone else out there will give her a job."

"Do you think I should talk to her? Say something?"

"Not right now. Scout's…well…let's just say she's got other things on her mind. Believe it or not, things more important than baseball."

Evan nodded. "Heard about that, too. Coach LeBec gave his notice. That's a ballsy move."

"It is," Sam acknowledged.

"I like it." Evan smiled. "If it was me and she was my girl I would have done the same thing."

Sam stiffened at the sentiment. It all sounded nice at first. Letting a man be strong and defend his woman's honor. Until it wasn't.

"How chivalrous of you."

She could see the change in his expression. As if he was aware that her attitude toward him had shifted. Which of course it had.

"You know," he said, "sometimes I don't know what to make of you."

Sam bristled. "I don't know that there is anything that needs to be *made* of me. It's not as if we will continue to know each other. The camp is over, you're headed back to your job and I'm headed back to mine."

His lips curled up again. "You said when I was at a point that I needed an agent you would consider taking me on as a client. So maybe we will continue to know one another."

"Mister Tanner…"

"Evan."

She looked at him then and could see she had pissed him off. Yes, he was definitely a man who carried that tone well. The tone that said do not mess with me. It probably served him well working with teenagers, too.

"Evan, as much as I respect my sister for doing her job and pointing out to her club that you have talent, the likelihood of you getting to that point of needing an agent is a slim one. I'm sorry, but you should be prepared for that."

"Ms. Baker… Samantha…you don't know me, but when I decide I want something I do everything I can to get it. So *you* should be prepared for that. Tell Scout…just tell her I said thanks. For everything."

With that he turned and left and Sam shut the door behind him. It really was her specialty, she thought. Chasing men away.

Evan Tanner. Could he seriously make it as far as the majors? It would be a baseball miracle.

Then she shook her head because she remembered there were no such things as miracles, fairy tales and happily-ever-afters. At least not for everyone.

CHAPTER TWENTY

Four years ago...

"YOU'RE GOING TO do this. You're really going to do this."

Jayson stopped shoving socks in his gym bag and looked at Scout. Her cheeks were red and she was in a perpetual state of trying not to cry. She had been in full-on howler-monkey mode since this morning when she screeched at him about who was going to make his coffee the way he liked it in the morning and who was going to go on hot-dog runs with him in the middle of the night in Houston.

He'd said nothing in response to any of it because what was the point? What did she think would happen? That he was going to change his mind, ditch his career and stay here like a good dog because that's what she wanted?

And what if he did? Wouldn't he always

know that he was her second choice? This life here in Minotaur Falls with Duff, this was number one for her. He was number two and he was going to be damned if he was going to spend his life with someone who didn't put him first.

He wanted someone who picked him above everything.

Like his mother had. Like his father hadn't. *Shit. Was this about his father?*

No, Jayson told himself. This was not about any issues he had. This was about Scout and her inability to leave Duff's apron strings. She was a grown woman, twenty-five years old, and she couldn't summon up enough courage to leave her daddy.

That was her issue, not his.

When he looked at her and he could see all the pain and the misery in her expression, the same pain and misery that was churning in his gut, he almost hated her.

Hated her for not being willing to take a damn risk on him. On them.

"I'm done having this conversation, Scout. I've been done with it for two weeks. I started out by asking you to come with me. I finished with basically begging you to come with me. You made your decision and I've made mine."

"No," she barked. "You can't do that. You can't put this all on me like I'm the one who is making this happen. We were happy here. You're the one who's leaving."

"Because of my job!" he shouted back. "Do you remember what my goal is?"

"To get back," she muttered under her breath.

"To get back! I had it for one day, Scout. One beautiful freaking awful day. I have to get back if for no other reason than that damn day doesn't define my life. This is how I do it. This is how I get back. By taking the openings when they come and where they come."

"But Duff could..."

He threw the socks he'd systematically been moving from his drawer to his gym bag at the wall. "Damn it, Scout, this is not about what Duff can do for me!" Jayson pushed his finger into his chest until it hurt, preferring the physical pain to the emotional pain. "This is about what *I* can do for me. I got to The Show the first time through hard work, passion and tenacity. I had to have more of it than anyone else because I knew I had less talent. But I did it once and I'll do it again. So you have a choice—you can either come with me or stay. What you can't do is stop me."

Her arms were wrapped around her stomach as if he'd kicked her. A sight that immediately stopped him.

"We're not doing this," he said calmly. "We're not fighting."

"I don't want to fight, either," she whispered.

"I've made my position clear, haven't I?"

"You have."

"Have you changed your mind at all about what you want to do?"

Her body trembled for a time but finally she shook her head. "I just…can't. It's too… much. Too soon. I can't…"

"Take the risk. I get it. I mean, after all your parents got divorced so relationships are impossible and unlikely to succeed. My dad didn't even bother with the divorce, right? He just cleared out. I shouldn't want anything to do with something permanent, either."

She didn't say anything to that. Just sat on his bed and watched him pack the last of his things. Which really wasn't much. His guitar that he never played because he just couldn't master the damn thing. Some pictures. The suit he'd worn to Pete and Jocelyn's wedding when he'd taken Scout on their first date. Everything else was T-shirts and sweaters. Boots and sneakers. Underwear and socks.

No, there weren't a whole lot of things in Jayson's life.

For the past seven months there had only been one thing, really.

The ache in his chest made him wonder if he truly was having a heart attack. Nothing in his life had ever prepared him for this kind of horrible emotion. Love was supposed to be happy. It was supposed to be simple.

This was excruciating.

"What happens when you get to Houston?" Scout asked, her voice cracking slightly.

"What do you mean?"

"I mean will you call or anything? Let us know you got there okay?"

Jayson sighed. This part wasn't going to be any fun, either. "I told Duff I would call him. Check in from time to time."

"Duff," she said with enough finality to make it clear she understood what he was saying.

"I think it's for the best. For both of us. A clean break."

"Yeah," she whispered, which in some ways was so much worse than her howler-monkey screeching. "Much better."

"It will make it easier for us to move on, I think." He had to force the words out of his mouth. Had to make himself believe that they could be true. That never seeing her again and never hearing her voice again was eventually going to make her go away.

And there would be a time when he would just remember this girl he used to date, who he'd thought was going to be *the one,* but she hadn't felt feel the same way about him.

Scout Baker. Just the first of the women he was bound to love. Certainly not the last. Or the only one. He was far too practical for that. Heck, by the time he finished his three-day drive to Houston, he might have already put her behind him.

"Okay then," she said, her chin jutting out. Those moist eyes refusing to let a single tear fall.

Is that what he wanted to see? Would the sight of her crying and sobbing at his feet, begging him not to go, make him feel at least that he mattered to her? That he wasn't as easy to let go as she was making it seem.

But she didn't do any of those things. She just stood quietly by while he filled his car with his stuff. He should have told her to go; he wasn't even sure why she stayed. He supposed she wanted to watch it happen. To see him drive away and know that he was committed to really doing it.

When everything was done and he had the keys in his hands, he didn't know what to do. One last kiss? No, it would hurt too much. In the end he just shrugged and said, "See you, Scout."

She nodded. "Good luck in Houston."

"Thanks." Then he sat in the driver's seat, shut the door and turned the ignition. The car rumbled to life, and there was nothing left to do except put the car into gear and drive away.

Nothing for Scout left to do but turn and walk back to her home and the life she shared with Duff. Jayson watched her make that walk in his rearview mirror. Waited for her to turn around. Waited for her to realize she was making the biggest mistake of their lives.

Waiting for her to shout... *Wait!*

She never did.

Present

KNOCK, KNOCK, KNOCK. "Elizabeth Baker, I need you to open this door now."

Scout stared at the ceiling. This was when she had to summon the energy to tell her mother to go away. Only she couldn't. She really didn't care if her mother stayed on the other side of that door forever.

"Bob!"

Scout couldn't imagine what her mother thought Bob was going to do. Sure, Scout had moved beyond her hatred of the man. She would even acknowledge that she sort of thought he was cool. That when he told her about his heartbreak, she understood now how much he had suffered. He hadn't just lost the woman he loved; he had also lost his daughter. That sort of blew for him. Plus, she imagined that their relationship was going to have to grow now that she knew about his connection to Sam. He wasn't just her step-father anymore. He was Sam's father and Scout wasn't sure why, but that made him seem more like family.

Which still freaked her out, so Scout decided she didn't want to go there, either. All she really wanted to do was keep her mind blank. Staring up at her cciling counting the cracks in the plaster. That was the only thing that worked.

So, no, nothing Bob said was going to have any more impact than what her mother said or Sam said.

Except then she heard some clicking and

scraping and metal against metal. Then the next thing she knew the door handle fell out of the door and rattled to her bedroom floor with a clang.

The door swung open and Alice leaned over to kiss her husband's cheek. "Thank you, dear."

Bob looked at Scout, the incriminating tools in his hands. He shrugged, "Sorry. But I was a navy SEAL."

Alice walked in and picked up the door handle. She set it on Scout's dresser and closed the door mostly shut behind her.

"I can't believe you did that," Scout muttered. "This is my house, my room, and you just violated any sense of privacy I'm entitled to." It was unthinkable. It meant that even here she couldn't hide.

Alice arched her brow. "You do remember I'm your mother, don't you?"

"Not likely to forget."

Alice came over, sat on the bed and rubbed Scout's thigh. "So you've had a bad day…"

Scout's mouth gaped open. "Are you serious?"

Alice had the audacity to chuckle. "I know. You've had an atrocious day. Followed by another and another. And frankly I'm surprised we haven't had to medicate you more often, although I suppose you self medicated last night."

"Mom…"

"My point is," she interjected, "you've gotten through all of it. You made it through your father's sickness, then his death. You're nowhere near recovered and you won't be for months or years. That's just grief. You'll have days where you think you're fine and you'll have days where you won't want to get out of bed. But you will. Because you're strong and you know Duff would have wanted you to be the type to get up off the mat after taking a hit."

"See, that's how wrong you two were for each other. Duff never would have used a boxing reference."

Alice chuckled. "You're right. There were times between us when I didn't think he knew how to speak anything but baseball clichés."

Scout closed her eyes and sighed. "What am I going to do without…"

"Baseball?" Alice filled in. "That's what I'm here to tell you. Your life in baseball doesn't have to be over."

"No, I don't care about that. I mean, I do, but I can't think about that right now. What am I going to do without Jayson? This morning it was like…having him back. Just those few hours were the best hours I've had in four years."

"Oh, I see. This is about him going to Arizona. Yes, it's a shame isn't it?"

Again Scout was incredulous. "A shame? I'm going to have to lose him again. Again! When the first time almost destroyed me… and you think it's a *shame*!"

"Well, if you're that upset about it, then why don't you go with him?"

"He didn't ask!" Scout screeched.

Alice winced. "Really, Scout, that sound you make. One would think you would attempt to get that under control."

"I'm serious. He said he was leaving but he didn't ask me to go."

"Would you have said yes?"

"No," Scout said. "I can't just pick up my life. Especially now. But…well…maybe I could. I mean, maybe I would because I can't stand it. I can't stand not being with him anymore."

"Why didn't you go with him last time? The real reason. Not because of your job or Duff. Why couldn't you take that leap if you loved him so much?"

"I was scared," Scout admitted. "I was so

scared that I couldn't make it work. That I wasn't going to be enough. That we would live together and it wouldn't work out and that the end of the relationship would kill me."

"So you ended the relationship anyway."

Scout considered that. "Well, when you say it like that it sounds so stupid."

Alice nodded. "Because it is. And it was exactly what I told Bob when he broke up with me. I told him he didn't have enough faith in me, in us. That ending things wasn't going to stop the pain. It was just going to start it sooner than we had to."

"Guess he didn't listen."

"No. He was quite stubborn. Quite sure of what he was doing and of course I had no shortage of stubbornness, either. I promised myself I would not wait for him, not even for a minute. Granted, circumstances changed when I realized I was pregnant with Sam, but my thought process didn't. Had I wanted to, I could have had her and waited for Bob to get back. But I didn't. I walked into that relationship with Duff, knowing I was going to give it my all."

"This is the part where you tell me how you screwed it all up by making the wrong choices, like I did."

Alice shook her head. "Nope, not even a little bit. I know you'll never believe it, but Duff and I were happy for a time. We really were. Then came Lane and you and I wouldn't have done anything different. Because I love you. I love all of you. And now I get to tell you that without you rolling your eyes at me. The future is bright indeed."

"Mom," Scout groaned.

Alice stood. "I'll leave you on your own with these last wise words. This is life, Scout. This is how it rolls. You get chances and you make decisions. And every once in a while you get a second chance. What you do with that is up to you. But not for nothing it worked out pretty well for Bob and I. He is amazing in the sack."

"Mom! How many times do I have to tell you? TMI!"

Alice waggled her eyebrows. "I'll have him fix the door for you, but really, Scout, aren't you a little old to still be hiding? If Jayson didn't ask you, maybe it's because he's waiting for you to tell him what you're going to do."

SCOUT HAD WALKED the few miles to Jayson's house. Being outside had cleared her head as she tried to think of all the things she wanted to say to him. When she knocked on his door and waited for him to answer, suddenly all those careful words she'd picked out to clearly articulate how she felt were gone. And it was just Jayson standing there in front of her.

"Hey," he said. "Come on in."

Scout followed him inside, thinking it was strange that he didn't seem angry or upset with her. After all, he'd declared his intentions to leave Minotaur Falls and what had she done?

Run away like the coward she was. Except she'd left her hiding spot behind and had come in search of him. That had to count for something.

"I'm sorry I took off so abruptly," she began. "It was a little shocking."

"I know. I'm sorry. I should have told you last night but…well…other things were more important."

Like making love for the last time? Is that what that had been? His way of saying goodbye to her forever. Scout felt like there was this shuddering in her chest. Like at any minute she might just collapse on the floor in front of him, clinging to his feet and begging him not to leave her again.

But that's not why she had come here. She hadn't come to fix the past, only to focus on the present.

"You didn't ask me to go with you."

"Nope," he said casually. "Want something to drink?"

He turned from her and walked into the kitchen.

This was not how this was supposed to go down. She had things she wanted to say. Big, important things. Except it was as if he'd already moved on.

Maybe because he thinks he already knows what you would say.

Scout followed him into the kitchen, gearing up her courage. He had two beers in his hands and handed her one. She could use a small amount of liquid courage right now.

"Are you not asking me because you think I'll say no again, or are you not asking me because you don't want me to go with you?"

He took a sip of his beer and shook his head. "Neither. I'm not asking because we're not doing what we did last time. This is the job. This is baseball. It won't be the first or last time I might need to move."

"I totally understand that."

Then he set the beer down on the counter

and crossed his arms over his chest. "So we're not doing this again. I screwed up last time, Scout. I thought I had to make you choose between me and your life here with Duff. And when you didn't pick me it was like telling me I wasn't good enough for you. Because of that I shut you down. As if it had to be all or nothing. We lost four years because I did that. I shouldn't have... I shouldn't have made you choose like that."

"But..."

"No, let me finish," he said so sternly she actually jumped a little. Jayson was the definition of low-key, but clearly he had his own agenda for how this conversation was going to go down. Scout held her breath.

"I'm going to move, but we're still going to be together. I'm going to call you and we're going to Skype and do all the things that technology allows for. Like sexting. We're going to do a lot of sexting. Then during the season you're going to come visit me. A lot. And in the off-season I'm going to come here. A lot. The point is we're going to do what we should have done last time and just find a way to make it work. Because without you, Scout, nothing works. You're it for me and you always have been. I love you."

She breathed in the words and smiled. "I guess this means you don't want to break up?"

"I don't ever want to break up with you again. And I never will."

Scout moved toward him. "Ask me."

"I told you. I'm not asking you anything ever again. This is what we're doing."

She moved even closer, setting her beer down on the counter and encircling his waist with her arms. Because she could. She could touch him and hold him because he was hers again. She heard it in his voice even more than in his words.

"Ask me what I came here to tell you."

"What did you come here to tell me?"

"That I love you. That I should have gone with you four years ago," she whispered. "I could have talked to Duff every day by phone, but I could have still been with you. You think I chose him over you, but it wasn't about Duff. It was about me. About how scared I was. You were always first for me, Jayson. Always. I should have been brave enough to go with you."

He caressed her face, brushing her hair back. "No regrets, Scout."

"No. I know. Because I did have that time

with Duff and I won't regret that. But I came here to tell you that if you want me, I'll go anywhere on this earth with you. I was afraid last time, but now I'm more afraid of what it would mean not waking up next to you every morning."

Jayson studied her face again as if he was desperately trying to read her mind. "You would leave this town? Your house? I don't know if you're ready for that, Scout. You're still grieving…"

"And I'll grieve in Arizona or California or wherever we end up. Just don't make me do it without you."

He kissed her softly on the lips. "Okay," he said before he took her mouth.

And when she felt his lips and tasted his mouth it was like feeling all the pieces of her life coming back together again.

"You came back for me, didn't you?" she asked him. "Not for Duff but for me."

"I came back for you. Even though I didn't really know what that meant. I just knew you were going to need me, so I couldn't be any-where else but here."

A whisper of a memory came back to her. It had been bugging her for weeks but now it made sense. She'd been at Duff's bedside.

Everyone had been surrounding him. Lane had checked for his pulse and said that he was gone. And Scout remembered falling…

"You caught me," Scout said. "The day Duff died I remember falling…but then nothing after that."

Now it came back to her. His arms, around her, carrying her. She remembered thinking everything was going to be okay even though Duff was gone because Jayson would never let her go.

"You fainted, love. I wasn't going to let you fall."

Of course he wouldn't. He was the man who'd come back for her when she needed him even though he had no reason to. He was the man who'd caught her in her darkest hour. He was the man she would follow anywhere.

"Are we really going to get a second chance?" It seemed almost too good to be true.

Jayson kissed her again. "Yeah. We are."

"So this means we're not exes anymore, huh?"

"Nope. You are now my official girlfriend."

Scout pouted. "Does that mean we can't have ex-sex anymore? Because I have to tell you, I sort of really liked ex-sex."

Jayson wiggled his eyes. "Oh, honey, if you

liked ex-sex you're going to love what comes next. Reunion sex."

"Reunion sex!" Scout threw her head back and laughed. "That's not a real thing."

Jayson cupped her cheek in his hand, his expression serious again.

"What?" Scout asked.

"You laughed. It's the first time I've heard you laugh, really laugh since...I've been back. I forgot how much I missed that sound."

She pressed her hand over his. "Promise to make me do it at least once a day."

"Now, that might be the easiest promise I'll ever make."

"Take me to bed now, Jayson."

"Yes ma'am," he drawled.

"I want to find out what this reunion sex is all about."

"How I do love teaching you new things."

And together they went hand and hand to Jayson's bedroom, where he proved to Scout as thoroughly as any man could the absolute virtues of reunion sex.

EPILOGUE

SAM WAS SITTING in her office, her eyes on the fifty-inch flat screen. She watched the rolling scroll bar on the ESPN channel and when she saw his name slide across she shook her head in disbelief. Immediately her iPad on her desk started to chime. Sam checked it and saw Scout wanted to FaceTime with her.

That was odd. Not that she was calling, but that she wouldn't have just called her phone. Instead she clearly wanted to talk face to face. No doubt to brag as much as she could about how right she'd been.

Sam figured in this case Scout deserved it.

She checked herself in the mirror and then answered the call.

"Hello, Scout."

"Hey, did you see it! Evan Tanner just got drafted."

Sam smiled. "I saw it."

"You know what I'm never wrong about?" Scout asked.

"Baseball," Samantha said promptly. "You are never wrong about baseball."

Scout beamed. "The third round, baby. Not bad. Not bad at all. By the Miners, of all teams."

"Well, he once told me that when he wanted something, he didn't let much get in his way."

"He was smart. He kept going to camps across the country. Everyone else saw what I saw and then his hitting numbers told their own story. Who knows if he'll make it, but at least he's got a chance. Which I'm telling you, I think he does. You should really consider signing him now."

"I'll consider signing him if or when he needs an agent. Right now he's still got a lot of ball to play before that happens. So why are you FaceTiming me? Did we really need to see each other to have this conversation?"

Scout shook her head. "No, but you know the other thing I'm really good at..."

Sam could see the mischievous smile on her sister's face. And it made Sam happy, really happy to know that Scout had come through their father's death and still found a way to be joyful.

"Well, let's see, I know you're really good at hitting people."

Scout frowned. "Are you still not over that? It was months ago."

Of course she was over it, but as sisterly ammunition it was something Sam was always going to have in her arsenal.

"Well, what is this other thing?"

Suddenly the picture was moving and it took a second for Sam to realize what she was seeing.

"I'm also good at loving Jayson LeBec," she heard her sister's voice say.

Then it made sense. She was looking at a beautiful engagement ring.

"It took him long enough!" Sam cried, thrilled for her younger sister. Truly happy that their second chance had paid off.

Scout's face was back on screen, but she was looking over her shoulder. "Did you hear that, Jayson? Sam says you should have proposed to me months ago."

Jayson's face came into view over Scout's shoulder. "Sorry, Sam, I had to wait and see if I could actually live with her and her howler-monkey voice for the long haul."

"Good point," Sam said.

No doubt Jayson had waited the perfect amount of time for Scout to be ready. To be at a point where she could be happy and feel good about their engagement rather than guilty that she wasn't still grieving.

Sam watched Scout hit him on the shoulder and then saw the two of them smile at each other.

So in love. So happy. It made Sam want to cry.

"Okay, we're going to go be in love now," Scout said. "Just wanted to show off the rock."

Sam laughed. "You go do that, little sister. And I'll look forward to the wedding invitation."

"Yeah, Mom's already on me about that. Jeez, it just happened today. Oh, and I almost forgot," Scout said. "The Miners offered me a job in the front office. Talent Evaluation Coordinator. They want me checking out all their top prospects. The management team here thinks the Rebels were fools for letting me go."

"They were," Sam agreed.

"I love you, sis."

Sam didn't know why, but the tears that had been threatening since she saw Scout's smile finally came. "I love you, too."

"Wait…are you crying? Sam, you know the rule, right? About crying and baseball?"

Yes. Sam did know the rule. But when her sister was this happy and in love, well, sometimes rules were made to be broken.

* * * * *

LARGER-PRINT BOOKS!

HARLEQUIN

Presents®

GET 2 FREE LARGER-PRINT NOVELS PLUS 2 FREE GIFTS!

PASSION GUARANTEED SEDUCTION